THE TRAVELING PRAYER SHAWL

JENNIFER LYNN CARY

"I loved reading this book! It had me intrigued from the first page, and as the stories began, I could hardly wait to turn the page to see what happened next! Love the mix of true facts mixed with some good, clean, fun fiction! Easy, quick read. I highly recommend this book!"—CatSmit

Relentless Heart

"This book was beautifully written and the best book I read so far this year."—Peggy Baldwin

"While I have read other retellings of Ruth's story, somehow having her character be Vietnamese in the middle of the Vietnam War was the most appropriate translation I have yet seen. "—Phyllis, Among the Reads

"This is a beautifully written story. It is full of emotions and you can feel every one of them. It hooks you on the first page and keeps you turning the pages to see what happens next. I hated to see this book end and can't wait to read the next book in this series. This is a book you don't want to miss."—Ann Ferri

"I felt as if Hien, the beautiful, brave Vietnamese heroine, was having tea with me while sharing parts of her life." —Ginny

"Hien's story helped bring alive the story of Ruth for me."
—Ruth Sand

The Patriarch: The Crockett Chronicles: Book 1
The Sojourners: The Crockett Chronicles: Book 2
The Prodigal: The Crockett Chronicles: Book 3

Tales of the Hob Nob Annex

The Relentless Series:
Relentless Heart
Wedding Bell Blues
Relentless Joy
Silver Bells Christmas

The Traveling Prayer Shawl

*Dedicated to my female cousins, all Johnson girls.
So glad we are family. Love you all.
Sheilia Behler
Linda Lehman
Suzy Baker
Darlene Burger
Vicki Schmitt
Jody Scherer*

You are from God, little children, and have overcome them; because greater is He who is in you than he who is in the world.

1 John 4:4

Chapter One

CAMI

Present Day

"Dearly Beloved, we are gathered here today…"

Yeah, yeah, yeah, let's do this. Cami Madison flipped a wayward curl off her shoulder and glanced about the church where family, friends, and the faithful wearing their Sunday best filled the pews. *Weddings or funerals, they're all the same. Experts yak and then the crowd gets a free meal while making nice to your face and smearing you behind their hands.* She had no time for this. Not with her schedule.

Yep, it was all the same.

This time it was a funeral.

Of course Cousin Morgan corrected her even in her thoughts — "Not a funeral, a Celebration of Life." Morgie did her famous eye roll in Cami's imagination.

Right.

Not according to Gram. She'd be all tapping her wristwatch declaring, "I say funeral and time's a-wasting. Drop me into my eternal rest, and let's get this show on the road. We've got a schedule to keep, folks." The mind video made Cami snicker. She covered her mouth, but not in time to keep

Morgie from noticing. That tiny squint used to send a shiver down Cami's back. Maybe it still did. A little. She fanned herself despite the air conditioning which fought with Phoenix's spring heat.

Yeah, Gram was known for her promptness. A body could set a clock by her. In fact, Cami learned to tell time by the schedule at Gram's house when she visited in the summers. Supper at five fifteen. *Wheel of Fortune* at six. *Jeopardy* at six thirty. Heaven help the salesperson who called in the middle of that.

But Gram also was there. For her. When she got trapped in the old orange tree while spying on Morgan and her first boyfriend (she ended up dodging the rotten oranges they chucked at her). When she needed a ride home because her prom date got fresh. When her parents were killed in the car accident. Cami rubbed her elbow that tingled weird at times, another reminder she'd been in the accident too.

Even when she should've grieved the loss of her only daughter, Gram still was there for Cami.

Now Cami was here for her. Which was only right.

But could we get moving? Please? The drive back to Tucson was long. Plus, this was harder than she wanted to admit.

"Kate Hanson was well known to all of us. Her quiet way of helping is legendary in our community. We've lost a dear friend with her passing. In the first two days after receiving the news, congregation members inundated my email with stories of how she had supplied a dinner, cared for a child, given a ride, or sent a card at the perfect time.

"Kate didn't crave the limelight. Instead, she served behind the scenes. I never heard of anyone having to request her help. Rather, she was the one to contact a leader when she learned of —or even suspected—a need."

Gram was special, all right. Cami knew that firsthand. But she had no clue her grandmother was that active in her church. Had she suddenly gotten religion?

She glanced around the room again. Many people attended, dabbing tissues to their eyes. They all seemed quite moved.

Well, Gram never let her skip that sort of training while growing up. Cami had done all the normal things—Sunday School and Children's Church, Youth Group, Mission Trips. All this time, though, she'd figured religious instruction was Gram's way to make her a better person. Guess maybe her grandmother had been more involved than she remembered.

The pastor introduced Morgan to come to the podium. He had suggested Cami speak too, but she declined.

She wasn't about to get all maudlin and fall apart in front of everyone. Besides, if she steeled herself to stay stoic, they'd know she was the horrible, ungrateful, snooty granddaughter Morgie claimed she was. No way to win.

"Thank you all for coming. I'd like to give you a little background on my grandmother, Katheryn Amelia Cummings Hanson. She was born—"

My grandmother too, Morgie.

Cami knew the stats. Born in 1949, she was a Baby Boomer. An early one. She embodied the can-do spirit. Through her grandmother, Cami developed a love for sixties music, especially the Beatles. "The Fool on the Hill" was her favorite. Not something Morgan was likely to mention.

"—she was preceded in death by her husband of twenty-five years, Andrew Jameson Hanson, and her daughter, Saundra Marie Hanson Madison." Morgan dabbed her eyes with a tissue.

Thanks, Morgie, I so needed that tossed in my face today.

Cami held her breath and counted to ten to hold herself together. Anyone other than her grandmother and she'd have found an excuse to not attend. But this was Gram. She owed her. Besides, Gram was the one who said she must be strong. It'd be a lot easier to be strong elsewhere. This was too reminiscent.

"Most of those who knew my grandmother realized she lived on an annuity from her husband's estate. This allowed her the freedom to help and serve her family and church.

"But most people didn't know Kate Hanson was an accomplished author, writing under a pseudonym. She penned many children's books, including the *Adventures With Stinkerella* series."

What? Who was this woman? Not her Gram? When did she do all this? More important, why did Morgan know this and she didn't?

"Gram was also a skilled craftsperson, excelling in crocheted items. She taught not only her daughter, but her son, her granddaughters, and her great grandchildren. My twins, Aidan and Addie, received lessons from her with single and double crochet stitches." She held up little granny squares to oohs and ahhs.

Cami remembered her own squares. Her mother had been there then too. She'd sat between Gram and Mom while they taught, guiding her into making her first. The memory brought a touch of moisture to her eyes, but she blinked before anyone noticed. She would not cry.

The sound of sniffing drew her attention. She glanced along the pew.

A tear scrolled down Addie's cheek.

Cami spotted a box of tissues poking out from under the seats and plucked one for the girl. She was only seven. Too young to understand that the world chewed and spewed the weak. Cami passed the tissue.

Addie peeked up with a slight smile. Bet she was having a tough time too.

An old memory prompted, and Cami dug a purple pen from her purse. She showed the child how to color the closed spaces in the letters on the bulletin. Like Mom did for her when she was young. And Gram during those summers.

One more song and the ordeal would mercifully end. Except for the meal. Cami hoped to hide out in the ladies' room during that event. She might check her messages. Chatting with folks was more than she could handle if she were to keep her composure. And she would keep her composure. Be strong for Gram.

A lengthy list of texts waited, she knew, but she'd still turned her phone off for this hour, even though shutting it down for updates made her as nervous as a salesperson without a voice.

The music leader led them in "Great is Thy Faithfulness," followed by an announcement inviting everyone to stay for a meal in the fellowship hall, and as a courtesy to allow the family to arrive first. That meant Morgan would know where she was, making it harder to sneak away. Cami sighed. Would her cousin insist on a receiving line? Just to be perfectly proper?

Cami followed Aidan and Addie, who followed their mom. It was the four of them now. She barely knew the kids who glanced back messages stating that fact. She read it in their eyes —who was this person? Perhaps if she and Morgan got on better, the twins wouldn't be such strangers.

Once Cami arrived at the fellowship hall, she started her circular path toward the ladies' room, crossing her fingers that Morgan didn't notice she'd disappeared inside its porcelain fortress.

It would be like Morgie to drag her into a conversation with some long-lost-twice-removed-fourth-cousin named Elmer.

She peeked over her shoulder as she grabbed the door pull.

Morgan headed her way.

Cami raised her index finger, hoping the signal would let her cousin know she needed the moment, and hustled to hibernate in a stall. She pulled out her phone and turned it back on. Just as she thought. Sixteen texts alone from Ray, her boss. She scrolled through before answering any. A new merger between the literary world and the movie industry that appeared to be a career maker called her name.

Literally, Ray was calling her. At that moment.

She answered.

"When can you get here?" No greeting or solicitudes.

Cami blew out a breath. "Give me a few hours. We just finished the service and moved to the dinner."

"Can you make it less?" Ray never allowed sentiment to waylay work.

"Travel will take two hours, at least. If the I-10 is clear. Once I'm out of the city, it should be fine."

He sighed. "If that's your best."

"Ray, it's not like I'm across town. I'm in Phoenix. I can't move Tucson any closer. And it's my grandmother's funeral, you jaded soul."

"Fine. But get here. I want my top person ready. This'll put Chukshon Advertising at a rarified air level of prestige. We've got to land this account." Not waiting for her answer, he just disconnected, expecting she'd climb every obstacle to be at his beck and call.

Yeah, he knew her too well. The problem was, he didn't know Morgan.

Cami slipped out of the restroom, scanning the room for her cousin.

Morgan stood chatting with the pastor while her kids sat at the nearby table picking at their tacos and enchilada casserole.

Good ol' after-funeral fare, prepared by the ladies of the congregation.

Mexican food was Gram's favorite.

No one tried to stop her to deliver their deepest condolences. Cami didn't know whether to feel relieved or insulted. Maybe no one recognized her, but it made getting to Morgan that much easier. "Excuse me, reverend. Morgan. Sorry, I've got to go. I realize I'm dumping this all on you, but Ray called."

Morgan's hand went to her hip and she shook her head. "Your boss? He can't even give you time to…Oh, what's the difference. You'd prefer to be gone, anyway. Just leave. But be here Monday. We're meeting with the lawyer and we must decide about Gram's cremains."

"I'll do my best. Again, sorry." She glanced at the kids who stared. "Gotta go." With a sigh, she faced the door.

"Do better than your best, Cam. Be here."

She exhaled blowing her bangs off her forehead and waved without looking back. Her exit was in sight, she dare not chance a retort slowing her down. She was outta here.

Kate

Fifteen years ago

Kate Hanson put the last item into the plastic drawstring bag. They'd done everything to make this hospital room homey and bright, but now they would leave. "I got it all, Cams."

Cami's eyes were bigger than normal, scanning the naked room, free of the get-well cards and posters. Even the gigantic window where the nurses let Kate paint fun cartoons gleamed scrubbed clean. "I'm not sure I'm ready, Gram."

"What's the problem, kiddo?" As if Kate didn't already stare down that beaten path where this conversation headed.

She'd worried herself about this day for several weeks and couldn't blame the child for being afraid.

"I don't want to ride in a car."

"I get that. It's a natural response. But you can't stay here. We've got to move you to my house in Phoenix. I'll be extra careful. We're not in a rush. We can do this."

Cami shook her head, the crocheted cap covering her starting to sprout hair flopping with the movement. "I know you'll watch out, but others won't, Gram. We shouldn't take the chance."

"So how are we to get home?" If she thought this through logically, she'd understand.

Cami sighed. "Um, why not live here in Tucson? You could buy a house close by, and we can walk."

Her thirteen-year-old granddaughter's logic produced something other than the right answer. "Well, that'd require me to sell my home, pack up, find one here in my budget, and hope that the sale goes through fast. And fast would mean in a month.

Normal would be longer. You don't have a month or even a week. They're kicking you out today."

"Can't you talk to them?" Now her eyes pleaded.

"Sweetie, they've got their rules and orders. Higher ups on administrative teams, along with insurance companies, are involved. Those in power get to decide. They gotta ensure their company has a profit, so everyone gets paid. No one'll ever agree with all their decisions, but someone's gotta make them. They look at what's most important."

"Most important to them. They've never been in a car crash like me."

Kate's heart broke. The trauma, though Cami still couldn't remember the event, fueled the fear that tinted her every word. Even in her sleep, the child cried out, often waking herself.

Kate spent the past six weeks at her side, sleeping in the convertible chair, and grabbing meals from the cafeteria and snack machines. She'd put on weight, her clothes told her that. But what's an extra pound or ten when her granddaughter appeared mummified with casts and gauze. Two broken legs, a crushed pelvis, a broken wrist, and traumatic brain injury. Thank God she lived.

The only person to emerge alive from that crushed vehicle.

She shook her head. Not the moment for memories of what she'd lost. "Sweet girl, it is time to be strong. You've already shown you are stronger than you imagined. Look how far you've come. Even tried a step in your PT class. And I have all that transferred to a Phoenix company, so you'll keep progressing. Pretty soon you'll be running." She glanced out the door to the empty hall. "They'll be bringing your wheelchair any minute."

"Gram, I can't. I can't get into a car." Cami broke into sobs.

She grasped the child's hand. "You can and you will because you are stronger than your fears. You rode in cars your entire life with no problems. People go their entire lives without an accident. It is more common to arrive at your destination than to have a crash. You tell yourself that. Remind yourself of the favorable statistics. We're going to make it. Together. We'll be fine. And once we're on the road, I'll introduce you to the best music ever written. We'll sing songs all the way home. This'll work, honey, I promise."

"But Gram—"

"No buts. I understand you're afraid. I would be too. But you'll be fine. You are stronger than your fear. You are. Keep telling yourself that until we get into the car." She kissed the crocheted cap atop her granddaughter's head.

Cami glanced her way, and then at her sheets, which were as white as her face.

Kate heard the mumblings as the child picked at her bedding.

"A little louder, hon. You want to scare your fear away."

"I am stronger than my fear. I am stronger than my fear." She sat a little taller. "I am stronger than my fear. I am stronger than my fear."

"Good girl. Keep going. I'll find out about that wheelchair." Kate stepped into the hall and spotted a nurse at the desk where she gave a brief explanation about her granddaughter's aversion to leaving.

Nurse Arlene checked on the wheelchair's ETA and shared that she'd seen this scenario before. With a sympathetic pat, she headed for Cami's room, Kate close behind.

"Got to tell you, I'm set to wave goodbye. You might be a sweet kid, but as a patient, I've seen you a little too much. It's time you hit the bricks, Cam." The nurse smiled and winked at Kate.

"You're sure I'm ready?"

"Abso-tively-lutely. You're healing so fast. It won't be long before you'll be running and jumping all over the place. You want to stop and say hi when visiting someone? Fine, but no more being a patient. You've used up all your points." She glanced out the door. "And your chariot awaits, princess. We'll get you into your chair and roll you out." Both the nurse and the aide worked to settle her in the wheelchair. Nurse Arlene rolled her out into the hall.

Kate walked alongside.

Cami reached for her hand and clung to it.

She squeezed some encouragement to the girl. "I need to bring the car around. Let me hurry ahead. I'll meet you at the door."

Cami held tight a moment longer. Then with a sigh, she released her hand. "Okay."

Kate's vehicle had remained parked here since the day she'd gotten the call and raced south to Tucson. Six weeks ago. Did she even remember where she parked? Would it start?

Her little Nissan Sentra turned over without a fuss. One thing going right. She drove to the entrance and pulled up where Alene waited next to Cami. This would be the hardest part. Once inside the vehicle, Kate would be able to help her, soothe her, comfort her. But until the child climbed in, she'd run out of options.

Leaving the car in park, Kate hurried around to toss the bags in the trunk while the nurse assisted Cami into the passenger seat and buckled her seatbelt. One last hug with Arlene, the no-nonsense yet compassionate professional who cared for them both, and Kate climbed back in the driver's seat.

Cami didn't even look up. Her eyes were closed, and she mumbled, "I am stronger than my fear. I am stronger than my fear."

Kate pulled out of the parking lot and punched the CD button. George Harrison's voice filled the Sentra with "Here Comes the Sun" from her *Abbey Road* album.

Cami glanced up. "What's that?"

"That, my dear, is the quiet Beatle showing he's not as quiet as everyone painted him to be. He's talented, thoughtful. Not my all-time favorite of his, but I do like it a lot, and *Abbey Road* is my favorite Beatle album. Have you listened to much Beatle music?"

Cami shook her head. "I might've read about them, maybe. I kind of like it."

"Shows you have excellent taste. They changed the face of rock-and-roll when their music came out. They're from England, and when American radio stations started playing their songs, along with those from other artists from over in the UK, they called it the British Invasion. The Beatles led it. They were only a group until 1970, but you can still find their music." She turned up the volume a notch.

Cami leaned her head against the seat, closing her eyes again. "I like this song, Gram."

"Good, I have most of their albums on CD, so we'll play all we can. Kick back and listen."

Cami did just that. For the next two hours.

Cami

Present day

Cami started the engine and plugged her iPod in to her speakers. Between the Beatles *Sgt Pepper's Lonely Hearts Club Band* and her phone showing her WAZE, she should be able to navigate this trip. Though she'd made this drive on several occasions, tingles still pinged in her belly every time. "I'm stronger than my fear."

If she kept the music going, she might not relive all the memories. Better idea to concentrate on the info Ray texted about the new client. This would be a test of sorts. If they came through this, they'd be tapped to provide the ads for all the rest of the projects this merger produced. From what she could tell, the first target would be something for the tween audience and *J-14 Magazine*'s heart-throb Liam Holsted.

Cami considered how to spin press releases and kits. Wholesome to the parent eye yet inviting to the teenaged girls who'd be begging moms and dads to spend cash on all the soon-to-be collectibles. She could see *Antiques Roadshow* in thirty years when someone brought in a treasured whatchamacallit. That made her chuckle.

By the time she'd pulled into the lot at Chukshon she'd come up with a list of ten fresh pitch ideas and only needed Ray to point her in the right direction to learn which to develop.

Though a Saturday, the door stood unlocked. She flashed her ID at the security guard and headed for the elevator. When the doors opened on the fifth floor, Ray paced the hall. "About time you got here."

"I realize you spawned from under a rock somewhere this side of Albuquerque, but even your rock would have the good grace to recognize the importance of a funeral."

He stopped pacing. "Yeah, sorry. But you don't enjoy that stuff anymore than I do. And I know you'd rather work than get pulled down into that feely rabbit's hole of muck. Consider this grief therapy. And you are welcome. Come into my office. I'll lay things out for you."

He only got away with saying that because it was true, and he'd known her since her intern days while at U of A. They'd toyed with dating for a brief second, recognizing a shared aversion to emotions, but Ray became her boss and her friend. If either of them possessed the capacity to be a decent friend.

An hour later, she'd uncovered only a bit more information.

The client never revealed what book they'd chosen for the silver screen, only hinted at "legendary."

Were any big fantasy or anime books ready for this step? The Marvel franchise still ran strong. Might they springboard from that?

She left Ray with a list of questions for the client, and stuffed a to-do list of her own into her planner.

Arriving at her condo, she poured an iced tea and pulled out her laptop.

She planned to brainstorm and flesh out ideas to pitch to

Ray on Monday while researching the publishing house's properties.

However, after narrowing her search on Amazon to middle school audiences, still pages of possibilities stared back.

Yet, that's not the first thing that jumped out, setting her pulse to pounding.

The number one bestseller, right up at the top of the page? *Adventures With Stinkerella: Book Nine: The Chat* by Amelia K. Sonhan. She'd found her grandmother as clear as day. Sonhan, Hanson. Amelia K., Katheryn A. Why hadn't Cami known?

She pulled up all the books, one through nine, and looked at the date of publication. Gram wrote for more than a decade.

Ten years ago, Cami still lived with Gram. Technically. On breaks and summer vacations. When had Gram started writing? Did she sell at once? Wouldn't she need an agent? Did the agent attend her service? Did Cami shake hands with him or her, never knowing the person?

Did that person know about her?

Cami had heard of the books. Hard not to when the ad campaigns popped up everywhere, and ads were her business. But, since they focused on the younger reader, Cami saw no reason to crack one open or download it either. She did now, though, and went to Amazon to get all nine onto her Kindle. The rest of the weekend she inhaled the words of a voice so familiar, so comforting. She'd lain awake until the wee hours to finish book three *The Code*.

These books were fun, insightful, and filled with enough clean adult humor that they could grow with a child. Gram was brilliant. More than once Cami ran across advice she should have heeded when the author's lips spoke those same words to her. That brought a chuckle.

What made her tear up, though, came when she spotted the dedication at the front of book one. *For my own Stinkerella and namesake.*

They named Cami for Gram. Katheryn Amelia. But rather

than have two Katies, her parents spelled Catherine with a C, and took her initials C. A. M., added an I at the end to come up with Cami. Though it didn't read *Cami* in the comment, she understood.

"I'm sorry, Gram. I never knew."

Sunday she made a cup of coffee, and started in on book four. By bedtime she'd inhaled the complete series. It might upset Ray that she didn't do more research, but Cami grew more at peace, as if she'd spent the weekend with Gram receiving one more hug and a lot more practical advice.

Monday she worked at the office prepping for a meeting with Ray when her phone buzzed. Morgan. Though tempted to send it to voice mail, she decided to get it over with. "Hey."

"Are you close? I'm in the parking lot. Thought we'd better talk before we go in."

In? Oh, no. The lawyer meeting. "I'm sorry, I got caught up in work. Can we make it a teleconference? I've got Zoom; I can start the meeting."

"I knew you'd do this. Never could count on you for anything. Well, just so you know, Gram made me the executor. Guess she recognized you'd flake on things."

Cami wanted to reach through the phone and rip out Morgan's photo-shoot perfect hair. "That's not fair."

"What? That Gram put me in charge, or that I stated the truth?"

Both, to be honest. "I don't care that you're in charge."

"Right. You never have cared about our family."

"I care, Morgan, though you don't make it easy. But if all we'll do is argue right now, we won't get to the important stuff. Tell me what you want to discuss before the meeting. What email address do I need from the lawyer to invite you all to the Zoom room?"

After a sigh, Morgan gave her the email address. "I just wanted you to understand that I'm executrix, but also that Gram added a strange bequest for you. You'll hear about it from the lawyer, at least part of it. I intend to follow Gram's wishes to the letter. You need to know that."

"I wouldn't expect anything less of you, Morgan. Tell me when you are at the office, and I'll send the invite to get the meeting set up."

"Fine. I'm there." *Click.*

Cami pulled up her Zoom account, set up the session, and invited the lawyer. She started to add Morgan but figured the feedback with them both in the same office might be too much, so she texted Morgan to keep her in the loop.

A couple minutes later she added William Jones, Esq. to her chat room.

"Ms. Madison, I'm sorry we aren't able to do this in person. Rather than read through the complete document, I'll cover the part unique to you. We should discuss this.

"Your grandmother remained adamant that things be handled in this manner. She bequeathed a package to you. Inside it are instructions for what you must do on a precise timeline. If you perform it to the letter, you'll receive your inheritance. I'm not at liberty to tell you more regarding that inheritance, only that if you do not accept the package and accomplish the task in the allotted time, you will give up your bequest. It will all go elsewhere. I cannot share with you where, either. Do you wish to accept the package and task?"

Gram, what possessed you? What did this task entail? Would she have time?

She envisioned Morgan with that smug Cami's-too-flaky-to-do-what-Gram-asked expression on her Dresden-doll-perfect made-up face.

She'd love to chuck a rotten orange at it. "Yes, I'll accept Gram's package and task. I loved my grandmother, and if she wanted me to do something, I'll do it."

A commotion started off-view. "Excuse me, Ms. Madison." Mr. Jones left the screen, but Cami could hear Morgan having a coughing fit, and the lawyer offering her a drink of water.

He returned. "Very well, Ms. Madison. I'll send the box. Will you take delivery at home or your office?"

"I'll be here late, so work is fine. What about a copy of the will?"

"You'll receive that upon completion or failure of the task. I'm to hold on to it and not file for probate until after you've finished the assignment. Once you've read the enclosed instructions, contact me with any questions. I want to add, aside from being my client, I considered your grandmother my friend. And I knew your parents. Please accept my sincerest condolences."

Cami's throat constricted. She reached for her water bottle and swiped a sip before responding. "Thank you Mr. Jones. I'll be in touch." She closed the meeting before he could add more.

Chapter Two

MORGAN

Present day

Morgan sipped more water and heard Cami's abrupt sign off. "Just like her. So sorry. I apologize for her rude behavior."

"Mrs. Pembroke, I took no offense. But I'm concerned for you. Are you better?" The lawyer stood behind his desk.

She set the glass on the floor next to her and nodded. "Much. Thank you. Mr. Jones, might I get a copy of the will?"

He cleared his throat. "I'm not at liberty to file it in probate court as a public record until Ms. Madison has either fulfilled or failed at the task."

"You mean that no one receives their inheritance until she gives in?"

Now he stared at her as if she'd grown another eye in the middle of her forehead. "Your grandmother was quite clear. She had faith that your cousin would come through."

"Of course she did. She always did, every time that little namesake flaked off leaving Gram to handle her mess." She shook her head at the absurdity. "But I don't understand why we all must wait. Mightn't we receive our share? The part that matches what it would be if she completes the task, and then, when, er, *if* she fails, you can disperse the rest?" A memory of what arrived in Friday's mail shot through her mind. She'd counted on today for help.

"I'm sorry. Once I'm allowed to file it, you'll have a copy and can handle your grandmother's affairs. She hasn't any outstanding debts, so no creditors are waiting. She made sure of that. If you have another question?" He glanced at his calendar, and she knew this was over.

But Morgan tried one more idea. "What if I took out a loan? I'd use the projected amount as collateral. Would you give me a round figure?"

He shook his head. "It sounds as if you need the money, but I'm—"

"I know, not at liberty to say. Thank you for your time, Mr. Jones. Oh, how long does Cami have to accomplish her task?"

"Two months from today."

Morgan groaned. She popped her hand to her mouth, her eyes wide. Now he'd be sure she was a mercenary. Two months? She needed the cash sooner.

"My secretary will see you out." He swiveled in his chair with a focus on his printer, aptly turning his back on her.

She glanced up at the forty-something administrative assistant with the reading glasses perched in her gray-less brunette pageboy, and wanted to slide under the desk. "Thank you, again." Purse strap over her shoulder, she stood, straightened her spine, and exited through the outer office to the hall.

There must be a restroom close.

Morgan spotted a You-Are-Here map on the wall by the elevator and located the ladies' room before making a mad dash.

The cramping in her gut almost kept her from arriving on time, but she did. Afterward, all the blood ran from her face, leaving her in a cold sweat. She wet a paper towel and dabbed the tepid water on her forehead, cheeks, and neck. Then she opened the towel, fanning it in the air to cool the moisture before resuming her dabbing. This was the reason she skipped breakfast. Still, she ended up in here.

The entrance to the facilities sported a waiting lounge where she might sit a moment. Good thing because her legs wouldn't hold her much longer. She plopped on a couch and pulled out her phone to check the time. Ten thirty. Her next appointment wasn't until twelve-thirty. Not knowing how long this one would take, she'd scheduled it to allow her to arrive without a rush. But now she possessed time more than she needed. Dare she get a bite to eat? Dare she even leave this room? With her luck, she'd make it to the elevator and pass out before it hit the first floor. How would that play on the evening news?

She sighed and dabbed. This was becoming a nuisance, besides a problem. She had little warning before things took a turn. The blood tests so far remained inconclusive. She needed answers.

That image spurred her on to try for her car. Once in there, she could crank the air conditioning down. The cold would help. Though a tad wobbly, she made it, started her engine, and put the AC at the coldest setting with all the vents aimed straight at her.

When she'd called Cami from here less than an hour ago, she expected her to back out of the challenge. Whatever pulled her away from her precious job and beloved Tucson got passed over. Why today? Why did she have to decide to honor Gram's wishes today?

Cami wasn't the only one left alone. Morgan's parents might be alive, but they weren't there to support her. With Mom on her third marriage traveling who knows where, and her dad embedded with the Marines in the Middle East, neither were available for her when she needed them.

Nor was her worthless ex.

There wasn't a single person on the planet she could count on now that Gram was gone.

The loneliness choked her as a sob rose in her throat. She

pulled a tissue from her purse, wiped her face, and gritted her teeth. She'd make it through, one way or another.

Her kids still needed her.

With a deep breath, she shoved the gearstick into reverse, backed from the space, and then headed out into traffic. The downtown area of Phoenix boasted amazing restaurants, but she required something with a drive-through so she didn't have to risk getting out of the car until she got to the next appointment. She settled on a cold chai horchata from Dutch Bros, hoping the line was as long as usual to eat some of her spare time. The line was. But those baristas were energetic. At least, now she held a cold drink to sip.

That killed a few minutes, but she knew she'd still be plenty early. Well, if she got sick at the appointment, that would give them more information. Ha!

The drive to the out-patient offices at John C. Lincoln Hospital wasn't bad. Of course. She'd hoped for traffic to consume more time, but the traffic up Central Avenue proved smooth and efficient. Was there anything she could count on?

And then the fact that Cami did the opposite of what she'd expected, depended on, if she were honest, only set her stomach to roiling. Why could't something today go right? Her nerves and stomach acid made her sicker. Why? She smacked her steering wheel. Why did Cami have to pick today to be noble?

Morgan heard Gram in her head. *You don't understand Cami. She's been through a lot. You've got to give her a break.*

Morgan would love to give her a break all right. Break both her legs. Then she gasped, remembering the visit she made to the hospital after Cami's accident. Her mom flew her in to see Gram and her cousin. But when she got to Cami's room, it horrified her. All the tubes and bandages. That included her two broken legs. "I'm sorry, Gram. I shouldn't have thought that. But why did you write your will so crazy? Put me in charge, but leave me in the dark? I don't understand?" She leaned her head against the steering wheel and pulled herself together. Anger at Cami wouldn't fix anything.

And they still never discussed Gram's cremains.

She locked up her five-year-old Pathfinder and started the trek for the building. Even great parking spaces were a hike from the entrance. So far, though, she held it together. If she kept her anxiety in check, that would be a tremendous help. Focus on pleasant thoughts. Good things.

Like the sweet faces of her twins.

Now they were a blessing. She'd live through that catastrophe of a marriage again just to be their mother. They both did well in school. And were such good kids at home. Not perfect. Heaven save her from a perfect child. She'd spend all her time waiting for the other shoe to drop. But her kidletts? They were perfect for her. Picturing them brought her blood pressure under control and her stomach relaxed.

That was enough to get her into the building and up to the second floor where Dr. Abernathy kept his office with a group of gastroenterologists. A nurse gripped a stack of file folders and bounced the bundle on the counter to straighten them as Morgan opened the door.

"Mrs. Pembroke, you're early."

Morgan smiled. "I've been to other appointments this morning. Perhaps I might wait here? Rather than go home and come back?" She glanced about the half-full waiting room.

The nurse returned the smile. "Of course. Let's get you checked in." She set the folders aside. "Maybe you'll squeeze in ahead of your scheduled appointment. Who knows?'

Morgan winced as her gut made another weird twist. She handed over her insurance card and Visa. A moment later she was at the chairs, filling out the forms. Again. Every time. Couldn't they at least update on an iPad?

She tried to focus, but the sweat prickles started at her scalp. Next came the nausea and dizziness. Morgan set the clipboard on the chair closest to her, closed her eyes, and breathed deep through her nose. Her hands, her arms, her shoulders grew heavy, and her eyelids did too. She felt herself falling.

Then nothing.

Cami

She slipped out of her office for the coffee room. Cami needed to gain control over her emotions before she did something stupid like bursting into tears over a simple remark. "And I knew your parents." Lots of people knew her parents. Nice people with loads of friends. But it was fifteen years ago. Most moved on with their lives, and didn't give Saundra and Kevin Madison another thought.

And if her thoughts kept running in this direction, she'd be back to bursting into tears.

She made herself a cup from the Keurig machine and wandered to her office. Their two o'clock meeting needed her focus. That's where she might gain a glimmer of what this big account entailed. Without knowing which property stood at the heart of the merger, she was limited. But the more ideas she generated, the better prepared she'd be.

A notion teased into her brain, more of a wonder. What if the property was Gram's series? Nah, that wouldn't happen. That only occurred in books and movies.

But what if?

Would she need to recuse herself? Would the client see it as a conflict of interest? Or maybe they'd like the personal touch she could add?

That's just a wild dream. No way it could happen.

She pulled up the client's list of new acquisitions and started through, noting possible campaign ideas for each. By the time she needed to head to the conference suite, she'd filled thirty pages of suggestions, and skipped lunch. Though her stomach growled, she promised to feed it well after the meeting, if it all went as she hoped.

The conference room stood open and she arrived first, setting up her iPad to take notes of what she gleaned. That was her number one lesson. Listen for the important—not only what's verbalized. When you pay attention, you'll discover the client's vision even when they don't see it yet.

Soon Monty Fuller entered. She nodded to him. He'd joined the company in the past month, but she recognized he wanted to move up and fast. Something about the way he kept inserting himself into conversations and tasks told her he'd made plans.

"Hey Cami, how's it going?"

"Good, Monty. You?" She glanced up long enough to acknowledge him and then back to her notes, hoping he took the hint. She could be polite, but it's another thing to listen to his life's story.

"Fine. Wonder who all's coming today?" He grabbed the seat next to her, peeking over her shoulder.

She switched it to desktop. "Ray and the client. Not sure who else."

The door opened.

Ray ushered in three executive types, two men and a woman, and began introductions.

"Vince, Doug, Felicia, this is my team for our project, Cami Madison and Monty Fuller. Cami, Monty, I'd like you to meet Vince Golden, Doug DeLise, and Felicia Meadows."

They shook hands, and the clients sat across the table from Cami and Monty.

Ray chaired the meeting. "I've not given much information to my team as I wanted them to hear it from you. They will catch your vision as you share, you can depend on it. Let's start with that."

The three execs glanced at each other until Felicia began. "First, we appreciate your willingness to keep this under wraps until the big unveiling. If things were normal, we'd need to create a buzz. And in some manner we still want to, but the teasers must only stir excitement, not give away our surprise. We purchased a small publishing firm for the sole purpose of acquiring the rights to this product. It's amazing. My daughter chattered nonstop about the first story. As a parent, I needed to learn what caused all the fuss. Let me tell you, I inhaled that story. The next book wowed even more. And I watched as my daughter's friends started groups. They enjoyed slumber parties with the themes of the books. I checked in with friends on my social media accounts and found they experienced the same thing. This series is a phenomenon. So, I let Vince and Doug know. They checked into it, and we found the pub house was small but choosy and promoted many great authors. If we start with this series, we should have a wealth of materials to someday launch most of the books in their library to the big screen. Our focus will be on YA, we'll serve that niche. We must promote the whole collaborative venture, and kick it off with *Adventures With Stinkerella*."

Cami gasped, and all gazes zeroed in on her. Great, she couldn't just be shocked. No, she must draw attention to it.

"Problem, Cam?" Ray eyed her like the wayward child who needed to toe the line.

She cleared her throat. Did she tell them? "No, it's nothing. Just remembered something I need to discuss after the meeting. I apologize. Please, go on."

Ray gave her another sideways glance as Felicia continued to share their hopes and plans. "I realize this is a tight timetable, but we'd like to do a big reveal in two months. We hope to loop things together with a casting call for the lead character, Stinkerella. We want someone new, fresh to give this a name. Liam Holsted is signed, though he agreed to do it blind. He's not seen a script, and reserved the right to back out if we can't get this set. That's why we've got to be ready then. It's all he'll allow before his people must have the particulars to lock in or reject the project."

Two months didn't allow much time, but the ideas she'd already generated could adapt to this. When Felicia sat, Ray asked for thoughts. Before she could speak, Monty jumped in. "We should hit every kid-centered social media site with teasers. Kids are the key. We get them hooked and they'll beg their parents for whatever."

Cami watched Felicia's eyes narrow and knew Monty chose the wrong track. Should she jump in and save him? Let him flounder or offer her own idea?

Felicia made it easy. "That's not our vision. Any other thoughts?"

Cami opened her notes. "I have a few. The big consideration is that these kids are preteen. Parent input is still important. I've read the series and noted that the author didn't talk down to the readers. In fact, an adult reading the books could enjoy them just as much. So, since the tweens are already on board through school and friends, we target the parents in a way that pulls them into the fun. Make it a family adventure that can bring them closer together, creating those memories that will last beyond the movie or media storm we manufacture. Make it personal to them. Instead of saying 'I remember where I was' when something bad occurred, they'll be saying 'I remember when my family and I did this or that' with the *Stinkerella* movies."

Felicia's gaze told her she'd hit the nail. Square on.

Cami continued to give examples from her notes on how to make this happen, all the while noting Monty's presence. Had she thwarted or embarrassed him? Wasn't her intention. But his stare remained anything but pleasant.

When she finished, Ray took over. "I can see by your faces that Cami's ideas are more what you envisioned."

Vince nodded. "Yes, I knew this must be a fresh approach, and admit I doubted whether it was possible. But Ms. Madison, you've done it." He looked at his colleagues and continued.

"We're in agreement. That's what we want. Can you have some prototypes and slides for us two weeks from today?"

"Yes, yes, we can." Ray rose, shook hands with the clients, then turned to Cami and Monty. "You guys wait here while I walk them out. We'll get this started when I get back." He exited with the execs.

Cami leaned back in the swivel chair and sighed.

"You pulled that out of the fire. Good job."

She stared at Monty. Did he mean that? "Thanks. I only read the signals."

"You did more than that. You guessed what property and read the books beforehand. That's pretty clever."

He sounded like he meant it as a compliment, but something in the way he said "clever" didn't match his demeanor.

Ray entered again. "Okay, kids, let's get busy. Cami, you'll take the lead on this. They love you, and you've got the proper feel for the project. Monty, you be her right hand. She has the ultimate word, but two heads are better than one. Oh, Cami, you got something you need to tell me?"

She glanced from him to Monty. Since they'd work together, he might as well be told. "Amelia K. Sonhan is my grandmother."

Ray's eyes got big. "You mean the one who just croaked?"

That stiffened her backbone. "Yes, Ray, that one. She used a pseudonym."

"So you've a conflict?" In character, Monty looked for a loophole.

"I can't think of one. I didn't even know she wrote until her service. Then when I saw the name with the clients' list, I figured it out. The dedication in the first book is to me, but she doesn't mention me by name. There isn't a money link at all, as far as I know."

Ray squinted. "As far as you know?"

"The will is waiting for me to complete some project. No idea what it is yet. When that's done, everyone gets their inheritance. Haven't a clue how she's set it up or any more information other than what I've said. Please do not share about my grandmother with anyone, I only brought it up because of this deal." That she needed to keep private.

"What about the client? Don't they have a right to know?" Monty's eagerness spilled.

Ray shook his head. "No. At this point we've no conflict of interest and they love you. If you were working to pay yourself, then maybe. But no. Plus, this connection should give you insights that no one else has. We're good." He dismissed them with a flick of his hand. "Go be brilliant."

Monty followed her to her office. "Want to start brainstorming?"

"What I want is lunch. I skipped to prepare. Give me an hour?"

He nodded and took off toward his lair.

"Hey, Cams, this arrived for you." The office manager, Lisa, ambled toward her carrying a large box.

"Let me help." Cami tried to take it.

"It's not heavy. Just open your door, and I'll put it on your desk." Lisa did, leaving without a hint of curiosity.

However, Cami couldn't make the same claim. Her inquisitiveness clamored for attention. This was from Gram. The task the lawyer and Morgan told her about. At the same time, she knew deep down she needed privacy. Was this her last gift from Gram? For sure it would be if she didn't complete the job. As much as she longed to know what lay inside, she didn't want to open it for fear of what her emotions would do.

"I'm stronger than my fear." She closed the door and grabbed a box cutter.

Just as she found the courage to put blade to tape, a knock sounded. Ray peeked around the door. "Busy?"

She set the tool on her desk and motioned him in. "What do you need?"

"Wanted to remind you to keep Monty in the loop. The only

way that kid'll learn is if he sees things done right. Let him pick your brain, and consider some of his ideas, but I trust you to choose what's best. He's got potential."

She plopped in her chair. Kid? Monty was at least twenty-three, and had his college degree behind him. When did Ray start acting so ancient? "Yeah, I get that. But…"

"But what?"

Cami shrugged. "I don't know. More of a feeling than anything. He irritates me. No worries, I can work with him."

"I know you can. What's in the box?" Ray approached, gliding a hand over a corner.

"This is supposed to be the project I must complete to receive my inheritance."

"So open it, let's see." His eyes grew and he rubbed his hands together.

She shook her head. "No. I'll wait. This is a private thing between my grandmother and me."

Ray's expression fell like he'd waited in a free ice cream line only to have them run out when he reached the window. "Oh, yeah, okay. Well, keep me posted." He turned at the entrance. "Any problems, let me know." With a brief tap on the jamb, he pulled the door closed behind.

She was alone again. Her finger drifted along the handle of the box cutter. Should she take a chance and open the silly thing? She could lock her door. But what if the contents called up… things… and she fell apart? Two weeks ago she would've better controlled her feelings. But ever since she got the call, her emotions turned rogue, like they were on steroids, and every bit of logic and mental acuity she pushed in front of them never seemed to hold back the onslaught.

After returning the box cutter to her desk, she set the light-weight package on the floor, and pulled up her notes from the meeting.

She needed a to-do spread sheet, so she organized columns

of tasks, and broke them into smaller pieces, color coding according to the timeline and priority/necessity.

That helped and only took forty-five minutes.

She emailed the spreadsheet to both Ray and Monty, knowing the latter would arrive before long.

And she still needed a bite to eat.

At least the building housed a cafeteria on the first floor. She hustled down, picked up a BLTA on white with a bag of chips and a Diet Coke, and returned to her office to munch while continuing to work. She opened the door to find Monty in her office, shaking her project.

"What are you doing?"

He set the box on the floor, not even having the decency to look embarrassed at being caught. "Oh, just curious about what you might have in there. Ready?"

"That's private property, mister. You will not enter my office when I'm gone, and you'll definitely keep your hands off my stuff. Have I made myself clear?"

Now he looked chagrined. A tiny bit. At least he stared at the floor like the bad boy in class. "Yes, ma'am. It won't happen again. Sorry."

Cami exhaled. "No harm done, I guess. Go sit at the table, and I'll bring my notes. We'll get started."

By four-thirty they'd produced a skeleton of a plan with steps A, B, and C to present. Now to flesh out the steps. The majority of her two weeks would be spent doing that. Then they'd need to build the slides for the presentation, and develop the prototypes to show for approval. The timeline was tight, but do-able.

Cami sighed as she packed up for home. With her purse strap over her shoulder, and her rolling pull-bag of technology and files ready to go, she stooped to pick up the box. Though large, about two foot high, wide, and deep, the package was light enough for one hand. The problem was getting it up onto one arm. She settled that by putting aside her purse and bag, and setting the box back on the desk. Then she reloaded, adjusted by holding the bag handle on the side with her purse, before swiping the box with her free hand. Now to get the door.

She had to let go of the bag handle to open the door and lock up, push the elevator button, and dig out her keys. But she got the box into her trunk with her bag, and collapsed into the driver's seat. She could've made two trips, but this lazy man's load was victory and she'd savor. Score one point for an independent nature.

Or she might've set the box on her rolling tech bag and pulled. She slapped her forehead.

Once home, she refused to suffer through that again. She took in her bag and purse, changed into comfy clothes, and then returned to the trunk for the box, setting it in the middle of her living room floor before retrieving her scissors. She knelt in front.

"Alexa, play *Abbey Road*." That would set the right tone.

After running the scissor blade through the tape, she inhaled, and pulled the flaps up. For a moment she could smell Gram's perfume. *Dawn* by Sarah Jessica Parker. Cami bought that first small bottle back when she was a senior at U of A, counting every penny. But it was for Gram's birthday. Who knew it would become her signature fragrance? She closed her eyes inhaling again, while tears burned from the memories. With a sigh, she pushed the thoughts aside and perused the box. Beneath a swaddling of bubble wrap, she found her project. Yarn. Six skeins. Plus, something already started, wrapped in tissue. And an envelope.

She drew that out, and removed the pages. A note in Gram's handwriting. Tears pushed free.

My sweet Cami,

You have worked so hard to claim your place, never relinquishing control of anything. I knew I could demand you complete the task, but that would only create resentment. I'm too tired for battles anymore. So I make this request. Finish this prayer shawl. I include the instructions behind the letter. When complete, find someone who needs prayer, who is going through a tough time, and give the shawl to her, or him (guess it could be a him). If you can do this within two months of taking possession of the box, you'll receive your inheritance. If you choose not to do this, I still love you, but there'll be no inheritance for you. Or anyone else. All proceeds will go to charity. I've informed Mr. Jones of which one.

Please understand I'm not doing this to be mean. You must release what you've carried inside for so long. I needed you to be strong, and you needed you to be strong to start over when you were thirteen, but now you are an adult. You know you are stronger than your fear. Stop trying to control everything and let love in. Sometimes strength is overrated.

I love you, and prayed for you while I made the first few rows. Start on row ten of the pattern. This is easy and I know you can do it.

One last thing, please be kind to Morgan. She needs you in her life, whether or not she realizes it. Don't let her push you away. This is one place where you can remain strong.

I wish I could hug you. I see your face and hear your exclamations in my head. Cami, love, it can be the best thing that ever happened to you. If you pick up the challenge. But if you walk away, I still love you.

Gram

Cami started the letter over again. She must have read wrong. Something. Gram couldn't put all this on her shoulders. It was one thing for her not to get her inheritance because of her choices. She lived with her choices every day. But no one received their inheritance? And, with this acquisition, the inheritance will be big. Big? Massive was more like it.

She pulled out the instructions and glanced through. The vocabulary of doubles, clusters, chains, and slip stitches were familiar but to try and remember how to do it all was scary considering what lay in the balance. *Gram, what were you thinking?* She scanned the letter once more, and the time frame jumped out at her.

Two months.

She had two months from today to relearn how to crochet and make the shawl.

If she remembered how, and wasn't under deadline at work, she might whip it out in a couple weekends.

At this point she needed to hire someone to get her groceries, do her laundry, and clean her condo.

She had no time for even basic necessities.

Hire.

That's an idea. What if she hired someone to finish the shawl for her? Everything would get done, and no one would be out their inheritance. She read the letter once more to check for a clause to prevent her from doing that. Nowhere did it state she couldn't. Okay. Where to find a person who crochets?

"Alexa, find me a crochet group."

Chapter Three

MORGAN

Present Day

Her eyes burned, hushed voices assailed her ears. Morgan raised her hand to rub her face and found she was under a sheet, or at least her torso and limbs were. Blinking against the lights, she focused on huddled figures turned away from her, and cleared her throat. "Excuse me, may I have a sip of water?"

"Good. You're awake. Of course, Mrs. Pembroke." A nurse stood at her side with a small bottle. She raised Morgan's head to be able to drink without spilling down the front of herself.

Water never tasted so good. She could've chugged the entire bottle, but she paused. No need to appear crude. She was embarrassed enough, her pulse pounding in her throat. "What happened?"

Doctor Abernathy picked up her wrist and gazed at his watch. "You passed out in the waiting room. I guess that's one way to jump to the head of the list." He winked, though his words stung as if she'd planned this whole debacle.

"I'm sorry if I caused a scene."

"You didn't. We're glad you were here when this happened so we can help you." The nurse understood. "How are you feeling?"

How did she feel? "Humiliated, stupid, mortified. Take your pick."

The doctor shook his head. "Don't worry about that. Physically. Are you having pain?"

Morgan did an internal scan of her body.

Nothing caused her discomfort other than her throbbing head. And she couldn't decide if that was emotional or physical.

"Only a headache."

He swiped his otoscope and peered into her eyes. The light added to the throbbing. "Need to rule out whether you hit your head as you landed. Where does it hurt?"

"The top of my skull, over my ears."

He cupped the back of her neck, searching from her hairline to her shoulders for anomalies. She wanted to rest her head in his cool touch, but that idea brought heat to her face. "Tight here. That's tension. Are you having a lot of stress?"

"Besides not knowing what's going on with my body, my grandmother dying, and being a single parent? No, not much." She regretted her sarcasm, but the bitterness broke her boundary.

He paused and gave her full attention. "That's a load to carry. I'd be surprised if you didn't have a tension headache. But it isn't related to your other health problem. We need to schedule some deeper testing. How do you respond to MRIs?"

She shrugged. "I've never experienced one."

"Do you get claustrophobic?"

The notion made her head pound harder. "Um, some."

"My wife's the same way. I've learned to ask. I'll give you a mild sedative before you go in. You won't sleep, but you'll relax." He pulled out a prescription pad, wrote, and then clipped it on her chart.

Something stirred in Morgan's brain. "Can I drive myself?"

He shook his head. "No, you'll need someone. Your reaction time will be like that of a drunk."

Great. Who could she ask? "What do you think you'll find,

or hope you don't find with this test?" She brushed stray strands from her face.

"I don't know. Something is going on. It could be your gall bladder. It could be a lot of things. We won't know until we look."

Gall bladder? That would mean surgery. But it could be outpatient. That would be better than other possibilities. But any surgery was risky. Dangerous. Scary. What would she tell the kids? What would she do with them?

"I see you're concerned. One step at a time. First the test. Find someone who'll be your ride. I don't recommend Uber or Lyft this time. You won't be in any condition for that service when you leave. A trusted friend or relative would work." He put out his hand. "You rest here a bit longer. Dottie'll check back to make sure you're safe to take off." Turning to the nurse. "Check her BP every fifteen minutes. When she can stand while you take it, she's good to go."

Nurse Dottie nodded and received the chart from Dr. Abernathy as he exited. "You'll be fine. It's just a precaution. Let's see how you're doing at the moment."

Her blood pressure was still a mite low when she sat, so Dottie helped her lay back. "I'll bring you some juice and crackers. Bet that's all you need."

Morgan tried to smile—didn't know if she succeeded—and closed her eyes. Another fine mess. How soon would the test be scheduled? She should've asked that. Would she need to schedule it herself, or would they call with the appointment? She couldn't ask for help until they gave her the information. How did life become this hard?

Dottie returned with the promised juice and crackers, and the prescription the doctor wrote. "We've called it in, so you are set."

"Must I set up the MRI or will he?"

"Doctor will, his office manager is already working on it. He wants you in as soon as possible." She straightened the counter as she spoke.

"Then he's worried."

Dottie shook her head. "He doesn't worry. He's cautious. Rather than let something get worse, he takes care of it before it becomes a concern." She patted Morgan's hand, and her unspoken "don't worry" came through clear. "I'll be back in about fifteen minutes, and we'll try your blood pressure again."

"What if it stays low?" Morgan needed to pick the kids up from school in a few hours.

"I don't see that happening. Your color is getting better already. Finish your snack and I'll be right back." Dottie exited before more questions slowed her down.

And Morgan would come up with more questions. She just needed to craft them. With a sigh, she opened the little package. Ritz crackers and cheese. At least they weren't peanut butter. She wasn't crazy about those. A twist and the tiny sandwich was in two parts. She licked the cheese away and reassembled the cracker pair before taking a bite. Who could she call? It'd be better having two people. Just in case. If the test ran long or got scheduled late, someone would need to get Addie and Aidan. What if she was too loopy to be alone with her kids? How loopy would the medication make her? Might she handle the MRI without the sedative? Should she try? If she didn't take it, and the procedure was in the morning, she would be fine. Right? No need for outside help since she could still drive herself.

What if they found something horrible, and wouldn't let her leave, and she got sent straight to the operating room?

Now she was just scaring herself.

But it might bring her blood pressure up to where it should be.

About the time Morgan had played out every likely scenario with the outcome figured, Dottie returned to take her blood pressure. Prone and sitting BP numbers were good. If the standing check worked, she could be on her way with the promise of going straight home.

The nurse made her stand away from anything she could lean on or reach. Hands at her sides, she focused on the tiny crack in the plaster coming down from the ceiling over the door. It was tiny, insignificant. And the building was older, despite the recent upgrades. It reminded her of herself. Upgraded to single parenting. Older, some tiny, insignificant lines she tried to cover with makeup and better breeding. One more marker to note she was aging. Not where she'd wanted her musings to run.

"You're good to go, Mrs. Pembroke. Here's your printout concerning the MRI. It directs you where to be, at what time, and when to take your medication." She handed Morgan a sheet of computer paper. "You got everything?"

Morgan slipped her purse strap over her shoulder and glanced about the room. "I think so. Thank you again. I'm sorry to have been a bother."

"No bother. We're here for you. You can head out this way." Dottie guided her to the exit sign. "Follow that hall."

Morgan nodded and waved as she went through the door. Let her make it to grab the kids and get home, that's all she asked.

Once at her car, she checked the time on her phone. She still had a couple hours before school dismissed. Perhaps she should head to the house for some rest. She could set her alarm in case she fell asleep. With a turn of the key, she started her ignition.

Or tried to.

This day just got better and better. She pulled out her AAA card and called.

Someone would arrive in the next twenty minutes. She sighed. Please let it only be the battery.

An hour later she was home, searching for the number of one of Addie's friend's mom. At this point, she'd better have backup for pick up time. Sara Cantu agreed to transport the twins when she got her own brood. A call to the school to ensure they knew she'd given Sara permission, and all was set. She could get into comfy clothes, lay down, and maybe even pull herself together.

But restlessness buzzed about her like a gnat. She found that page from the doctor. They wanted the MRI on Wednesday. Day after tomorrow. Great. Should she impose on Sara once more? But then she remembered, Sara worked from home most days, but on Wednesdays she worked from the office, and her husband handled the school taxi service. She didn't know him, and wouldn't trust another man to watch her kids.

That brought only one name to mind. She dreaded the idea. *No, please be another answer.*

After the kids came home, did their homework, and helped her celebrate the first ever Monday night pizza night—she wasn't up to cooking—she let them watch some TV. They each got to choose a show from the allowable channels, and they checked the schedule to see whose turn it was to pick first. Aidan's.

Morgan didn't even wait to hear what he chose. Instead, she climbed the stairs to her room and closed the door before bringing out her phone.

"Lord, if You've ever cared about me, please help me through this call, and make Cami say yes."

Cami

Cami made a list of the Alexa suggestions. Some club met this Saturday close to her. She Googled their contact information, crafting an email to ask if she could join them. A church group, so they're required to let people in, right?

With that off her shoulders—and that's all she could do since she'd forgotten most of her crocheting skills—she opened her laptop to work on the *Stinkerella* project.

And stared at a blank page.

This campaign pieced together unlike anything she'd attempted before.

But if she could pull this off, show Ray that she knew what she was doing, she'd get that vice-presidency promotion.

They'd been considering a new vice-president role to help guide in creative acquisitions. This would be ideal. She'd be the one in control, not asking permission. Instead, she'd be giving it. Making choices and living with them, sink or swim. A much better arrangement. She and Ray would no longer be boss and employee either. They'd be equal level colleagues. She never wanted to date him again, but as her supervisor, he was less than perfect.

The phone's chime pulled her from her thoughts. Morgan. "Yes?"

"Um, hi, Cami. Did you get the box?" She sounded strange. Morgan's normal was not subdued.

"I did. Please thank Mr. Jones."

"Good. Good. What'd they send?" Morgan didn't know? But she's the executrix.

"Just a project. I'll get it finished in no time." Cami didn't need Morgan to stick her perfect nose into Gram's last request.

"Oh, I figured you might pass."

Something's way off. "You want me to choose not to?"

Morgan's sigh came through the speaker. "I just figured you'd prefer not to put yourself through all that."

And then it dawned on Cami. Morgan didn't realize that everything went to charity if she didn't complete the shawl and instructions. Should she tell her? Nothing in the letter prohibited her from saying. But if Gram wanted her to know, she would have explained it to Morgan. Okay, she did say *something* —to be kind to her cousin. Fine, she'd do her best. "I've decided to accept this as a special gift from Gram. I want to fulfill her last wishes."

"Oh, I see. Well, um, I've another reason for calling. I need a favor."

Morgan never asked for favors. Cami would've bet money her cousin's tongue would roll out of her mouth like Richard Pryor's in that old Mel Brooks' movie if she asked for help from anyone. Maybe that's a family trait they shared. They both craved control. "What?"

Things got quiet for a while. Cami wondered if she'd lost the connection. Then she heard Morgan's muffled cough. "I have to have a medical test run on Wednesday morning. I'm required to take a sedative and won't be able to drive after. The only person I know here to help, I can't ask."

"So you phoned me? All the way in Tucson instead of burdening someone local?"

"I knew I couldn't count on you."

Ouch! Unfair! Phoenix was two hours away versus some local person she didn't want to inconvenience? And Cami's the flake? "How can you say that? You're asking me to lose a day of work in the middle of a major project on a tight timeline, and I'm the bad guy?"

She grew quiet again.

"Morgan?"

"You're right. I'm sorry. Too much to ask."

Never once had her cousin attempted to see her side. Before this. Cami sighed and heard Gram's voice. *Be kind to Morgan.* "Are you sure no one else can help? I don't want to leave you in the lurch with a medical situation, but…"

"You could come up tomorrow night and stay with us. Once we're home from the procedure, I'd only need you pick up the kids from school. Then you're done. I realize you'd miss an entire day at your office, but shouldn't you have on-line stuff? I have great wi-fi, you can work while I recover from the medication." Morgan had never invited Cami to her house. Ever. She must be desperate.

"It's possible. I gotta talk to Ray. Let me text him, and I'll call you back." Cami heard Morgan's sigh. "Hey, what's the test for?"

Morgan's pause grew endless. "They're doing an abdominal MRI. More exploratory in nature. Need to learn what's going on." The fear in her voice filtered through the speaker.

"What has been going on?"

Morgan paused again. "Nothing much. They just want to make sure." So she didn't care to share about her medical stuff anymore than Cami wanted to share about the shawl.

Fine. She wouldn't pry. "Well, let me touch base with Ray. I'll call you back in a few."

"Sure. Thanks, Cami. I appreciate this." Morgan had never uttered those words to her before. One call, three new experiences.

Morgan must be in a bad way.

They hung up and Cami stared at her cell. To text was the coward's way, but she could control her written words.

Cami: *Got a family situation in Phoenix. Will be gone Wednesday, back Thursday. Should be able to work online so the day won't be a total wash. Will keep Monty apprised.*

She set her phone on the counter, and rummaged through the freezer for a mini ice cream sandwich. Before she could close the door, her cell chirped.

Ray: *Did you tell them you're doing something important and time sensitive here?*

Cami: *Yes. This is important too.*

Ray: *Did you tell them about the project?*

Cami: *RU kidding? Of course not.*

Ray: *I hope you're taking this serious. I'm counting on you.*

Who didn't? Ray, Morgan, Gram. Face it, anyone mentioned in the will, whether or not aware, counted on Cami. The load grew heavier by the minute.

Cami: *I won't let you down.*

Ray: *You'll be in tomorrow?*

Cami: *Yes*

Ray: *We'll talk then.*

Oh, great. She looked forward to that.

After peeling the wrapper off her treat, she asked Alexa to call Morgan. "Got things all set. I can leave here about four-thirty. With traffic, no telling how late I'll be." She thought a moment. "Perhaps I should eat here and take off after seven tomorrow night. I'd avoid the rush, and would arrive around nine."

"If that works for you. I'm just relieved you're coming. Thank you."

Morgan's attitude was way off. She was always so reticent that expressing relief was out of character. Politeness was her trademark. She polished that first impression to a high shine. Every black hair of her below the shoulder curls always in place. Her manicure impeccable, and her makeup flawless. Morgan groomed herself to be the perfect executive's wife. And instead she ended up divorced with her two kids.

Cami never understood what happened with that marriage. They split a little more than a year ago. Not that she'd ever been that fond of Morgan's husband. Ex-husband. Okay, not a bad guy but blah. Nothing to make him stand out. Did she recall his first name?

Bruce. Yeah, now she remembered. Bruce. *Well, Bruce Pembroke, you should be taking your wife to the procedure. Not me.* Great. Now she was getting irritated with clueless people she hadn't seen in years.

She got a second ice cream sandwich. Even if they were a once-a-day treat, and mini, she'd miss one day this week. This would make things equal.

After unwrapping her ice cream, she opened her laptop, and stared at the blank page. *I'm stronger than my fear.* Didn't she read that line in the first *Stinkerella* book? *I'm bigger than my fear?* That would make a great slogan. She played with images to set the stage. A little girl, sketched, wind blowing her hair backward, standing tall. This could be the ticket.

Now to develop an outline of branding items.

Cami worked for an hour listing viable products before contacting their regular suppliers.

She wrangled ballpark pricing and delivery without having to mention any details.

The exact figures could wait for now.

After a while, things fell into place. That slogan would be a strong pull and great branding. *I am stronger than my fear.* Ray would dance a jig and forgive her for skipping out on him for a day. She and Monty could Zoom conference about what she came up with and any ideas he could add. This would work.

So why'd she have a sour stomach?

Was it too personal? Was it her concerns for Morgan?

Yeah, she had to admit to worrying for her cousin.

Especially with Morgan unaware of the charity clause.

Or could it be that unsettled feeling from working with Monty?

She closed down her laptop. But she couldn't turn off the acid racing to her belly.

Kate

Seventeen years ago

"Gram!"

Oh, those girls! What now. Kate wiped her hands on her apron and glanced out the kitchen window. Cami was in the old orange tree. Morgan and her friend were pelting her with over-ripe oranges that last night's storm blew free.

Kate thundered out the back door. "Stop that. Right this minute. Morgan, you're too old for that kind of behavior."

"Gram, she was spying."

The whine grated on Kate's nerves, but she was determined to be fair. "Catherine Amelia Madison, why are you up that tree? Get down before you break your leg."

"I hope you do." Fourteen-year-old Morgan stomped her foot for emphasis.

"If I do, I'll land on you and smash you." Eleven-year-old Cami stuck out her tongue.

"Just lovely. And when we have company too. Joey, you'd better go home. Seems like my granddaughters don't know how to be good hostesses." Kate opened the side gate to her yard so the neighbor boy could pass through.

"That's not fair, Gram. Why does Joey gotta leave just because Cami's such an infant?" Morgan balled her fists at her side. Tears streaked her cheeks while Cami, who had yet to obey and climb from the tree, made kissy noises.

Kate sighed. A visit to Grandma's house was supposed to be fun. Plus, this was a chance for her granddaughters to become lifelong friends. Both came from single children homes. They were as close to being sisters as possible. "Joey is a nice enough boy, but he's spending too much time here. I want us to do something together. The kitchen is close to clean. How about you both help me finish, and we can pull out a puzzle? The weather's going to be too hot out here real soon." Already the thermometer was in the eighties. By noon it would cross to the nineties. This Spring Break was a scorcher.

Morgan wiped her hand over her face and straightened her back. "Sure, Gram, I'll help you. Some children are too immature to behave as a proper guest."

Cami jumped to the ground. "I'm a proper guest, right Grams? I make my bed and help you when asked, don't I?"

"You are both lovely guests when you aren't fighting. Let's go in. If you'll finish the kitchen, I'll get the puzzles down."

Twenty minutes later, after giving each other the silent treatment, the girls entered the family room where Kate set up a table and picked a puzzle.

She would've let them choose, but realized they'd argue for the sake of arguing.

"Gram, Morgan redid everything I did like it wasn't good enough. Can't you make her stop?"

Kate caught the older one's gaze. "Is that true?"

"But it wasn't good enough, Gram. She leaves bits of grit on the floor when she sweeps, and doesn't dry the glasses all the way. Someone's got to?"

"I dried them enough, and getting a wet paper towel to pick up the last bit after using the dustpan is extreme."

"It's not."

"Is too"

"It's not, right Gram? Right? If you do a job, you should do everything in your power to make things perfect, right?" Morgan's dark blue eyes were wide with her plea to be vindicated.

"Gram, there's a limit to having to be perfect, right? Nobody is perfect, right?" Now Cami's hazel eyes were as wide, hoping the adult in the room would side with her.

Kate sent up a plea for wisdom. "You realize, when my kids grew up here, they fought on occasion, but they'd try to understand the other's point of view. If what they did or said hurt feelings, it wasn't worth it. Morgan, you are older, and I understand you feel the pressure of doing things right. All your role models are adults. That is a heavy burden. But what you might not realize is that Cami admires you." Both girls snorted, but Kate continued. "If you are too critical of her, you'll push her away. And Cami, Morgan is trying to do what she's been taught. In the military, they must keep things spotless, and training is everywhere. I know you two are capable of getting along. You are both so bright, and I love you more than I can say. For me, will you try to be kind? Please?"

Morgan opened her mouth to argue, but then rolled her lips tight between her teeth.

Cami sighed. "Fine, Gram. What puzzle are we doing?"

Kate beamed at them both, knowing full well the truce could explode at any moment. "I found this one at a garage sale a few weeks back. I liked the picture." The label showed a thousand piece puzzle of a kitten tangled in yarn with a crochet hook and a half-way completed granny-stitched something in the background.

"Aw, that's sweet." Morgan stroked the cover.

"So, let's sort the pieces. First, find all the edges. After we can group according to colors and shapes."

The girls nodded, so she dumped the puzzle on the table, and turned the box halves up. "Put edges in this side, non-edges here, and leave the corners on the table."

Ten minutes later, the pieces were sorted, the frame together, and Kate thought it safe to leave them to get some cookies and paper plates to help sort their groups.

She was wrong.

"We need to sort by color. It's easier to see." Cami held up two pieces to emphasize her point.

"We need to sort by shape first, then color. That'll cut down on our search."

"Gram!" They screamed in unison.

Kate pushed through the swinging door with her tray. "Yes, ladies?"

"Do we do color first or shape?"

She sighed. "What does it matter as long as we're agreed? If we do color first, then we do shape. If we do shape first, then we do color. Either way, the result is the same. I say paper, rock, scissors." *And then I won't need to take sides.*

Morgan's rock broke Cami's scissors.

"Two out of three." Cami wanted better odds.

"Girls, are we going to argue or put this puzzle together? Once is enough, and no pouting." That last was added as Cami huffed and crossed her arms.

"Fine, shape first. Let's sort into no knobs, one knob, two, three, and four. That's five plates. We can sub divide those as to right, left, top, and bottom." Morgan smiled at her plan.

Kate knew the child couldn't hear how bossy she sounded. In

fact, the girl would throw a fit if anyone (other than her parents or grandmother) dared talk to her that way. One day she might learn, at least that was Kate's prayer. She picked up one of the sorted plates, the two-knobbed pieces, and began grouping according to knob placement.

Cami followed suit with the three-knobbed ones.

Morgan's hand shot into the air as Cami pulled away. "Not that plate, Cami, can't you see what you're doing?" Micro-managing again.

"What now, Morgie?"

"My name is Morgan. Stop calling me Morgie.

"Stop telling me what to do, Morgie Porgy."

Morgan squinted eyes at her cousin. "So do things all wrong Camalama Ding Dong, and I'll fix them for you."

Cami stood, hands on her hips. "What did you call me?"

Morgan twisted her sweet face into the perfect gargoyle imitation and stood. "I didn't stutter Camalama Ding Dong."

"Sit down, both of you. I wish we'd never come up with those nicknames for you girls. We used them in love, but you are just acting mean. What happened to being kind for my sake?"

The girls stared at Kate like she just didn't understand, and the truth was, she didn't. Both of her granddaughters were smart, and beautiful, and full of life. To see them behave in such a petty manner broke something basic and foundational inside, making her worry where she'd gone wrong. With her own children? Had she taught them unacceptable behaviors that they passed on to these lovely girls?

She had no time for guilt. This must stop. "Morgan, we're sorting the way you chose, but within those perimeters we've got some wiggle room. Let Cami do it her way."

Morgan plopped in her chair and crossed her arms with a pout.

"And Cami, you know that nickname irritates Morgan. To purposefully upset her isn't kind. She's only trying to show you what she considers a good way."

Cami plopped, imitating Morgan, though she'd deny she ever did such a thing.

"Let's just keep sorting. This'll be so pretty when we're finished. Okay?"

They sighed at the same time. "Fine, Gram." "Okay, Gram."

Kate exhaled blowing a curl off her forehead. Life was hot enough without tempers raising the temperature.

Once they'd organized the plates, Cami looked up. "Now how do we sort for color?"

Before Kate could answer Morgan grinned and piped up. "We shouldn't need to now. This is so much easier to follow."

Cami stood, tipped the table over, and ran for her bedroom.

"Gram, just look what she did!"

Chapter Four

CAMI

Present day

That went well. Not. Cami packed her tech bag.

Even the brilliant idea about the tag line for the promo blitz didn't get stamped as genius. Ray was too focused on Cami being away from Tucson for the day to comprehend. But she still felt the client would sing its praises. She only needed to prove herself to Ray. And to Monty, who grew creepier by the minute.

That man didn't want to give her space, and for all intents and purposes had about moved into her office. She didn't mentor this way. And if he didn't back off, she'd go full Arnold on him.

As a bit of an olive branch, Cami packed and brought everything she'd need in Phoenix, so she could stay and work until seven, leaving from the office. Ray grunted when she pointed out she wasn't slacking. Good grief, the man remained tunnel-visioned. She agreed to go the extra mile, but he wouldn't give her a chance to pull off the driven road to the scenic view for a single moment. Hadn't she shown with her track record how she was responsible and hardworking and creative to boot? Man, she needed this promotion so Ray would quit driving her to Crazyville.

Seven oh one she clocked out with the guard downstairs and headed for her parking space. With her tech bag in the backseat, she climbed in, started the ignition, reminded herself of her strength, and clicked *Rubber Soul* on her iPod.

At 9:10 she pulled into Morgan's driveway. She almost backed out and returned to Tucson. This many hours near her cousin could require a visit from the homicide squad. But she remembered the desperation in Morgan's voice when she phoned. More was happening here than her cousin shared. Maybe she needed to stay. Besides, at this late date, her leaving would only give Morgan more proof of her unreliability.

Cami popped the trunk, grabbed her tech bag from the backseat, and her carry-on from the back. *Beep!* Everything locked. She hauled it all to Morgan's front door, which flew open before she could ring.

"You're here." The anxiety in her cousin's voice couldn't be missed. Morgan, still looking perfect in drapey pink pajamas and a messy bun, stepped aside while holding the door. Then she kind of did a sort of side hug. At least Cami figured that's what she attempted.

"I said I'd come. Hello to you too." Cami dragged her tech bag while her purse and carry-on hung from her shoulders. She glanced about, seeing the inside of Morgan's home for the first time. "Nice place. Where should I put my things?"

"Follow me." Morgan led the way upstairs and down the hall. "You can bunk with me."

Cami stared at her. Sleep in the same room? Maybe if they were best friends, or twelve again and having a slumber party. Where was Morgan's brain?

"My bed is enormous."

Cami continued to stare, at a loss for words.

"The sheets are fresh, I did laundry today." There's that

familiar huff in her voice, the one she showed when she didn't get her way.

"I'm sure they are. I'm just surprised you'd want me in here. That's all." Shocked was the better word. Cami shrugged and put her stuff on the floor. Gram said to be kind. She'd do her best.

"Oh, over here, I have a travel table for you." Morgan reached for Cami's carry-on and plopped it in the correct spot on the other side of the room.

Cami followed, wheeling her tech bag and purse to the proper location.

"Did you bring the project? I'd love to see." Morgan's smile seemed a tad forced. She was trying too hard.

"No, I left it at home. I have some research I need to do before I can finish. So, what is our plan?" Cami sat on the edge of the bed, ignoring the disappointment in Morgan's eyes.

"I can make us some tea, and we could sit up here and talk. We haven't in a long while."

"Morgan, we never have." The moment the words escaped, Cami wanted to shove them back. "But tea sounds lovely. Maybe we could start something new." She smiled, hoping that would pacify. Just one night. She could make nice for Gram for one night. Tomorrow Morgan would be drugged for her procedure, so that would be easier.

"Okay, do you want to pick out your tea or trust me?"

Why did that sound like a challenge? "I'll trust you. Anything but chamomile."

Morgan chuckled. "How did you know I planned to fix chamomile?" She shook her head. "Even when we try, we can't win."

"I'm sorry. It tastes like soap to me. Honest, anything else is fine. I appreciate you doing that."

Morgan cocked her head to the side and peered. "You're telling the truth, aren't you. Not just trying to be polite. I appreciate that." She blinked. "Be right back. You can get comfy while I'm gone." And she left.

Cami glanced about the room. Everything appeared in perfect order. Not even a speck on the baseboards or ceiling fan. She didn't need a white glove test for proof either. Cami twinged with disappointment. She'd hoped something misaligned somewhere. Photos of the twins stood on her nightstand. A painting of a phoenix rising in blues and greens and purples hung above her bed. The soft gray walls and the pale plantation shutters gave a restful ambience while through the open door, perpendicular to the hallway door, she noted the master en suite in shades of teal. A very peaceful retreat.

She unzipped her bag, taking out her pajamas and socks before shucking out of her clothes and getting ready for bed. As she debated whether to brush her teeth, Morgan arrived with a tray—mugs of steeping tea and a bowl of microwaved popcorn. Somehow that seemed so un-Morgan. Cami figured her cousin only served popcorn made from scratch on her stove top. But the night remained stuffed full of strange things. What's one more?

"Figured a little snack might be nice." She set the tray on the bed. "Do you have everything? Can I get you something?" That perfect hostess.

"No, thanks, I'm good. Is this side okay?" She pulled back the Moroccan patterned comforter and dove gray sheets.

Morgan nodded.

Cami shared her discomfort, and knew her cousin was doing her best on unfamiliar territory. Made it easier to be kind in return. She climbed under the covers and waited for Morgan to serve.

"I have a lovely lavender lemon tea, no caffeine or chamomile. Do you want honey? I forgot to ask."

Cami shook her head. "No thank you." She reached out to steady the tray while Morgan climbed in from her side before taking a sip. "This is nice. Thanks."

Morgan beamed. "Good. So what shall we talk about?"

"You could tell me more about tomorrow's test. What's the problem?"

"No, I can't think about that. How about the project? What was in the box?"

Gram's box was the last thing Cami cared to discuss with Morgan. And not only because it was private. She didn't want to explain that everything rested on her shoulders, that the only way anyone, including Morgan, could receive their inheritance meant she must complete the task. The burden weighed heavy enough without Morgan adding pressure. "Actually, I'm not supposed to talk about it." A white lie. But for a good cause.

"Not supposed to talk about it? Why?"

"Gram put some conditions on it. But you'll learn every-thing once I'm done. She's given me two months." She crossed her fingers, hoping that tidbit would buy her some time.

"I know that part. Mr. Jones, Gram's lawyer, told me that. But he wouldn't say more. All that not at liberty to say. I wanted to choke him."

Cami snorted, sloshing her tea. "Oops, let me—"

"Oh, look what you've done. Get up, I'll change the bedding." Morgan jumped out of bed, setting the tray on the floor by her closet, before tugging at the sheets.

"Don't worry. It's not much. I can dab with a napkin."

"It will stain. Get up, Cami. I've gotta put this in the washer."

Cami stared at her. Was she that OCD? "You're going to wash a load tonight?"

"I must or the stain will set. I've got another set in the hall linen closet. You can grab that while I remove the bedding." Morgan had already pulled the pillows from the cases.

"But it's just on the comforter. And I ought to be able to get the spot out with a damp cloth and dry with a hair dryer."

Morgan stopped, hands on her hips. "I must wash it all together, or the fading will be different. Are you going to help me?"

Cami shook her head in disbelief before heading to the hall. She found the linen closet, pulled out an identical set of bedding, and brought it to Morgan. "Go do what you have to do. I'll make the bed."

Morgan stared.

"I can make a bed, Morgan. If you are dead set on doing this, get going."

Her bossy, OCD, gotta-be-in-control cousin glared and scooped up the bedclothes before heading into the hall.

Not even ten o'clock and the cuckoos had already flown over the nest. Cami made the bed. But she would not speak to Morgan for the rest of the night.

MORGAN

Morgan stuffed the sheets into her washer and wanted to climb in after, wash away her words and anxiety. Having nice things while she grew up meant taking special care because nice things didn't come around often. Her stuff came from the Goodwill or Salvation Army stores close to the bases where she and her mother got dragged each time Dad got a transfer. That's not happening to her kids. Ever.

Which explained why she was alone the night before her procedure, scared out of her wits, and making a mess of things with her cousin. The cousin who'd dropped everything at work, and drove two hours to come help.

She didn't want to like Cami. But truth? She'd not been fair to her either, and that grated. It'd be so much better to harbor a righteous dislike. Morgan wanted to scream. If her kids weren't sleeping, she would have.

By the time she'd put the first load in the washer—the comforter and shams would go next—Cami had the bed about done. And she did it the correct way, military corners on the sheets even. She was spreading out the extra comforter, so

Morgan grabbed a pillow and started stuffing it into a case. "I'm sorry. I shouldn't get all upset. I know it was an accident."

"No worries." Cami didn't even look up. Great.

"I can finish if you want to enjoy your tea."

"Away from your bedding?" She did glance up that time.

Morgan shook her head. "I'm sorry. It's just…" How did she describe to anyone how she got to this point in life? She didn't understand it herself.

"Just what? I can't do anything right?" Cami grabbed another pillow and crammed it into the case.

"No, that didn't even cross my mind. I want to tell you. I don't know if I can explain things." A tear slipped free. Morgan swiped it away, angry now since she couldn't talk without losing control.

"It's fine. My temper is pretty edgy too. Life is…" Cami heaved a sigh. "Between Ray's dogmatic philosophy on work, a new client who has more importance than anyone I've dealt with —for my future as well as the company's—and a sleazeball I must mentor on the job, life's been a little stressful. Throw in that the client's timeline coincides with Gram's and you've an idea of the pressure. I will make this happen, for Gram and the client. And when I'm through, I'd better get my promotion or, so help me, Ray'll wish we'd never met."

Morgan laughed. The first real sharing Cami had done, and it felt normal, like they were building a bond of sorts. "I get it. And…" she paused for fear she wouldn't be believed.

"And?"

"I'm proud of you, Cam. I should've told you before. But I am. You took your degree and ran hard with it. Now look at you. Great job."

Cami's jaw dropped. Was she even breathing?

"Are you okay?"

Cami nodded. "Yeah. I keep looking for Rod Serling to jump out."

Morgan remembered the late nights staying up at Gram's,

huddled with her watching old Twilight Zone episodes. "You watched with Gram, didn't you?"

Cami nodded.

"That must've been a granddaughter thing. We did that when I'd stay over too."

"Yep, Friday Night Frights. The only night I was allowed to stay up late. She didn't let me watch with her until I was a teen, and by then we lived together." Cami tossed the last pillow onto the bed's head and sat on the foot.

Morgan joined her. "Yeah, Mom's first divorce happened about that time. Afterwards she couldn't afford to send me to Gram's for a while, since Gram wasn't her mother, anyway. When she had cash, and got remarried, I'd left for college. That's why I chose ASU, so I could at least visit."

"And I chose U of A so I could still visit but be back in Tucson where I grew up. Funny how we determine our choices."

They sat silent.

"Morgan, may I ask you something? Why can't Bruce take you tomorrow? What happened?"

That's asking a lot. Cami had shared and figured it fair. But would she be judgmental? "He's out-of-state now. We don't talk. This summer I must put the kids on a plane to go see him, and I'm terrified." Morgan swallowed and ran her hand over her face. "In my mind we were good. Then he got a job offer. A too-big-to-pass-up one. But it meant we'd have to move away, change locations every couple of years. I did that as a kid, and I said I couldn't put our twins through all that instability. He made me choose between him and his job, or Phoenix and our kids. I chose Addie and Aidan and Phoenix, so he divorced me. He found someone else pretty fast, and is happy living all over the world."

Cami patted her knee. "I'm sorry, Morgan. That stinks. But you are the best mom I know."

A pat on the knee, a compliment, Morgan would lose it big time if she didn't watch out. She cleared her throat. "Thanks. I love them more than I could ever imagine loving anything. But hey, you'll find out about that someday. Just need to meet the right guy. But make sure you're heading in the same direction." She flashed a smile.

Cami chuckled. "I've got to hire out my grocery shopping, laundry, and housecleaning. Doubt that hiring out dating will work. Maybe one of these days, though."

Morgan glanced at her cousin. Perhaps it was time. Be honest with her. She took a breath. "I've run into some recent expenses. Between the house payment that went up, the home-owners' association fees going up, the kids' tuition… and the cost-of-living expenses all rising versus Bruce's child support and alimony staying the same. I'm getting pinched." She ran her hands over her legs. "Tomorrow I might find out I need surgery and will need to pay a lot out of pocket for that because I haven't built up the deductible this year. And if it turns out to be something more than a little outpatient gall bladder thing, I'm sunk. I spoke with Mr. Jones in hopes he'd tell me how much I'm supposed to get, so maybe I could take out a loan against it, but he wouldn't divulge a confidence. I hate to ask, but would you consider not doing the project so I could receive my share of the inheritance?"

Cami stared at her.

"I'm sorry. Honest, it's not about me. I have to consider the kids. And I'm plain scared." Morgan's heart hammered in her chest at divulging those private fears.

Cami stood and walked to the window before turning around. "I shouldn't tell you this. But I'm out of options. Morgan, I gotta do the project."

And there it was. "Just like always. It's all about you." Morgan couldn't fathom that she'd poured out her heart. She'd not been that vulnerable with anyone since before Bruce left. Maybe ever. She'd never explained to him how she couldn't leave Phoenix. All he saw was that she chose the kids over him. But now, Cami chose what she wanted over helping her. How could she have been so wrong?

"You don't get it. I'm not being selfish. I've no idea what our inheritance will be."

"Then why, Cami? Why can't you help me? I am desperate. I'll do anything for you. But please, I need the cash. Please help me."

Cami stared out the window. She ran her hands through her long blond curls before clasping them behind her head. When she turned around, Morgan saw tears in her eyes.

"You've got to understand something. I've always looked up to you. When we were kids, I know I gave you a hard time, but I wanted to be like you. You got the looks and talent, and Gram sang your praises. She'd tell me you did this. Or made that. Or won such-and-such. She wanted us to be friends. But the more she pushed, the more jealous I got. Instead of drawing us closer, I couldn't stand to hear anything more. But the truth is, I still admired you, and couldn't help but imagine everything you touched came out perfect. I mean, look at those faces on your nightstand. Can you envision cuter kids?" Cami pointed to the framed school photos and sighed. "Morgan, I don't want to hurt you. Honest, I don't. But if I let the project go, if I don't complete it, I will hurt you. Worse than you can guess."

Morgan stood, fists balled at her sides, and her gut twisting into knots. "How? How would that hurt me?"

"If I don't complete the project on time, all the inheritance goes to charity. You, me, everyone but the charity receives nothing."

Cami

She offered to drop Morgan off in front of the hospital entrance, but her perfect cousin insisted she could walk from the parking lot. Which, in a weird way, disappointed Cami.

A few things changed last night. That's an understatement. Morgan tumbled from her pedestal, no longer perfect. Though, the Venus de Milo lost her arms and was still considered a treasure. Maybe the cracks in Morgan's shield added to her value. But pondering all that would be easier if she weren't sitting in the passenger seat with perfect makeup and hair. No jewelry, though. An info sheet rule.

She found a shady slot and parked. "Got everything?"

Morgan patted her jeans pocket. "Insurance card, Visa, and my pill." She exhaled. "Let's do this."

Cami nodded and turned off the engine. After locking up, she followed Morgan through the automated doors to the check-in desk. She found a chair to wait out of the way while Morgan signed her paperwork.

"Have a seat and I'll bring you back when they say. Do you have your medication with you?" The check-in nurse sounded all business.

Morgan nodded and pulled out the small vial.

"Good. You may take it now. It won't take effect for about twenty minutes. That'll give you time to change into a gown." The nurse, or whatever her job description labeled her, pointed to a water fountain, and exited to another room in back of the reception desk.

Cami noticed Morgan's hands shook as she tried to open the small bottle. Should she offer to help? Would Morgan pull her gotta-do-it-myself routine? Before Cami decided, the lid popped off.

A moment later, Morgan sat in the next chair, her hands clasping and unclasping.

"It's going to be okay, Morgan. Don't worry."

"Worry? I'm not worried. I just want to get this over. I hate waiting is all."

"Okay." Cami sighed. Had all they'd shared last night fled with the first rays of dawn? She chalked it up to nerves on her cousin's part. The more frightened she became, the more stubborn, pig-headed… No, that wasn't fair. Cami guessed she was also embarrassed for sharing so much. Morgan was the most private person she knew, and that was saying something since Cami saw herself in that light.

The nurse returned. "Mrs. Pembroke, you can follow me."

Morgan stood, and then glanced back at Cami. "You come too. I don't know what will happen when the medicine kicks in. I want you… sorry, I'd like you with me."

Cami followed them through some doors and down a hall. The nurse indicated where she might wait, and showed Morgan where to change out of her clothes.

The waiting room stood empty but for the chairs, all ready to assist friends and family with their lonely vigils. Cami chose one close to the door.

By the time Morgan came out, Cami grew concerned she might have to catch her. The girl wobbled like she'd imbibed a few too many. If she were still eleven years old, she would video it to use as insurance to keep Morgan behaving nice. Ha! But Cami had matured. For now, it remained a diabolical notion. Not a plan. "Here, Morgan, have a seat." The poor kid wore two gowns, the patterned under one with ties in the back, the over one a solid green like a robe. She'd been given beige socks with rubbery treads as well. This must kill that internal fashionista.

Morgan locked gazes, cocking her head to the side. "You didn't run away."

Cami helped her to a chair. "Of course. I told you I'd help you."

"But you know…" Morgan paused, blinked, and acted like she saw Cami for the first time. "Oh, you are here."

"Yes, I'm here. I've got your back, Morgan."

"Oh, I'm so glad. I's afraid I'd do this alone." Morgan slurred worse with each word. Then her eyes grew big. "Will you go in with me? Can you hold my hand?"

Cami chewed her lip. "I doubt they'll let me go in, but I'll wait right here. I'll take you home and make sure you are safe."

Morgan sighed and leaned her head against the wall. "Okay. I want a nap." She closed her eyes and her mouth dropped open.

The nurse came out. "Mrs. Pembroke, we're ready for you. Mrs. Pembroke?"

Cami jiggled Morgan's shoulder. "Morgan, it's time for your test. Go with the nurse"

She sat up straight. "I can do dis. Where's my pencil?"

The nurse tried to hide her smile and touched Morgan's elbow. "Come with me, Mrs. Pembroke. I'll take you to the room."

"Oh, okay." Morgan stood, swayed, and smoothed at the wrinkled hospital gowns. "I'm ready." She linked her arm through the nurse's and walked away from Cami, though the conversation still floated back. "You're so nice to take care a me."

Cami settled back to wait, pulling out her phone. She scrolled through seven text messages from Ray. And she'd checked before they left the house. She scanned them. None were earth shattering, and all could wait until she arrived at Morgan's to answer.

"Excuse me, are you Morgan Pembroke?"

Cami glanced up into clear blue eyes that she would swear were smiling even if the rest of the face didn't show it. Those amazing eyes made her gums sweat. She gnawed her lip and choked. "Um, I'm her cousin. C-Cami. She's inside. Can I help you?" *Or will you help me? Oh my!* The fact that he also wore two hospital gowns and white athletic socks without shoes didn't detract one bit—the guy was hot.

"She dropped something in the changing room. Just wanted to return it." He took the seat Morgan vacated.

"You can give it to me. I'll make sure she gets it." She held out her hand.

He leaned back. "No, that's okay, I'd rather give it to her. I'm next anyway."

Cami returned to her phone, not sure if she was disappointed because hot guy didn't trust her or because he didn't seem interested.

It'd been so long since she'd even met anyone to spark her imagination, and within seconds of doing so, he squashed her dreams before they bloomed.

She glanced his way.

He watched her.

She flicked her gaze back to her phone as her neck and face grew warm. Sauna warm. Midday in the Phoenix desert on the fourth of July warm.

"It's not that I don't trust you, but she might prefer I give it to her. My name is Jeff, by the way. You said you are Cami?"

She nodded, afraid to let him see her embarrassment.

"You're Morgan's cousin, you said?"

"Um, yeah. So you're getting an MRI too?" She glanced sideways at him. He didn't seem to be extra amused, just friendly. However, she knew to be aware of those types. They considered Ted Bundy friendly, she remembered.

"Yeah, me and Irene have an annual date."

She turned in his direction now. "Irene?"

"I've been here so many times, me and that machine are on a first name basis."

What did one say to that? "I'm… sorry."

"No need, I'm used to it. I can block out the hammering noise and practically fall asleep."

Now she stared.

He winked. "Practically. But not quite. It's no biggie."

"Oh."

"So what do you do?"

"I work for an ad agency, Chukshon Advertising. How about you?" She tucked her hair behind her ear.

"I work down the street at Desert Bloom Community."

She stopped and mused. Was that a school, a community center? Then she remembered. "That's a church, right?"

"Yep."

"What do you do?"

He smiled bigger. "I'm the pastor."

And she'd worried he'd be like Ted Bundy. Could she misread any better? But wait, she'd only his word that he was a pastor. He might be an escaped psycho for all she knew.

"That's not my usual lead. Don't get me wrong, I love my job, and will talk about it for hours on end, but once it's out, conversations change." He shrugged.

Now what did she say? "Have you been doing this long?"

"About a year as lead pastor. I started as a youth minister in Payson, but the opportunity to take this position appeared, and I'm loving it."

"That's good. What's your family think of the change? I mean, it's different here than in the mountains." Must be family, right?

"My parents are in Wickenburg, and my sisters are all over the place, but I'm the only one here." He grinned, and she knew that he knew why she'd asked that.

Her face got warm again as she risked a peek at his left hand. "That must make you a great workaholic. Or someone who's discovered all the little-known nooks around the valley."

"A little of both. But hey, if you're looking for a great church with a loving congregation, you won't find better."

She grinned. "You should write commercials."

He laughed.

Somehow they landed on out-of-the-way places in Phoenix. He knew spots she'd never heard of, and she told him about some he said he'd like to try. Before she knew it, the doors opened, and the nurse walked Morgan out.

"You ought to help her change her clothes. She's not steady enough to do it herself."

Morgan waved her hand in the air. "Oh, no, I can do it. Don't need help—" She fell forward.

Cami jumped to catch her.

So did Jeff, er, Pastor Jeff.

The nurse still held on, too, so together they righted Morgan.

"I'll help her. Thank you so much." Cami guided the wobbly and unfiltered Morgan to the dressing room. Her clothes were in a bin under the bench Cami helped her sit on. Piece by piece, she got her ready while Morgan went on and on about how kind everyone treated her. Then, holding her about her waist, Cami drew Morgan close and helped her walk out.

The nurse brought a wheelchair. "She's going nowhere without this. I'll push her to the front while you go after your car. Pull up at the curb."

"That sounds like a plan. Oh, wait." She turned back to Jeff. "This is Morgan, if you want to give her what you found."

"On second thought, maybe I should give these to you." He handed over Morgan's insurance card and Visa. "Nice meeting you."

Cami sighed. *You have no idea.*

Chapter Five

CAMI

Present day

Cami pulled into Morgan's driveway and shut off the igni-tion. This time she had no wheelchair to help, but at least Morgan had handed her the house key after she locked up this morning when they left. They weren't stuck outside. But it'd take some maneuvering to get her cousin into the house. That was a given.

She slipped the long strap from her purse over her head so it crossed her body, and unlocked the front door, leaving it wide for when she returned with her unwieldy load.

Next, she needed to coax Morgan into cooperation. The girl slept the entire ride. "Morgan, we're here. Let me help you."

Morgan's eye cracked a bit. "No thank you, I'll stay right here." She was asleep before she finished her sentence.

Cami sighed. "Sorry, Morgan, I can't do that. Let's get you inside, and you can sleep for the rest of the day in your own bed."

"Um, don't wanna move."

It was too hot to leave her in the car. Besides, Gram would

say it wasn't nice. Or kind. "Come on, sleepyhead." She unbuckled Morgan's seatbelt, and pulled her by her upper arms.

"Wait, wait."

"Put your hands on my shoulders, Morgan, and I'll guide you out."

"Okay." She sat and smiled at Cami but didn't raise her hands into position.

Cami pulled again and then pressed down on Morgan's crown as she was coming out the car so she wouldn't clobber her forehead. Once her head was clear, she drew the girl to her and used herself as a leaning post until she could walk Morgan out of the way of the passenger door. So awkward.

But at least the hard part was past.

Cami got her into the house, but after that ordeal, she decided the couch was the better choice. Managing the stairs grew too much to contemplate.

She slipped Morgan's shoes off her, placed a pillow beneath her head, and pulled an afghan over her. One Gram made, no doubt. Or did Morgan make it? She was big on crocheting.

Maybe she should reconsider and tell Morgan about the project. She'd jump at the idea of finishing it and do it in record time without charging a fee.

But then she'd hold it over Cami's head for the rest of her life. The only reason everyone got their inheritance was because Morgan fixed everything just perfect. Again.

She sighed, and wandered to the kitchen for a sandwich before sitting at the table and starting up her laptop. As she settled in she set a reminder to get the kids from school on time. It was one thing to work through lunch and dinner because you're so into a project, but another to leave two elementary schoolchildren stranded. And she knew someone would tell Morgan the entire story, and it'd be one more point of proof that Cami could not be trusted.

With a sigh, she searched her mind for anything else she

needed to handle before delving into work. Nothing popped in her brain, so she pulled up the file.

Two hours later she'd generated a list of ideas on how to capitalize on the tag line, and started a set of presentation slides to introduce that. She was on a roll when a phone rang. It was Morgan's cell.

Did she answer for her? Did she wake her?

She answered. "Hello?"

"Mrs. Pembroke?"

"No, this is her number, but she is sleeping. May I take a message?" She ran to her laptop and pulled up Evernote.

"Please. Have her call Doctor Abernathy's office as soon as possible. Thank you."

Cami's fingers hovered over the keys. "Wait, what is the number?"

"She has it. Have her ask for Dottie."

"Dottie. Okay, I'll give this to her when she wakes."

"Thank you." The line disconnected.

Cami blew out a breath. That was a fast call. Normal was a few days. A week. Perhaps more before hearing on a test. This can't be good news.

Her alarm reminder sounded. Time to get the twins. She found a piece of paper and scribbled a note to Morgan.

Gone for Addie and Aidan. Be back in a few minutes. C

She gave one more glance at Morgan, who lay curled to her side, arm wrapped around another pillow, before tiptoeing out of the house, and locking the door behind her.

The school wasn't that far, as long as one drove. It was a private academy, and Cami was pretty confident the last thing Morgan wanted to do to cut expenses was to pull them out and put them in public school. It wasn't snobby enough. She smacked her hand. *Bad thought.*

A queue of cars lined the parking lot, picking up students. Cami scanned for instructions, making certain she was in the right place. When she pulled to the front at her turn, the kids waved and smiled. They popped into the back seat. "Be sure to buckle up."

"We know. Mom made us promise to always buckle our seatbelts." Aidan spoke for the two of them.

"Your mom is wise. Oh, and speaking of her, she's asleep on the couch so when we go in we need to be as quiet as possible."

"Is she okay?" That was Addie.

Cami adjusted the rearview mirror to glimpse the girl. Her bottom lip quivered a tad. "She's fine. They gave her medicine to help calm her for the test. It can get loud and feel awfully close inside the machine, so it helps to be relaxed. Now she just needs the medicine to wear off." She stole another glance.

Addie smiled.

"So what is your routine when you get home?"

Aidan spoke up again. "We change out of our school clothes and have a snack while we do our homework. After that we can play until dinner if we did our chores for the day. Once dinner's over we each choose one TV show before we get ready for bed." He made a point to mention that last part.

Good thing Cami never planned things to mess with his plan. Wonder if he's as single minded as his mother? "Well, depending on how your mom is doing, I might be gone by dinnertime. At least soon after. I don't want to deal with the traffic rush, but I need to be home tonight."

Someone groaned in the back. Cami was sure it was Addie. It was nice to imagine they might miss her.

She pulled in the drive. "Now remember, we go in quietly."

The kids were so solemn, such serious faces, tiptoeing to the front door. Cami covered her grin as she let them in the house.

Morgan sat on the couch. Not what you'd call lucid, but awake. "How was your day guys? Come, give me a hug."

They both did, though Addie held back. Most likely she'd not seen her mom with sleep scars on her cheek, mascara smears under her eyes, and her hair a tangled mess. Cami never saw Morgan like that either.

"Oh, the doctor's office called. I told them you were sleeping. They didn't want me to wake you but asked for you to call them when you woke. Said you knew the number and to ask for Dottie."

Morgan's eyes grew wide. "Thanks." She swiped her phone and went upstairs.

Cami rubbed her hands together. "Guess that means I'm getting your snack. You two go change, and I'll see what I can find. Everyone like PB and J's?"

The kids nodded, less than enthused, and trudged to their rooms.

Now to search the cabinets for peanut butter. She'd spotted strawberry jam earlier in the refrigerator. By the time Aidan bounded into the kitchen and opened his backpack at the breakfast nook, she had two plates of sandwiches ready, cut into triangle wedges. "How 'bout some milk to go with?"

He nodded. "Thank you."

Addie wandered in about then, agreeing to milk too.

She set them up and headed into the living room as Morgan came downstairs, looking more pale than Cami had ever seen her.

"What's wrong?"

Morgan opened her mouth and then closed it. At once, she threw her arms around Cami and sobbed.

This was the last thing she expected. Cami froze until a part of her brain suggested she pat Morgan on the back. What could be wrong? The phone call. Oh, no. "What'd they say, Morgan?"

Morgan pulled away and ran her hand over her face. "They say I need a specialist. A liver specialist. I have a mass on my gallbladder, and they can't tell if it is connected to the liver or not. They can't tell if it's malignant or not. They kept saying that. They don't know, can't tell. But I need a specialist. Cami, this is so much worse than I feared. Now what do I do?"

Cami possessed a great imagination. It was what fueled her advancement in advertising. Yet this situation, Morgan sick, maybe fighting cancer? Not an inkling. What would she do? What could Cami do to help?

Oh, no. Not possible. She couldn't keep making the trips up here. That would tank everything she'd worked for. To start over in another city? And if she did, what'd Morgan expect? For Cami not to work, stay home, and care for the kids?

Whoa, now her imagination kicked in. Talk about getting ahead of herself. She couldn't tell what went through Morgan's brain. From her expression, her cousin was too overwhelmed to contemplate her name.

"You're not awake yet. I see it. Can I get you something to drink? Maybe you want to splash some water on your face?"

Morgan nodded. "We've got bottles of water in the refrigerator. I'll be back in a minute." She headed for the downstairs' bathroom.

Cami fetched the bottle and sat in the living room. The kids' heads were bent over their school work, so she guessed they heard nothing. Which was a good thing.

Morgan returned looking more herself. She'd fixed her hair, wiped under her eyes, and powered a more awake gaze. "They gave me the name of a liver specialist to contact. What do I do? When do I schedule my appointment? I don't even know the next step." She dropped to the couch.

Cami took the wing chair across from her. "The first step is contacting the specialist. He'll know what your MRI found and be able to advise you." To break projects down into parts and prioritize was her job. It was the same thing here. Only different.

Morgan pulled out her phone and glanced at the kitchen. "Are the kids doing their homework?"

"Yeah, they're busy. I made them PB and Js like Gram would do and gave them each a glass of milk. They were working hard last time I checked."

That seemed to help. Morgan placed her call, and then stepped outside to her porch.

Cami used the moment to peek in on Addie and Aidan.

His arm draped around his sister, who cried on his shoulder. "Hey guys, what's going on?"

They both glanced up, startled.

Aidan stood. "What's wrong with our mother? Something isn't right. She doesn't act that way."

"She's a little stressed taking care of things. She needed to sleep off the pill from the doctor, and now she has to catch up on what she missed. Sleeping with medicine is a whole lot different from going to sleep. It can be harder to wake up and get it out of your system." She almost added that it would all be okay, but she couldn't bring herself to make that kind of promise. Some things weren't okay. And never would be.

The front door closed. "You two finish your homework so you can play. I'll check on your mom." She smiled and hoped that helped.

Addie smiled back, but Aidan searched her face like he studied for a test. Then he nodded and returned to his chair.

Cami tried to look casual as she sauntered to the living room, but inside her heart raced. How bad was this?

"So, they want me as soon as possible. The next step is a CT scan. Dr. Brennan, the specialist, says he'll note more contrast this way. And now that they've a better idea, they can search with more purpose. I asked what comes after that. He said that depending on what they find, most likely a biopsy. If it is malignant, I'll start chemo right away to shrink the tumor. Then if it's operable, I'll have surgery." Morgan captured her gaze. "All I heard after chemo is I'll be bald. I'm going to lose my hair."

"It's better than losing your life."

Morgan's lips drew tight and she sighed. "Yeah, I know you're right. Maybe if I tell myself a million times, I'll believe it." She shook her head and swallowed. "But what to do about the twins? They'll call me when the CT scan is set, should be in the next few minutes. They want me in yesterday."

Cami needed to tell her she couldn't come back. Please do not ask. And she wanted to say she'd help. Like she'd developed a split personality, wanting to do the right thing and being resentful for needing to do what she'd been working on for years. It'd only get worse, she could tell.

Morgan's phone rang. She stepped outside to take it.

Cami slid back in her chair, and something in her pocket poked her. Morgan's Visa and insurance cards. It reminded her of that waiting room. This morning it'd been so easy sitting, talking with Jeff. She'd laughed and felt like a person again. That was what she wanted. To live that way. And be in control of her career. Now that would be perfect.

Jeff. She remembered those twinkling blue eyes, that grin. That he was a pastor…

A pastor, that's it. She googled his church and found the phone number. A lady answered, so she asked to talk with Pastor Jeff. A moment later she heard his grin in his hello.

"Hi, don't know if you remember me or not. Cami, Morgan's cousin?"

He laughed. "Sure. Great conversation. How can I help?"

She swallowed. Morgan would go ballistic if she gave out too much personal information. But she needed help. "My cousin got news from her test today. She's going to need assistance. I live in Tucson. Work prevents me from driving up too often. Do you have a program or someone reliable who might help her? Things like transportation, and maybe some babysitting? She's very private, and asking will about kill her, but she needs it."

He got quiet. She could hear him tapping something. "Um, I might have your answer. We've a lady in our congregation who loves to do this kind of thing, it's her ministry. How about if I bring her over and introduce her to your cousin? Then they can decide if they want to work together?"

"That sounds great. I'm here until seven tonight. Might be wise if I'm around." Plus, she'd get to see him again.

"This is your cell number? I'll text you when to expect us. Let me call Nohemi."

"Good. I'll watch for your text." She said her goodbyes and disconnected as Morgan came in.

"They want me to go in tomorrow. Can you stay?" Morgan appeared defeated, no begging in her voice.

"Sit down. I have a plan. It isn't final, and you have the last word so no freaking out."

Morgan's eyes grew wide. Not good.

"When you were doing your test, this guy came out. He'd found something in the dressing room that belonged to you. Wouldn't give it to me, insisted on the owner. We got to talking and he's a pastor near here. His name is Jeff. When you wandered out, he could see you weren't in any condition to take back what he discovered, so he gave it to me. Your Visa and insurance cards."

Morgan started patting her pockets before reaching in and coming up empty.

Cami held up the cards for her.

Morgan swiped them, holding them to her chest. "Sorry. I don't know what I'd do if I lost them too."

"I understand. I'd forgotten they were in my pocket. They reminded me of Jeff, and that gave me an idea. I called him and he suggested a solution. He's coming over in a little while and bringing someone who might help you when I can't." Cami waited for the disapproval.

But Morgan only sat, staring.

"Is that okay?"

"You're not leaving me in the lurch. I knew I was asking too much, but you said, 'when I can't' and that means sometimes you can." The waterworks started again.

"Now I haven't met this woman. You might not like her. But I got the notion Jeff is an excellent judge of character."

Morgan snorted. "You figured that after how many minutes of chatting?"

Cami smiled. She was taking this better than anticipated. "I know. I could be way off. But meet her. You decide. I don't know how often I can get here, for sure I can't tomorrow. But we'll take it as they set your appointments. I'll do my best, Morgan."

"I know you will."

Cami glanced at her cousin. Did those words come from Morgan's mouth?

Morgan

Morgan wasn't one to surrender. She always went down with a fight. But her fight had evaporated. Emotionally drained waved a white flag in her face. It's as if someone reached inside and removed her will to battle. She lay on the battlefield too wounded, and maybe beyond repair.

Cami attempted to make concessions for her. Just knowing that tipped her world all out of whack. If she didn't need the help, she'd have challenged Cami's step over their well-established boundaries, but in this instance, it would be worse than the slicing off of one's own nose for spite adage.

Who knows? Perhaps this woman might be suitable. Morgan glanced toward the kitchen where the kids remained. At least she hoped they did. She couldn't spot them from her vantage point, and only silence flowed from their part of the house. They needn't be included in this. She would dispense information on an as needed basis to keep them safe from worry.

Cami's phone buzzed and she checked the text. "Jeff is bringing the lady, Nohemi, over in a few minutes if that works for you."

None of this worked for her, but she nodded anyway. Oh, let this woman help, and not create a problem. Morgan couldn't take another. "Maybe I should make myself more presentable."

"You look fine. The mascara smears are gone, and your hair is cute in the ponytail. Don't worry." So easy for Cami to say.

"That's all I do anymore. Worry. I've nothing here I can

control. Cami, they're going to find cancer. I know it. I could die. I could die bald." Fear rose up her throat as if she would vomit. "What'll happen to my kids? I'm terrified."

"Morgan, I don't have answers. I wish I did. Too many people told me it was okay when things weren't, so I won't lie to you. This is not okay. But you'll come through it, and I'll help however I can. Jeff impressed me today—"

Morgan could imagine.

Cami spotted the thought crossing her face. "No, not like that. Well, maybe. A little. He is handsome and single. But that's not why I remembered him. He's got an air of integrity and transparency I found refreshing. I know we didn't talk long, but when I called his church, it wasn't from a number he gave me. I googled it and he picked up. That told me something. Maybe next time I'm here on a weekend, we can attend his church, and see what it's like. Gram would like that. Hers is so far, across the valley. But that was important to her. We should check it out."

Morgan nodded. She couldn't imagine past the next few minutes to going to church with Cami. Would she get a weekend like that in her future? How was she going to handle it when they started all this treatment stuff? How would she pay for it? She'd meet her deductible fast, but what about that part she must produce that remained out of her means? And what price would this woman charge for her help? That's something she'd ask up front.

Unless Cami planned to pay for it for her. No, even on the remote chance that that was her plan, Morgan wouldn't allow it. She was already too indebted to her cousin and didn't like it one bit.

The kids wandered in. "Mom, our homework is done. Can we ride bikes for a while?" Aidan approached, but Addie held back.

"Would you mind playing a game inside instead? We've some company coming, and I might want to introduce you. You can play something on the patio, if you prefer, but I need you home. Okay?" She peered into his eyes first, then hers. Worry and fear stared back, and it crushed her soul. How she craved to wipe that away from them. It's bad enough that they didn't comprehend why their father left. Well, to be fair, their father didn't understand either, but now in their world that should be safe, things were growing more chaotic. She'd sacrificed a lot to build security for them. "Would you do that for me? Please?" She smiled to make it seem less like begging.

"Sure, Mom."

Addie nodded in agreement, and they headed out through the Arcadia doors.

Morgan tipped her head against the couch back and closed her eyes. Whatever this storm was, it kept coming. The sprinkling had started, and she knew the downpour was next.

Car doors sounded, followed by a quick *beep-beep* of an automatic lock. She sat straight.

Cami stood. "They're here." She opened the door. "Hi, come in."

A Hispanic lady in her fifties entered first, followed by a guy who could double for Chris Pine. He stood tall and smiling, and Morgan caught the glance between him and Cami. Did she hallucinate? They'd just met for Pete's sake. Not that she'd blame Cami. Why didn't she ignore her cousin's advice and make herself more presentable?

"Morgan, this is Jeff. I didn't get your last name." Cami glanced at him, her head tipped to the side.

He grinned, and Morgan could see why Cami forgot to ask. "Brooker. Jeff Brooker." He reached out to shake hands with Morgan. "And this is my friend, Nohemi Sanchez. She is a wonder in our congregation, and vetted for work with children. Our insurance requires all our children's church volunteers to be fingerprinted. She's a retired teacher and a true gem."

Nohemi smacked his arm. "Come on, pastor, I can't live up to all the hype you're spouting." She also shook hands with Morgan, and then Cami. "I'm retired, like Pastor said, but since my grandkids are out of state, and my husband has passed, I've a lot of time to help where needed. I'm happy to do that."

Morgan remembered her manners. This was her house, she needed to be a proper hostess. "Please, sit. Cami, we've some iced tea in the refrigerator, if anyone is interested."

Cami took a step for the kitchen but glanced at the guests.

"Sure, thank you. Nohemi?" Jeff looked at his companion.

"Yes, please. That would be nice."

Once Cami left, Morgan felt her intelligence drain away, and stared at her hands.

"And you are Morgan. I doubt you recall meeting this morning." Jeff grinned.

What did she do?

Her fear must have shown on her face.

"No, you did nothing. I could tell the medication was still active and you wouldn't remember. First time I experienced an MRI I freaked from claustrophobia so the next time I took the meds. Now I'm so used to it, nothing fazes me."

"You've had several then?"

"Yeah, more than I want to count. But let's let you and Nohemi talk." He crossed his leg over his knee, and looked more comfortable on the loveseat than Bruce ever did.

"Yes. Well, where to start? It looks like I need a CT scan tomorrow. The time frame's rushed. I didn't get to make it early enough to be able to pick up the kids from school. That's first, I guess. Afterward, they want to schedule a biopsy. That is outpatient. I don't have a date yet. I won't know what's next until those results." She shared such private things with perfect strangers. She'd rather vomit. If it weren't for Addie and Aidan, she wouldn't be doing it at all.

Nohemi nodded. "I'm happy to pick up the kids. Do they have a house key? I can bring them home or do whatever you prefer. I live about a half-mile from here. They are welcome to wait at my house. How would you like to handle this?"

The tears prickled, but she'd not cry in front of them. That line she would not cross. "What do you charge, and what is the difference between being at my house or yours?"

"Oh, I couldn't take payment. I do this to help. Please, whichever way you'd like is fine with me."

Morgan glanced away, struggling to pull herself together. No tears, no tears. Then she got drawn into an embrace.

Nohemi had left her seat and settled next to Morgan.

So much more than she could fight. Her tears rained.

"I'll help you, don't worry. Check all my references. We can do this." Nohemi rubbed Morgan's back as she spoke the comforting words.

Morgan pulled away and swiped a tissue from the box on the end table. After drawing in a couple breaths, she gained more control. "Would you like to meet my kids? I have twins. They're in second grade. Addie and Aidan."

"I would love to."

Morgan stood.

Nohemi and Jeff did too.

"They're playing out back. I'll go call them." She headed for the Arcadia doors off the dining room. Was she making a big mistake? These people seemed trustworthy, but it'd been what, five minutes? If she'd ever taken up praying, now would be the time.

Chapter Six

CAMI

Cami poured four glasses of iced tea and found a tray to carry everything. She was just returning to the living room when Morgan passed her, headed for the Arcadia doors. Must be getting the kids.

She brought the drinks to the guests, and set the tray on her knees until Morgan returned for hers. Difficult to tap her feet in the moment's awkwardness.

Jeff cleared his throat. "So you don't live here?"

She shook her head. How'd that get missed this morning? "No, I live in Tucson, and have to return tonight. I'm working on an extensive project, and my boss is already steamed I left, though I got a bunch done while Morgan slept when we got back here." What compelled her to explain that? Who cares whether he saw her as industrious? Maybe she did.

"Oh, but you came anyway to help. That says a lot." That was from Nohemi, but the words still brought heat to Cami's face.

"Morgan needed help. It's what family does. But I hope you can be here when I can't. My plate's never been this full. Timing is everything, I guess."

Jeff grinned at that. "Sure is. Good thing Morgan dropped her cards this morning and I spotted them."

"I agree." Her fingers grew restless, so she clutched the tray tighter.

The silence grew until Morgan reappeared, holding hands with the twins.

Jeff and Nohemi stood.

"Kids, I'd like you to meet Pastor Brooker and Mrs. Sanchez. Pastor, Mrs. Sanchez, these are my twins, Addie and Aidan." She leaned in toward the kids. "Go shake hands."

Addie followed Aidan, who shook hands like a perfect gentleman. "Nice to meet you."

"Pleased to meet you both too. You can call me Jeff."

"What lovely manners. You may call me Ms. Nona." Nohemi's gentle smile encouraged one from Addie. "Perhaps we might get better acquainted. Would you like that?"

"Yes, ma'am." The twins replied in unison.

Morgan perked up. "You could sit at the breakfast nook and chat." Cami realized her plan was to keep an eye on things that way.

"Sounds like a lovely idea. Addie, Aidan, would you please show me the way?" Ms. Nona and the kids wandered out. Nohemi tossed a smile over her shoulder as she left the room, giving Cami the impression she enjoyed this opportunity.

Jeff sighed. "Nohemi is wonderful with kids. To help others like this brings her great joy. I'm thinking this was a God-send for all of us."

Morgan accepted her iced tea.

Cami was able to set the tray to the side of her chair. "Sure seems that way. I'm grateful for the conversation this morning. It made the wait much shorter."

"So where do you go to church? Looking for a new one?" He chuckled. "I guess if you had a church home you'd have called them first." He still leaned back with his leg crossed over his knee, looking so relaxed. And handsome.

Morgan spoke up before Cami could gather her thoughts. "We used to attend Community of Desert Grace, but it's so far on the other side of the valley. It was one thing when we'd spend the night at my, er, our grandmother's house. That was her congregation. But she recently passed."

"Oh, I see, I'm sorry. You are more than welcome at Desert Bloom. Hope you'll make it. I know Nohemi would enjoy having the kids in her Sunday School group." He paused. "No pressure, just an invitation." His grin made his eyes twinkle.

"We talked about that before you got here. Discussed maybe if I'm up here for a weekend, we could stop by." Cami tried to return a grin, but her stomach fluttered so much, she was afraid she looked like a fool.

"Where do you go in Tucson, Cami?"

Great, what did she say? That she was a heathen who'd not darkened a church door since college when she went with Gram? Aside from that funeral last week. "I'm not attending. At the moment." Then she remembered. "But I searched and found a group that meets on Saturdays that I'm checking out."

Morgan stared at her.

Well, she wasn't lying. The crochet group met at a church and it met this week. She stared back. "Mount Lemon's Shadow Community." So there, Morgie.

"Oh, I know the youth pastor. Great congregation. You'll like it." He smiled too. "I sometimes need to travel to Tucson. Would you be okay if I texted you when I'm in the area?"

Cami's tummy fluttered so loud the flaps pounded in her ears. "Um, that'd be great. Maybe I can show you some hidden gems in my area."

"I'd like that." He uncrossed his leg and leaned forward. "Before we go, though, I'd like to pray with you all. I can tell you're worried, Morgan. If you're okay with it, I can add you to our prayer chain. I'll only say what you approve."

Morgan still seemed in shock for Cami's mention of the church. She shook her head and blinked. "Ah, sure, but maybe don't give my name, or what tests. Maybe say I'm… concerned about…" She weighed her words. "medical things? Keep it broad? I'm sorry. I don't share like this. Privacy is important to me and I feel invaded. Sorry. Not a good word, I realize, when I've been the one to share, but it's how I am."

"No problem. I understand." He glanced at his watch. "We didn't intend to take up all your time, either, so maybe I can pray for you now." He stood.

Morgan rose, so Cami did the same.

"It's okay, Morgan. Just sit. We'll come to you." He motioned for Cami to join him as he stood over Morgan, placing his hand on her head.

Not sure what was proper, Cami touched Morgan's temple with her fingertips and glanced at Jeff.

He remained straight-backed with his shoulders squared, but tipped his chin to his chest and closed his eyes.

She closed hers too, but then peeked a few times. To make sure she did this right.

He breathed in and out before starting. "Father, we bring you Your daughter Morgan. From what she has shared, a lot has landed in her lap that she's not prepared for. But we know You are. None of this has surprised You, and though she may wonder if she's out of control, You are not. We ask You, Lord, to walk her through this valley. If You can take her away from this fire before it happens, we thank You. If You need to stand with her in the fire, we praise You. And if You need to carry her through the fire, we rely on Your presence to do all that is needed. Bring her peace, give the doctors and staff wisdom beyond their ability and knowledge. And let all the glory and honor for this outcome go straight to You, Lord. Thank You for how You brought us together. We love You, we praise You, and thank You in Jesus's name, Amen."

Cami echoed Amen and opened her eyes.

Morgan's shoulders shook.

Cami sat next to her cousin, empathy overwhelming her, and embraced Morgan.

All this touchy-feely stuff was foreign.

Jeff sat on the arm of the sofa. "One last thing. I have Cami's number, but it might be a good thing if we exchange numbers before we leave so you can reach me. Nohemi will need to do that too."

On cue, Mrs. Sanchez and the twins arrived from the other room. "They are so smart. You have brilliant children, Mrs. Pembroke. I'd love to help you." She gave Morgan her cell number and address. They agreed to have Nohemi take the twins to her house tomorrow until Morgan could bring them home.

Everyone said their goodbyes.

Cami offered to walk them to the car.

On the sidewalk, after Nohemi climbed into the gray Altima, Jeff paused and touched Cami's elbow. "I need to tell you something. You already know I'm not married. I seldom date, the primary reason being because church life keeps me busy. I've even considered skipping this whole love life thing so I could concentrate more on being a better pastor. But sometimes God brings a person across my path and I notice a tug to want to get to know them. I figure we both shared that tug, Cami. But I have to be clear. I don't date just for fun. And I won't consider a future with someone who hasn't a relationship with Jesus. The Bible says not to. Both people would end up miserable." He patted her arm. "Just wanted you to know." He climbed into the driver's side, waved, and drove away.

Cami had never been so confused in her life.

CAMI SPOKE HER MANTRA ALOUD, put the car into reverse, and backed out of Morgan's driveway. It was tough leaving. She and the twins got along, and it was fun being a surrogate aunt.

Though they didn't call her Aunt Cami. Morgan didn't respect her enough, she guessed.

But things improved some between them in the last twenty-four hours.

Reminded her of an old movie, *Enemy Mine*.

Funny how desperation can force someone to cross that No-Man's-Land in a relationship.

She'd plenty to reflect about on the trip home. At least she felt less guilty about not staying to help, knowing Nohemi was available for Morgan. And she's a much better choice. Cami realized the compassionate woman knew the correct words to say in the perfect moment. Morgan needed that—perfection. It was how she gauged everything.

And then that last comment from Jeff. What did he mean? That he was interested in her, but she must join his church? Or despite being interested, was walking away? Did he realize she wasn't big into religion? Well, he's gotta make the first move. Not only was she swamped between the work project and Gram's project and more trips to Phoenix (Morgan would call for her to come, she knew), but adding dating to her schedule would require giving up something. She already hired out necessities like housecleaning, laundry, and grocery shopping. She wasn't about to hire someone to date Jeff for her. If he dated anyone else, she'd rather remain ignorant. At least with her in Tucson, she didn't need to worry about running into him and another girl out on the town.

Those thoughts, and *The White Album*, kept her going until she reached home minutes before nine. Once in her condo, she sent Ray a text to let him know she was back and would be in the office come morning. She'd even arrive an hour early, to prove she was serious.

Despite her great intentions, though, Ray met her at the lobby. Either he spent the night, or he knew her too well and showed up two hours early to cow her. That man! Oh, to be on equal footing with him, a peer. The vice-presidency position couldn't come through quick enough. He was making her life so miserable she might lose her head and do something rash. Homicide. Or quit.

By lunch, both ideas were more appealing. She closed her door and turned off her light to work in peace without Ray's constant dropping by to see if she was busy. How did interrupting her help? Did he hope to catch her slacking? Even when she'd showed him everything she'd put together at Morgan's, he didn't look impressed.

She'd pulled up her app to try some rough draft copy for the big release when another knock sounded. If she stayed quiet, maybe he'd go away, figure she was in the break room.

The knob turned. She watched as a hand snaked over the edge of the jamb as it inched opened. It was more like viewing a movie than sitting in her own office seeing it happen.

Monty's face peeked around the corner and saw her.

"You always enter offices you assume are empty, Monty?"

He sputtered.

"If I cared to talk with anyone, I'd have asked you in. But entering when you think I'm gone raises some serious flags. What do you want?"

"Sorry, just wanted to see if I'd left… ah, no, guess I didn't. Sorry, I'll go." He started his escape.

"Oh, no. Not that easy. Get in here. We both know you left nothing. And this is the second time I've caught you. Am I not making myself clear?" She almost added that she should report him to Ray, but she didn't want to appear a tattletale who couldn't handle her own problems. "Why are you here, Monty?"

He sighed, and plopped in a chair, raking his hand through his hair. "Honestly—"

"Drop that opening, I've no reason to imagine you're being honest. Just tell me."

"Fine. Where are you with the project? Maybe I can add to it."

"Steal my ideas, then? Monty, I am supposed to be sharing

and teaching you. All you have to do is ask if I'm not passing information fast enough." She came around her desk and sat on the corner closest to him. "Look, I get that you're hungry for this to be big with your name on it. But you gotta understand how I process things. I need to mull them in my head, follow the threads before I can spit them out for us to develop more. Ray is someone who talks it all out, mistakes, rabbit trails, all. That works for him, and he gets excellent results. It doesn't work for me. So if you want the best from me, you must let me get to where it's ready to share. Trying to scoop me wouldn't do either of us any good. Do you understand?"

He nodded. "Yeah, I, ah, yeah. So where do we go from here?"

She pointed him toward the table. "Let's sit, and I'll bring my laptop over and show you what I have. I'm not where I wanted to be, but I'm close."

A couple hours later, she was glad she'd shown it to Monty. They brainstormed on what she'd done—he liked the tag line—and designed twenty mock print ads for their presentation. They'd be easy enough to adapt to Facebook, Instagram, Twitter, and any of the other big social media sites. The next step would be video presentations. She pledged not to leave him out, and he agreed to stay out of her office when she was gone.

Not that she trusted him. He'd promised before. No, she'd seen that hungry look in other colleagues' eyes, and was aware of the backstabbing that occurred when trying to climb that career ladder over former "friends." She wouldn't trust him to bring her a Diet Coke instead of Diet Pepsi. But she would keep her word.

Friday things returned to normal with Ray. Or as normal as Ray ever got. He at least asked about Morgan, and when Cami explained her cousin faced possible surgery, he revealed a moment of humanness and said, "That's tough." Then he moved on with his priority list. Ray would never get nominated for humanitarian of the year, but he was honest, and you always knew where you stood with him.

That evening Cami arrived at her condo overwhelmed. It seemed as if it'd been years since she'd relaxed and done something for herself. She decided on a protein shake for dinner, too tired to even order delivery, and pulled out the box. Gram's letter and the started shawl were just as she'd left them. Tomorrow was the crochet group. At ten. She'd googled the address and found it would only take about fifteen minutes to travel from her place.

Morgan didn't need her. She'd texted that the results from her CT scan showed she'd need exploratory surgery to determine about the tumor. They'd do that with the biopsy. Which wasn't yet scheduled.

So Cami returned her thoughts to Saturday's meeting.

Should she store Gram's shawl and yarn in a canvas bag? That box was too unwieldy to carry. She searched her bedroom closet shelf, taking down things she'd forgotten she'd saved. This was her first place. Gram helped her buy it with money she'd inherited from her parents. It grew in a trust until she finished college. Cami never knew it existed until Gram presented her with the news at graduation. Now she owned this place free and clear, making her bills much smaller.

Gram also helped her move in. That had been a fun weekend, and the memories made her smile as a tear escaped. Now, eight years later, Cami realized she'd not gone through most of the stuff on her shelf. She was a creature of habit. If she didn't use something with some regularity, it gathered dust. She could toss many of these things. Or give them to charity.

As she grabbed more from her shelves, Cami started stacks—Keep, Toss, Give. She could add some of her clothes to those piles too. It was about time she cleaned her closet.

Then her hand swiped something. Far in the back. A familiar tingle traversed her arm. She pulled it to her and sat on her bed, brushing her hand over the canvas bag. It wasn't that she'd forgotten about it. That would never happen. But she'd chosen not to remember. It brought too much mingled happiness and pain. At least it did as a teen. Then it overwhelmed her. She couldn't even open it, even when Gram begged her to.

But she did now as tears streamed her cheeks. It was the crochet kit Gram and Mom put together for her when she first learned.

Kate

Fourteen years ago

Kate could hear Cami in the kitchen, grumbling about not getting to go to the state fair with friends from school. If she'd not let it slip about no adult supervision, Kate might've said yes. But the fairgrounds could be dangerous for young teen girls alone. Her job was to keep the child safe. Nothing said Cami must like it.

"I still don't get why you won't let me go." Another cabinet door slammed.

"Go easy on my cabinets and stop yelling. Vanna just turned a P and I'm trying to guess."

Cami stood in the doorway. "Gram." How could she turn those four letters into three syllables?

"Yes?"

"Didn't you go places when you were my age?" Her fists propped on her hips like she'd just uncovered the key to the mirror of truth.

"Yes, dear, I did. However, if I went to the state fair or some other such event, I either traveled with my family or a trusted adult." No need to recount the time Kate and her best friend sneaked out of town to hear the Beatles at Convention Hall—in Las Vegas. Her best friend's older sister drove the three of them the four hours to Nevada, where they had the time of their lives, and drove the four hours back. Somehow her parents figured things out, and her father waited when she came home. She'd been grounded and stripped of car privileges for a month.

Having just gotten her permit, that hurt. And she was two years older than Cami when she pulled that stunt.

So it didn't matter if she sympathized. Her job was to protect and guide Cami to adulthood. The risk was too great.

Cami ducked back into the kitchen with more slamming.

"Catherine Amelia Madison, please do not slam my doors. I'm sorry I upset you, but my cabinets are innocent." Kate finished the row she'd worked and held up the project. Soft baby yarn stitches variegated in shades of blue and green were coming together to create a shower gift for a young lady at church expecting her first boy. She rubbed the created fabric next to her cheek. Yes, a baby would be lovingly swaddled in this.

Vanna turned another letter. This episode touted a jungle theme night. "*The Lion Sleeps Tonight.* Yes!" Fist pump.

"What'd you say, Gram?" Cami was back in the doorway.

At least she was speaking. "I figured out the puzzle. Come, do them with me. Jeopardy comes on in a minute. Wanna guess who figures out more questions?"

"Nah, you always win."

"Then keep me company while I beat the TV contestants." Even if she was right to stop Cami from going, she hated to have a rift between them. With every glance at the child, she saw her daughter. She'd not lose this connection too.

"Fine." Cami plopped in a chair in time for the last puzzle.

The middle guy used his turn to get vowels. "E please."

Vanna turned letters as Pat announced, "There are three Es."

Before the guy could guess, Cami and Kate spoke together. "*The African Queen!*"

TV guy couldn't conjure an inkling. But the lady next to him figured the answer. She became the night's big winner.

"You came up with that one on your own, sweetie. Good job."

Cami shrugged. "Not hard. We watched it last weekend."

Kate smiled. "Yeah. Did you like it?"

Another shrug. "All right, I guess. Had some funny parts.

Humphrey Bogart was no Brad Pitt. And Katheryn Hepburn's no Julia Roberts."

Kate captured her granddaughter's gaze. "Cami, are you saying movie stars should be flawless? Most people I know don't fall into that stepped-out-of-a-magazine pose. Besides, what we see on TV and in magazines comes after a makeup artist has worked miracles. For my money, regular-looking actors are far more interesting." Where did these kids get that idea?

She tried to have the same conversation with Morgan. Only Morgan's mother insisted on appearing as if she should model for Vogue. Made it difficult to instill the message. Maybe Cami would catch her meaning, though.

"Yeah, I guess so. I'll never look like Michelle Pfeiffer."

"No, you are prettier."

"Aw, Gram. You have to say that." But her attitude softened.

"No, I don't. And you are. When you're an adult, you'll be stunning. But remember, genuine beauty is on the inside."

"You tell me every day. But I'll still never be a model with my legs." Cami wouldn't go swimming with her friends because of it. Kate overheard her one night telling someone she couldn't swim. That was a whopper. Kate taught her when she was six. The girl swam like a fish. But rather that confront her for lying, she let it go knowing the disfigurements on her limbs were only the outward signs of the markings on her heart.

Kate set her crocheting on her lap, giving her full attention. "Honey, those scars are bigger to you than they are to anyone else. So what if someone asks? Just say you were in an accident, but God healed them."

"He didn't do a great job. Not if I can still see them."

"Maybe they are little signs of His mercy to remind us both that He took care of you."

Cami crossed her arms. "I don't want to talk, Gram. Let's watch your shows."

Kate studied the girl a moment. Even after counseling and moving on, anger remained. She understood. That was not only

Cami's parents who died in the crash, it was Kate's only daughter. But anger wouldn't bring healing. And Kate's healing couldn't be complete until Cami's was.

Must be something she could do to engage her granddaughter. Something that would bring hope and peace and comfort.

A memory dawned. Kate left for Tucson to visit and was crocheting with Saundra when Cami burst in from school. She and Saundra talked on the phone before that visit about how Cami was mature enough to learn to crochet. Kate made the special trip down with a new set of hooks, some yarn, and a little kit of stitch markers, tapestry needles, a tape measure, and yarn nippers. They would teach her while she sat between them on the couch.

Cami took to the craft like a natural, first learning to make a slip knot and chain. When she'd done that several times, she advanced to making single crochet stitches.

Kate spent the weekend, and Cami made little squares of single crochets before she left on Sunday. The next time she visited, Cami was ready for the double crochet stitch. After making a couple five by five potholders, Kate showed her what it looked like to alternate the stitches, single, double, single, double. Cami ran her hand over the bumpy fabric and beamed up at her. Kate's heart had swelled at the sweet connection.

It swelled again at the memory. Only Cami never crocheted once since she'd moved in. Kate made a point of bringing Cami's crochet bag to Phoenix along with any other mementos the girl might long for in her new home. But she'd yet to bring out the bag, though she surveyed Kate working her hook for long spells.

"Honey, let's crochet together. It's always more fun that way. I'll bet you could make a giant granny square throw for your room. I've got plenty of yarn. Want to pick your colors?"

Cami shook her head. "No, thank you." Her arms remained crossed, but somehow the child looked like she retreated deeper into the chair.

She laid her own project aside. "Why not? You were getting good, Cams. Bet you could make something real pretty."

"No, I don't have my stuff anymore."

That was a lie. Kate knew. Cami must realize that. "Are you sure? I could have sworn I put it on the shelf in your closet. Let me go see. Maybe you didn't notice."

The girl popped out of the chair. "No, that's okay, Gram. I can't remember how, anyway."

"But I'm the one who taught you. I can always teach you again. And you know what I said about muscle memory? It comes back."

"No!" Cami trembled. "No, Gram. I can't."

Kate stood and pulled the girl to her. "What do you mean?"

Cami drew back and ran her forearm across her eyes. "I can't do it, Gram. Remember what it was like? You on one side. Mom on the other? That's my favorite vision of her, the three of us together. So I tried to make some stitches a few months ago. It was like my right arm was missing. I can't do it without her. I can't."

Kate tried to draw her close, but she pushed away, ran down the hall, and slammed her door.

Chapter Seven

CAMI

Present day

Cami swallowed hard as she slipped the crochet kit bag over her shoulder with her purse and locked her car. The beep made her jump. *Doggone it, Gram, why'd you have to tie Morgan's money to all this? I could walk away if you hadn't.* Truth was, she was ready to bolt, toss it all to the back of her closet again, and move on with her life. But knowing what she knew about Morgan and the terms, she couldn't. Not fair.

Signs directing her to a modular room at the rear of the parking lot showed her where the crochet group met. They called themselves Needles of Hope. Must mean they included knitters too. She trekked to the building and sighed before grasping the door handle and crossing the threshold. If she was going to save her family, she needed to find some help. This was the place.

About seven women sat in various types of chairs pulled into a circle as conversation stopped mid-sentence and she became the center of attention.

"Welcome! You must be Cami?" A lady in her fifties put her yarn aside and stood.

Cami plastered on a smile. "I guess I must be. Hello. I found the right place."

"You did." The woman smiled in return while others peeked up from their work. But their faces were friendly enough. A few smiles beamed here and about. Guess she wasn't an intruder. "Let me introduce you to the girls." She started with the grandmother type closest on the left and went around the circle, each waving as she called her name. "This is Opal, then her granddaughter-in-law Dericka. Flossy, her daughter Chrissy and granddaughter, Lori. That's my daughter Ellen, and I'm Nell. Ladies, this is Cami and she found us on line. Guess that means we've gone viral."

Several chuckled as Cami glanced about for a seat.

"You can sit here." The second one she'd met—Dericka?—pulled a bag of yarn from the chair next to her.

"Thanks." As she sat, she tried to come up with an opening to explain her presence. But everyone was back to their tasks, and talk about Nell's latest adventure with her sons resumed. Cami was fairly sure it was sons, but it took a minute to figure it out. In the meantime, she held the crochet bag on her lap.

"What are you working on?" Dericka's voice was soft, so she almost missed it. The girl was thin with wispy long blond hair pulled into a braid and wire-framed glasses slipping from her nose that she peered over.

"Oh, I need to finish a project my grandmother started. I haven't crocheted in years." She fished into the bag and drew out the shawl and instructions.

Dericka put her own project aside and fingered the edge of the shawl. "That has a nice touch. Looks similar to a virus shawl, at least from the start. May I see the pattern?"

Cami handed it over. Maybe Dericka could be talked into completing the shawl. "Been a long time since I read a pattern."

"Oh, it all comes back, just like riding a bike." This came from Opal. She peeked around Dericka to make contact. "Who started this for you?"

"My grandmother. She passed and left it to me."

"I'm sorry, hon. So, Dericka, is this something you might teach her?"

Dericka nodded. "This is pretty simple if you know the basics. You could try a few practice pieces to regain your rhythm. But you can do this. I'm happy to explain things if you have a question."

Cami's fingers slipped through the lacy designs of the shawl's fabric. "Well, I was hoping to find someone to more than help me remember." She coughed as embarrassment slithered up her throat and her face heated. "I sort of imagined asking someone else to finish it."

Opal and Dericka's eyes grew wide.

"I'm happy to pay."

Opal patted Cami's knee. "Oh, honey, you wouldn't want that. This is a family thing, special."

"I don't want…" How did she explain without over sharing? "I'm so swamped at work. And I need to get this finished. I might have a lot of trips to Phoenix. For my cousin. So paying for help would be better."

Opal continued to stare, well, not exactly stare. Something like Gram used to when she waited for the rest of the story.

"Like I said, I'm happy to pay. It's time that I don't have."

Now Opal leaned back. "I thought you looked familiar. I used to live in Phoenix too. You're Kate Hanson's granddaughter. Between your name and the other stuff, I pieced it together. Well, I'll be."

It was Cami's turn to stare. This woman knew Gram?

"Kate spoke of you and Morgan so often that I felt like I knew you both. I was sorry to hear about your grandmother's passing. I moved down here with Dericka and Thomas a couple years ago, but I stayed on the prayer chain."

"Yeah, I wasn't ready for that." Cami blinked hard, keeping the tears at bay. "So, since you knew Gram, would you be willing to help me? Would either of you please complete the shawl for me? Please?"

Dericka picked that moment to finish going through the instruction pages. The letter from Gram sat on top. Both Opal and Dericka stared at the handwriting.

Cami started to snatch it away but remembered where she was. "May I have that back?" She trembled, her voice a notch above a whisper. How could they read through her private message?

Dericka handed the sheets over. "I'm sorry. I never meant to snoop."

"But I'm glad we did. Cami, you're in a tough position. I didn't get it all, but read enough. You must do this. It was important to your grandmother. And since she was my friend, we'll abide by her wishes."

Cami stuffed the papers and yarn into her bag and ran her wrist under her eyes. "Yes, well, I'm not sure I can handle that pressure."

"Of course you can. Your grandmother realized it would be a challenge, but she also knew it wouldn't be too hard for you. What if Dericka came by to help you a few evenings a week until you are ready to solo?"

Dericka looked like someone had thrown her into a fight she wasn't ready for. "But Gramma, what about the kids? What will Thomas say?"

"Honey, I'll watch the kids. You've gotta get away on occasion. I know Thomas will be supportive since I'll tell him you need it." Opal grinned like she'd solved all the world's problems.

"You'd be willing to come to my house and help?" Cami focused on Dericka. She couldn't force her into something she didn't want to do.

But the girl's face relaxed. "An evening away from my children, for a short time, sounds lovely. I'd like to help." The more she spoke, the more she smiled.

So it was settled. But not the way Cami wanted. Even with

the support, she remained stuck making the shawl. Not what she'd intended.

"Why not get your things back out? Dericka can show you how to practice your stitches until you are ready to tackle Kate's project."

Cami pulled out a separate skein and a hook. Would she be able to make it create what Mom and Gram taught her so long ago? It took three tries to get the slip knot right, not because she forgot but because her hand shook so.

Dericka leaned over. "If you start your chain with a larger hook, and then switch to a size smaller, your bottom border won't be so tight."

Yeah, she'd forgotten that. Cami chained about fifty loops before grabbing the next smaller hook. She'd noted that most of the stitches in the pattern called for double crochet, so decided that's what she should practice. But it was torture poking into the chain, creating the stitch. Her hands twitched, her eyes watered, and she hurt as though each insertion of the hook stabbed into her heart. "I can't. I just can't."

She shoved it back into her bag.

Opal rose and stood in front of her, placing her hands on Cami's shoulders. "I understand this is more than you getting out of finishing the shawl. That's why Kate wanted you to do it. She'd say something about facing your fears, right?"

"I am stronger than my fears." Cami sniffed.

"Maybe you are. Or maybe you need Someone Who is stronger than you and your fears to fight for you."

Cami glanced up at the woman. That differed from what Gram taught.

"May we pray for you? That's our big thing around here, praying. Prayer goes into everything we make. Are you okay with it?"

Since she was stuck, and everyone depended on her, she'd better get some help. And she was willing to try about anything. Including prayer. "Sure."

"Girls, Cami needs our prayers. Let's gather 'round."

The ladies all put down their crafts and circled Cami, placing their hands on her head, shoulders and back.

It was a little much being touched by so many at one time, but she swallowed, bowed her head, and squeezed her eyes tight. This was her last option.

THERE WAS no concentrating on the work project this evening. Something Opal mentioned made her second-guess the tag line. And that was the heart of her campaign. Gram always told her she was stronger than her fears. Even when Cami doubted, repeating the words gave her courage. When she said them enough, she believed them.

But what if she wasn't stronger than her fears?

What if that's why she couldn't face picking up a crochet hook?

This entire day differed from all Cami anticipated. First her plan fell like a dud. Next, Opal turned out to be one of Gram's old friends. And that praying over her thing. Talk about strange. She couldn't remember that happening before.

Or could she?

Something about it reminded her of the hospital. Gram said her church prayed, and she imagined people standing around her bed saying words that weren't medical. More dream-like than anything. Did Gram's friends pray over her when she was in the coma? Was Opal one of them?

Nah, she would've mentioned that. She and Gram must've become friends later, maybe after Cami left for college.

But she woke from that coma.

Would she wake from this nightmare?

Cami shook her head and grabbed a bottle of water before plopping on her couch. She needed to rethink this campaign. That was one thing Gram drilled into her. Integrity. She needed to show integrity with the products she endorsed. Maybe she should reread the books again. Did that tag line jump out because she knew the author was Gram? What if her grandmother included another message or theme throughout?

With those print ad mock ups ready, starting over would be a pain, but if she focused, she could binge read every other book for the continuing thread she knew Gram would have put in them. And maybe if she put them on Audible, she'd have a different viewpoint while she tried to practice a few double crochet potholders.

She pulled out her kindle, started the Audible version, and then pulled out the skein and her hook. With a deep breath, she yarned over before pushing the hook into the chain, yarned over again, pulled up the loop, and then pulled through two loops, creating a double crochet. She'd made one. Not much, but she'd done it.

The voice came through the speakers, making her drop her work as she covered her mouth. Gram read the story to her. Gram's voice, here in her living room. With her one more time. Saying things she'd said when Cami was a teen. Guiding her once more. If she'd wanted to know what her grandmother thought, well, here she was telling her straight out.

Only Cami couldn't take it. She stopped the book, tears streaming down her face. *Not fair, whoever you are, God. That was mean. And painful.* She curled into a ball, sobbing into her couch pillow. How would she ever get through this? The campaign? The shawl? She needed more than just being stronger than her fear. She needed help. Someone to give her strength and guidance. Someone to make these problems go away. She experienced enough problems in her life. And why make her the champion for her cousin? Morgan didn't even like her. To shove them together, making Cami the one to help Morgan's life come together? Not fair.

At once it dawned. If Cami came through with the campaign, this wouldn't just be that she was out from under

Ray's thumb and capturing a promotion she'd more than earned. This would be a sizable payment to the estate of the late Katheryn Hanson. And that would make everyone's share of the inheritance grow. A lot. Morgan wouldn't have to worry about her bills or anything happening to the kids.

And Cami, well, she'd have enough capital to start her own ad agency if she wanted.

But nothing would happen unless she finished the shawl. Without that, all the inheritance, all her hard work would give some charity an early merry Christmas.

Talk about pressure. The stakes grew in her mind. Now she wasn't just helping Morgan get her needed share. Oh, no, this was far beyond that.

Which meant something else. She might not have any conflict of interest in any technical sense, but potential conflict abounded. If she were successful, the client would be pleased and make lots of money. They in turn would pay the author whatever was negotiated in the contract, with residual royalties paying long into the future. That income would go to the author's heirs. And she was one of them. She worked for herself. Basically. And that was the conflict.

This was too much. She needed to talk with someone. Someone who could advise without bias and keep confidence too.

Mr. Jones came to mind. He was Gram's lawyer, so that made sense. But he might pull his "not at liberty to say" bologna. Which would help. Not.

What about Morgan? Well, she wasn't unbiased, per se. And having Morgie tell her what to do would send her up a tree. A memory of Morgan pelting her with rotten oranges while she tried to hide in the orange tree's branches flitted through her mind. No, by now she was a bigger target, and Morgan might recruit the twins to help her. That brought a smile.

She could call Ray. But he was biased for other reasons.

Cami sat up. Why not? It's what Gram would've done.

And others did for her today. She closed her eyes and inter-laced her fingers. "God, if you hear me, and give a hoot, I need help. I guess I'm not stronger than my fear. In fact, I'm terrified of failing both projects. I'm terrified of letting Gram down, and I guess Morgan too. Maybe a little of letting down Ray. And me. I don't want to fail, and prove I'm as inept as everyone tells me I am. So, if you can help me or send me someone to help, that would be great. Thanks. Oh, and amen."

She wiped her hand over her face as her phone's chime rang out. A text. From Jeff.

Jeff: You're on my mind tonight. Okay to call?

Cami's hands shook, this time in disbelief. She typed sure, took a deep breath, and hit send. Her phone rang a second later.

"Hey."

"Hey, yourself. How are you tonight?" His voice soothed, hitting all the right tones.

"I'm a little, oh, stressed. Strange day. Made some even stranger observations. Feeling like I'm having to hold a bench press a lot longer than I'm able." How did she explain he was an answer to prayer? A pastor can't share what's said, right?

"Want to talk? I'd be happy to listen."

"Sure is a lot. Do you have the time? Plus, you might hear a few unflattering things about me." That's another problem. But maybe it's better he saw how selfish and wounded she was now instead of later.

"I've plenty of time. It's a quiet evening. Tell me what's weighing you down."

You asked for it. "I'll give you the big picture first before I fill in the details. But I gotta ask, please don't share any of this. I'm breaking a rule, or ten, to tell you. But I'm stuck and need to trust someone. In fact, I prayed about it and you texted, so I'm figuring God sent you."

"Thank you." He chuckled. "It goes no further. I promise."

She sighed and told him about Gram's passing, the will, and

the work project, and that she learned the author from the big new work campaign was her grandmother.

He didn't interrupt but gave an occasional uh-um, so she knew he listened.

"Still hanging with me?" She wanted to be sure before she filled in the rest concerning why crocheting was the hardest thing Gram could ask of her.

"I'm here. But you've got a kicker, right? What is it?"

It took another ten minutes to get through all the details, living with Gram, and her aversion to crocheting. She had to mention the crash, but since her emotions were on steroids at the moment, she referred to it briefly. Relating those details would wreck her. She ended by explaining about the meeting that morning. Some. She didn't need him to know she was such a novice with prayer.

He got awful quiet. Did he breathe? Then he exhaled, and she knew he'd help.

"That's a lot on your shoulders for sure, Cam. Add in taking care of Morgan through that, and I can appreciate the load. But since you asked for my advice, I say you're headed in the right direction. First, you already told your boss about the connection. It might be fair to inform the client too. Let them decide if you belong on the team. And I tell you this from experience, you must set-up times for each project. You know your schedule best, but what if you say, keep work that you'd do outside the office to two hours when you get home, and then put in an equal amount of time into the shawl after? On weekends, set a specific amount of time for each project. Be sure to allow rest time. You must recoup or otherwise you'll burn yourself out. This is more important since both have the identical deadline. With Morgan, you have Nohemi to help. And I can step in as needed. So you put your concentration on the two projects, but set up time goals for them. Give yourself rewards for sticking to the goals for the week."

"Like what?"

She could hear his smile through the phone. "Well, I'd toyed with the idea of driving down next Saturday. Can I take you to lunch?"

His smile was contagious, even through the phone line. She couldn't help but return it. "I'd like that. I know a place. Might never have heard of Migi's, but you'll like the menu. I can't be long, though. Not if I'm setting up a schedule. No tempting me away from my duties."

He laughed. "Deal. Text me your address, and I'll let you know when I'm on my way."

They talked a while longer. He even prayed for her before they said goodbye. But when they hung up, Cami realized she had a plan. She could make this work.

Morgan

Morgan stretched. Morning came so early. As an army brat, she was used to that, and as a single mom, the habit helped. But some days it'd be nice to sleep in. Especially when you expected a call from your doctor with information you didn't want to hear. If she slept in, she might dream it all away.

"Mo-o-m! Aidan won't give me my Trix!"

The twins were too young to appreciate sleeping in during Spring Break. The sole thought that occupied their minds consisted of playing all day with no homework.

"Aidan, let your sister have her cereal. I'll be down in a minute." She knew better than to yell down to them, it only meant she set a poor example and they'd continue doing it. But she was tired, too tired to go straight there.

After tossing on some jeans and a cute T-top, Morgan pulled her hair into a ponytail. Something about standing at the mirror, seeing her reflection with swinging black hair, made her chest grow tight. Was she about to lose it? If they found cancer, and started chemo, and she went bald, how long before she could pull it into a ponytail again? That was the least of her worries, she knew that. The bigger question was would she survive? Would she live to see her kids finish grade school, high school, college, get married, start families?

And here she worried about her hair. How vain could she be?

She tossed the brush on her vanity, and just to prove she wasn't as wrapped up in her appearance as she knew she was, she forewent any makeup before slipping into her sandals and taking the stairs to her life in the kitchen.

"Everyone got something to eat?"

They both replied around the food they chomped. "Yes, Mom."

"Don't talk with your mouths full, it's not appealing guys. Okay, I'm going to mix up a shake and maybe we can figure out a plan of fun for today."

"Yay!" Filled mouths still.

Morgan checked the fridge for healthy items for her breakfast drink. Maybe she needed to make sure she put better things into her, cut back on coffee, sugar, and fats. Maybe she was too late.

But maybe she wasn't, and she'd grab at any hope.

Once the blender had stopped, she poured the drink, and took her seat at the breakfast table. "What shall we do today?"

"Go swimming?" Aidan looked hopeful.

"Kiddo, we've got the pool in the backyard. We can do that anytime. I'm thinking of something that we don't do often, something special." To create a memory for them, just in case.

"Could we go to As You Wish?" Addie grinned, and she'd made a point of swallowing first.

Aidan perked at the idea. "Yeah, I like that place."

"Me too. Okay, let me set an appointment." Morgan stepped away to call the design your own pottery store. She discovered it a few years ago, and the kids loved going. They could pick out the green ware, the paints, and do whatever they liked. The people there were patient and sometimes held classes. Plus she had the points to cut the cost. This wouldn't just create a memory, but would give them a souvenir to hold too. She reserved a table for ten-thirty.

"We got a place saved. So make sure you finish your chores. I'll check your rooms as soon as I'm finished with my shake. Aiden, it's your turn to unload the dishwasher, and Addie will fill it today and wipe the table. Whose turn is it to sweep?"

"Addie's." Aidan was a born supervisor.

"Fine, then Aidan, you are on trash, and recycles detail. Get them out. Once chores are done, play until time. We'll leave about ten, got it?"

"Gotcha, Mom." They echoed each other as they raced off to put their rooms into order for inspection. Sometimes her military upbringing helped with organizing the basics. They could run the vacuum and dust on Saturday. If she was here.

That was the hard part. Today was Monday. She couldn't say what the rest of her week held. Until she heard from the doctor that they'd scheduled her surgery, life was without a plan, only contingencies. Just in case.

But thank God for Nohemi. And she meant it. The woman had been a Godsend. The only church Morgan ever attended was Gram's. Her mother hadn't had time for it, and her father never had time for her. But Gram did, and Gram believed. That was enough to know it was special. But with Gram's church on the other side of the valley, nearly an hour's drive away, and not knowing about the surrounding churches, she hadn't gotten into that habit with her kids.

Of course, she could have pursued it, googled at the very least, but she worried she didn't know enough to keep from getting mixed up in a cult. That was the excuse she told herself.

But yesterday, she and the twins had attended Desert Bloom Community. They were welcomed and treated as family. Jeff, rather Pastor Jeff's sermon was clear, funny at times, deep at others, and caused her to want to read her Bible. Except she didn't have one. But some of the congregation used an app on their phone. She checked with Nohemi, who showed her how to download it. Morgan fell asleep reading through Psalms last night. First good night's sleep she'd had in months.

Another reason she didn't want to start her day.

She rinsed her glass and set it in the sink before heading to her own room to double check. Fair was fair. If she held the twins accountable, she needed to hold herself too.

Then it was onto their rooms. They each did good jobs. She'd never had a lot of trouble about them pushing things under the bed or cramming into the closet. Could be because she started the training early. Or perhaps they hadn't thought to try it yet. The teen years were down the road. But probably not as far off as she hoped.

That gave her time to read. She got comfy on the couch in the family room while the kids drew with chalk out on the patio. She pulled up the YouBible app on her phone and went to the next Psalm—Psalm twenty.

May the LORD answer you when you are in distress;
may the name of the God of Jacob protect you.
May he send you help from the sanctuary
and grant you support from Zion.
May he remember all your sacrifices
and accept your burnt offerings.
May he give you the desire of your heart
and make all your plans succeed.
May we shout for joy over your victory
and lift up our banners in the name of our God.
May the LORD grant all your requests.

Morgan shook. She couldn't stop the tears. It was as if someone heard her. Someone saw what she faced and cared. Someone peered into her heart and said it would be all right, somehow.

She needed these words where she'd see them often. Then

she had an idea. After glancing at her watch, she figured there was enough time. She pulled out her computer and typed the words into a Word doc. She could've cut and pasted the verse, but she wanted help to commit this to memory. Once written, she played with the font until she found something she liked that she could replicate. Then she hit print.

Another glance at the time showed they needed to leave. She called the twins to wash up, get all the colorful chalk dust off themselves, and then head for the car.

The West Gate location was the closest to her house. They arrived about ten minutes early, but that was fine. The kids got to search the shelves for the new ideas, decide what they wanted.

As for Morgan, she'd already formatted a plan. There were square tiles she could get, putting one verse per tile. She could mount them across the top of the mirror in her bathroom. She'd have to raise her eyes each day to read them, but that went with what Pastor Jeff spoke of yesterday, how God is the lifter of her head.

They'd gathered their supplies—Aidan designed a mug and Addie a keepsake box—when Morgan's cell chirped. She told the kids to stay in their chairs, and stepped outside the door to take the call. From her doctor.

"Mrs. Pembroke?"

"Yes, this is she." Morgan's hands sweat over her phone so much she was afraid it would slip and crash on the concrete entrance.

Waiting for the details made her heart stop mid-beat. Guess she was just one more person to call to relay information. The all-business voice continued. "You're scheduled for outpatient surgery Thursday, this week. You'll need to arrive at seven in the morning. Eat nothing after six Wednesday evening, and only sip water after that until midnight. Are you taking any regular medications?"

Isn't that in the file in front of her? "No, I'm not."

"Good, just needed to double check. So nothing by mouth

after midnight. I'll send you an email with all this information." She checked to make sure the email address was correct.

"Please let me know if you have any questions. I know they can occur after we hang up. Just call me." This nurse was no Nurse Dottie, but she was astute.

"I will. I'll look for the email. And thank you."

Morgan pocketed her phone as the weight of the words stole her breath. Thursday. She had two more days to give the kids normalcy. And then what?

Chapter Eight

CAMI

Present day

Dericka would arrive in a few minutes. Cami scanned her living room. She wasn't used to having people over, so though the place was comfortable for her, she wasn't sure how someone else would view her living space.

Did it matter?

Well, it shouldn't. But Cami rarely made long-term friends. She stayed connected with the few she retained from college on Instagram, and that's about all. She never had time to do social things. And now that her classmates were married with little ones, social media worked best. But that meant no visitors darkened her condo door.

This could be a test run. What if Jeff came in her place? Would he wait outside her door? There's a lot to consider when dating a pastor.

Was she dating a pastor? This might be a onetime thing.

No, she hoped for more than that. She wanted to get to know him. Just the notion brought a smile, plus a niggle of fear at the nape of her neck.

The doorbell rang.

Dericka.

Cami held the door wide. "Come in."

Dericka appeared as shy as Cami remembered.

"Can I get you something to drink? I've got iced tea."

"No, thank you. I've my own." The girl held up a metal travel cup.

"Okay." Cami shrugged.

"Oh, nice of you to ask. But I'm picky. I'm a dietitian, and if I'm going to tell others what to ingest, I need to follow my own guidelines." Dericka smiled and tipped her head to the side. "Thanks anyway."

"No, I get that, no worries. I've also got water if you need any. Just let me know."

Her guest nodded, though she had yet to take a step into the room past the entryway.

"Well, come in and have a seat. Anywhere is fine. I've got my stuff over here." Cami picked her bag up off the parson's table. "I tried pretty hard yesterday and finished this potholder. It's a little wonky, but guess I improved the more I did.

Dericka sat on the couch, so Cami joined her and held out the pot holder for inspection.

"Yes, it's a matter of keeping consistent tension. You already knew that, though. But since things are coming back to you, want to try working on the shawl?"

That sent a tingle up Cami's spine. But she must begin soon, or it would never get done. "Sure." She pulled out the start and the pattern.

"The letter says you are ready for row ten. Let's see what that row looks like." She studied the instructions. "You know, I'm thinking, this pattern is great for learning how to read charts. That would make things easier to follow. Have you ever read a chart?"

Cami shook her head. "No, never even tried. Are you sure? It's one thing to remember past skills, but a whole 'nother to learn a new one. And we've so little time."

"You'll find this helps. I get a sense you are a visual person." She glanced around the living room.

Cami followed her gaze, noting with fresh eyes the colors, patterns, and art that created her comfort zone. She'd always considered herself an auditory learner. But Dericka could be right. "Okay if it isn't too intricate."

The girl shook her head. "It's not. The only symbols you need are for the double crochet, the single crochet, and the chain. Just those three, really. And with a chart, when you've got it on a tablet, you can make it as large as you want. This is a four row pattern. I'd pull it up on my phone, but if you have your tablet available, I wouldn't need to send it to you."

Cami grabbed her iPad, and as per Dericka's instructions, googled Virus Shawl crochet chart. Boom. A bunch of thumbnails of increasing fan sketches came up. She clicked on one and increased the size.

"See? Here along the bottom are the row numbers. The odd rows start on the right. The even on the left. Find row ten." Dericka already pointed to it. "This is where you will start by chaining three. That counts as the first double crochet. Now add a double crochet in the top of these." She pointed to stitches Gram made. "Once you have ten, counting the three you chained at the beginning, stop and show me. See here in the pattern? You will single crochet and chain four between these clusters, but I'll show you that next. Go ahead. I brought something for me to do while you're working." She pulled out a similar shawl, only the pattern changed partway down. Cami recognized the granny stitch for a few rows before morphing back to the virus pattern.

"What are you making?" It was in a creamy white, and the yarn looked so soft.

"The pattern is called Virus Meets Granny. It combines the two. This is my new favorite prayer shawl." Dericka stroked the yarned fabric.

"I can tell why. May I ask you something?"

"Sure." Dericka stopped, folding her hands in her lap over her work.

"You called it a prayer shawl. Gram called this a prayer shawl too. What does that mean? I don't understand."

The girl stared at her hands. "Well, they are very personal gifts. You pray for the person you're making it for."

"What if you don't know who that is? I'm supposed to give it away, but I've no idea to whom. How do you know?"

Dericka smiled. "Often I don't know. I turn them in to our group. When I pray I try to imagine all the things someone might deal with—illness or death of a loved one, financial troubles, anything that'd makes them overwhelmed and alone. The shawl wraps around them, and they experience the embrace of God's love, realizing we prayed for them and they're not alone anymore."

"Oh." Cami all at once recalled how Gram often wrapped a shawl about her when she sat in the living room and crocheted. She'd not seen Gram's shawl in years. Wonder where it went? "Okay, I understand. Do I have to pray out loud? Not sure I can do that."

This time Dericka chuckled. "No, you don't have to. I can't pray out loud with others in the room either. But God hears even when it's in our heads."

Cami took a deep breath, slipped the correct-sized hook into where the place holder kept the last stitch safe and chained four before making a double crochet. When she'd made ten, she showed Dericka who showed her how to make the little single crochet-chain four-single crochet part, and told her where to stop again. Thirty minutes later, Cami completed row eleven. And the stitches appeared okay. Maybe not as neat as Gram's, but passable. But she'd completed the last row of the pattern. She was ready to start the repeat. Dericka stayed until she'd done three more rows, but then needed to head for home. By that point, Cami had experienced each row of the pattern and grew a tad more confident.

She walked Dericka to the door and thanked her for coming. They made a plan to meet each Monday until the shawl was finished. Cami breathed a little easier.

Now time to work on the campaign. She had important changes to make after listening to Gram read on Sunday. That was one of the hardest things she'd ever done. But also she recalled Gram tucking her in bed, or stroking her hair, or wiping a tear just by hearing her voice again.

Cami searched her purse for the jump drive she'd purchased after the last episode of Monty trying to sneak in to her office. Not that she didn't trust him.

Well, that was it. She didn't trust him. After getting all the files moved onto the new drive Sunday night, she felt more secure.

And with all the meetings she'd attended today with her regular accounts, there'd been no chance to even open the big project. But that was okay. That's what tonight was for.

She got comfortable at her kitchen island, powered up her MacBook, and popped in the drive. Her laptop scanned it for safety. All good.

Until she opened it.

The drive was empty.

Cami stared at the empty file. No way. Could she have been so careless as to lose the entire campaign? No, she was positive she'd moved it all to the drive. But if she did, where was it?

Monty. Would he have stolen all her work? He couldn't be that stupid. Could he? Didn't he consider she'd take this whole mess to Ray? Or was he counting on the fact that Cami wouldn't want to be viewed as weak and needing her boss's help?

What possessed the man?

Or did he do it?

She couldn't go pointing fingers without proof, and as of this moment, she had none. And with the presentation in two days, should she spend her time tracking down the thief? If one existed. It still might've been her own clumsiness.

Or should she plow through? Work as if her changes were the original plan?

The second choice made more sense, though it fought with her spirit of justice. Doggone that Monty! She knew he did it.

But instead of dwelling on it, which was quite tempting, she pulled up a fresh Word docx and typed her brainstorming notes. Then she redid the spreadsheets with the current information. At last she created the new mock up ads for social media. That put her about halfway caught up—and it was midnight. The rest would need to happen tomorrow. However, she'd never leave her jump drive alone in her office again. That was for certain. And her door would remain locked no matter what.

The brief night's sleep did nothing to dampen her sense of injustice, though Cami still figured pushing ahead with the new ideas the best way. She now understood that Gram's use of the stronger than your fear phrase carried another component. One that explained how to be stronger. It was through the strength that faith shored up inside.

That brought up all sorts of thoughts. Ones that challenged her own stand on faith, made her study hard on what might come of a relationship with Jeff. Still, she had no time to follow those rabbit trails. This presentation must be ready for the clients, who would arrive at the conference room tomorrow morning expecting to be wowed.

As Cami worked behind a locked door, it hit her. Monty must realize she'd discover the problem. And she was sure he counted on her being too proud to rat him out. But what did he hope to gain?

If he knew she'd discover the theft well before the meeting, did he hope she wouldn't have time to build the campaign again? Or that she'd be so rattled she'd defer to him to present? Why was he so eager to make her look bad?

Then she realized.

He wanted the vice-presidency promotion too.

If he was that hungry for it, what else would he do?

That question put a halt to her musings, sending a shiver down her back. Perhaps she had underestimated him.

No perhaps about it.

Her phone rang. It was Morgan. "Hey, Cam."

"Hi, Morgan, did you get a date for your surgery yet?"

Pause. "Yeah, it's tomorrow. I realize this is short notice, I tried to figure another plan. Nohemi will have the twins. But someone must drive me. Can you do it?"

Tomorrow. She couldn't. "Morgan, I'm sorry. The biggest presentation of my life is tomorrow. But I have an idea. I'll call you back. Don't panic, 'kay?"

Morgan's sigh said more than her words. "You'll call me?"

"Yes, trust me." *You've got to trust me, Morgan.*

Cami promised two more times before Morgan let her go. Then she texted Jeff, asking him to call when he could.

A minute later she explained her dilemma.

"Sure, I can pick her up and take her home. If Nohemi brings the kids back to Morgan's once I have her settled, she'll care for the whole bunch. It's not a problem."

"Looks like I owe you when you arrive Saturday." Heat crept up her cheeks as she imagined their first date.

"I might hold you to that. But no worries, I'm a pastor, remember?" He chuckled, and she wrapped the sound around her.

"I'd better get to work." She started to tell him what Monty did, but held back. What if it'd been her own stupid mistake? Not that she believed it, but still, without proof…

They said their goodbyes, and she called Morgan, who sounded a bit breathless as she answered.

"Cami! Thank God."

"Morgan what's wrong? I told you I'd call." Did she regard her so little? Why did that pinch so much?

"I know. I'm trying to relax, and it seems as if everything that could go wrong will. Bruce texted. Seems he somehow heard that I've been sick. I mentioned something in my email to

Mom. I should've remembered that she and Bruce's mom are friendly, so I'm guessing that's how he found out. He wants me to send the kids to live with him. I can't catch a break." She sobbed.

Great. But somehow, she never blamed Cami. Instead, she turned to her for… what? Help? Advice? Encouragement?

So little she could offer in the moment, but she'd give what she had. "I spoke with Jeff. He's going to pick you up in the morning, and coordinate with Nohemi so that once he has you home, she can bring the kids back and watch over all three of you. Can't do much about Bruce. But I'll listen if it helps. I'm sorry."

Morgan's big breath came through the speaker. "No, you helped, Cam. Thank you. I didn't feel like I knew Jeff well enough to ask. I'm not so panicky now. But I've got to duck Bruce's messages until I know what's going on. He's a good father and loves the kids. He deserves time with them. But pulling them out of school to move across the country? Never. I can't live without them. Especially after he…" She sniffed, and Cami heard her fight her tears. "Thanks for helping, Cami. I'm glad I can count on you. I'll let you go. Bye." *Click.*

She's glad she can count on me? Cami never imagined she'd ever hear those words.

Oh, she needed some air. After saving to her jump drive, she ejected and pocketed it. And then for further security she locked her door before heading to the break room.

Someone must be celebrating a birthday as a platter of cupcakes airbrush-tinted with pastel colors sat on the table with a note. Help yourself.

She did. To a pink one. Whipped cream frosting on a choco-late cupcake? Too good to resist. She poured herself a cup of coffee too, and headed for her office. As she slipped her key in the lock, she noticed a hint of blue on the door handle. She ran her finger over it, smearing the speck. It was fresh and smudged like butter. Or whipped cream frosting.

She glanced down the hallway noting all the opened rooms. But no one headed to or from their office. It could be anyone.

After getting her door unlocked, she closed and latched the bolt. And kept off the lights. Still enough sunlight streamed in her windows from the strong desert sun, so she didn't need them, anyway. Let everyone figure she was gone. Maybe she'd catch the sneaky varmint, whoever that might be.

Like she didn't already know.

She popped her jump drive back into place, opened the file, and continued her work. An email popped up from one of her suppliers who asked a question regarding some of the giveaways she'd planned. From her queries, it looked like Monty might have reached out.

Cami crafted a well-worded response, including the changes she wanted made, and ended by instructing her supplier to only respond to her with regard to this project.

As she hit send, she glanced up to see her door handle move. Not much. She'd locked it. But enough to spot someone wanted in.

Cami hopped from her desk and pulled her door wide.

Ray stood on the other side. His face startled. "You're here."

"Where else would I be?" She turned back and let him follow her inside.

"Hmm. Phoenix?"

"Ray, I went one day last week, and I kept working while I was gone. Why are you so worried about me not doing my job."

He plopped in a chair. "Maybe because I know you. This is getting to you with your grandmother being the author. Or maybe because I told you to keep Monty in the loop and you haven't."

"Who says I'm not keeping him in the loop? Monty? I've met with him several times and laid out my plans as well as explained my way of doing things. I even brainstormed with him and noted some of his ideas, not that they were all that brilliant." Boy, she wanted to tell Ray about the break-ins and theft, but something held her back.

"Okay, maybe he's overzealous." He patted the arms of his chair and stood. "But why the locked door? Lights out?"

"So I can concentrate. You want my best, right?"

"Right." He sighed. "Fine, I'll catch you later." And he left.

She followed to the door and relocked it, leaning her head against the polished wood and drawing in a ragged breath. These changes better be worth it.

CAMI THUMBED THROUGH HER CLOSET, searching for the perfect blouse. She wanted to not only look professional, but capture the feel of someone who understood the *Stinkerella* stories and appreciated their depth. She also figured today was the day she'd come clean with the client and let them know who she was, or at least who her grandmother was. That notion made her stomach clench. With a hand to her gut, she slid the next top down the bar.

Yes. Found it. Soft, drapey off-white silk with a crossover front. She'd wear the gray pearl on the silver chain that Gram bought her for her seventeenth birthday, and her charcoal heather slacks, tailored with cuffs. It was classic, professional, and feminine. It said experience and style.

With that settled, she texted Morgan to wish her good luck, and then Jeff to say thanks.

He sent back a smiling emoji.

She'd practiced her presentation three times last night and once more over coffee this morning. Nothing left to do but get there.

At her car, as she turned the ignition and started to quote what she always did, she paused. If her strength came from inner faith, then what did she have faith in? She shut off the engine. Did she believe in God?

She had no time for self-discovery. For now, she'd be stronger than her fear, and when this was over, she'd figure it out. Because strangely, she feared bombing the presentation more than crashing on the way to work. Too much depended on this.

Cami restarted the car, spoke her mantra, and pulled out of the parking lot. Fifteen minutes later she settled into her designated spot and locked up, dragging her tech bag behind her.

Once in her office, she breathed a sigh and loaded up her bag with the handouts she'd prepared.

"Going somewhere?"

She spun at the voice. Monty.

"Just hauling things to the conference room."

"I've got it all set up. Figured that gave me something to do when you kept cutting me out of the project."

"I didn't cut you out. And you didn't need me to tell you about it all, did you? Not since you hunted for the information yourself." Two could play his game.

"I don't know what you mean. But I did my best to follow what you parceled out and got us ready." He held the door as she pulled her bag to the hall.

"Well, thank you for that. I appreciate it. Something happened to my work, or I'd have shared more yesterday. Instead, I needed to use my time to recreate the campaign from the beginning."

He looked surprised. Maybe he didn't do it. Maybe she'd dumped it herself.

Maybe she would one day accept that. Ha.

"If that's the case, I can take the lead. I know what to say." He seemed a little eager. Wonderful, she'd be questioning his motives forever.

"No, I've got it. But thank you. This will be great." She pulled her bag into the conference room to find the clients and Ray already seated. She did a fast glance at her watch. No, the time was correct.

"Guess you didn't get my message. We're starting a little

earlier." Ray shot her a gaze that said she'd messed up before things started. Fan-freakin-tastic.

"Good thing the room's setup. So if you want to skim the pages while I pull out my iPad and link to the SMARTboard—"

"No need, Cam. I've got this." Monty stood at the front of the table and preceded to go through the original plan.

Ray's mouth pressed into a hard crack. She'd never told Monty that Ray wasn't thrilled with the tagline.

And the clients? Vince and Doug looked unimpressed, but Felicia was downright unhappy.

And Cami realized why. Felicia possessed a personal link to these stories through her daughter's experience. She understood there was more than just "You're stronger than your fear" and didn't want to send the wrong message.

At the earlier meeting Cami spoke up, saving the day. Today she saw her moment. She'd allow Monty to fall flat on his fuzzy face. She owed him nothing, and he wasn't able to read the crowd well enough to know he was bombing. So let him. Served him right for sneaking in and stealing her work.

"And so you can see, with these as the basis for our print ad campaign, and the video I shared for our commercials, the tagline can take the lead. You are stronger than your fear. It'll be iconic like Just Do It. Questions?"

Felicia leaned forward, her hands clasped on the paperwork in front of her, eyes focused on the SMARTboard screen behind Monty. "Did you even read one book?"

Monty's jaw dropped. "Ah, well, I helped Cam here with the project and we built this based on her knowledge of the product." He threw a *help me* glance her way.

"Then the answer is no. You didn't bother."

Monty must've burned like an inferno inside because his face grew as rosy as a flame. He sputtered a moment more until he found his words. "Cami's the granddaughter of the author. She oughta know what's in those books."

That wasn't the way she planned to share that piece of information. Now all eyes focused on her. "Yes, I recently discovered that my grandmother wrote under a pseudonym. However, I've not received one dime from any book, nor have I any holding in her estate. I let Ray know about it as soon as I learned of the connection. It is possible I could one day be an heir, but that's not been determined yet. I've not sought legal representation to fight to make it so."

She glanced at those around the table. Did they believe her? She figured Ray did, but she didn't know these clients on a personal level. Nor did they know her. "If you'll give me a moment—"

"We've given enough time. Thank you for your presentation. This isn't what we want." Felicia scooted back her chair and stood. Vince and Doug did as well.

"Let me walk you out." Ray held the door, and Cami knew he'd use his last idea to save this deal.

The door closed. Monty turned on her. "You changed the plan, didn't you?"

"Yes. If you didn't break in and take things before they were ready, I'd have shared it all with you."

"Right. No way I trust you. You were going to shut me out this whole time." He ran a wrist across his mouth, and she could almost smell the anger that steamed from him.

"Monty, no one planned to shut you out. You did that to yourself. You were supposed to tell me about the time change too, weren't you? And you planned all along to hijack the presentation. If you read the room, you'd have seen early on that this wasn't the way it should go. You've no one to blame but yourself."

Ray stepped in. "She's right, Monty. You're fired."

"What?" Monty glowered like he might throw a punch at Ray.

"I had security called before returning. They'll take you downstairs. My secretary is packing your office and will bring the box to you."

"You can't do that!"

Two burly guards walked in.

"I just did. Get out."

Monty shook the guard off from touching his arms, glared at Cami, and stormed out.

Once the room was clear, Ray motioned for her to sit again. He took the next chair. "And what do I do with you?"

"What do you mean?" Cami went from relieved at Monty's departure to a gulp of fear choking her.

"I mean, the clients don't know what I do. I figured out who was being truthful with me. You realize you could've come to me." He leaned back in his chair.

"I almost did, but I didn't want to appear like I was tattling to Daddy."

"We've been friends longer than I've been your boss. Tell me what happened."

So she did. Each incident of Monty getting into her office, of the jump drive disappearing, and how she couldn't prove any of it. "So it would have been my word against his."

"It would've been. But I trust your word. Now I'm not sure what I'll do. The clients suggested I fire you. The promotion is off the table. Can't fix that. We lost a big one, Cam. This is bad." He looked as sympathetic as she'd ever seen.

And that scared her the most.

Chapter Nine

KATE

Fourteen years ago

The kitchen door slammed, followed by books crashing on the counter. Kate knew the sound. Cami was home, and something was wrong.

"I'm in here, sweetie." The late February days were pleasant, so kids required no coats on the walk home from school, but still cool enough that the lovely prayer shawl her Sunday School class had presented to her after the accident comforted without getting too warm. She pulled the crocheted fabric closer, knowing she needed wisdom to handle whatever set Cami off again. "Come in, tell me about your day."

"I hate school." She plopped in the chair and kicked her shoes off. "Gram, why can't you homeschool me, so I don't have to deal with all those morons."

"What morons are you referring to, dear?"

"Kenny Blackstrom. He's plain mean. He wants to get me in trouble with the teacher." Cami's arms were crossed, and her chin tucked while her face squinched.

"What kinds of things has he done?" *There's more to this story.*

"He keeps poking me in the back with his pencil, trying to get me to squeal when we're supposed to be quiet. And…"

"And what?"

"He told me I gotta give him my answers to the homework, or he'd…"

"He'd what?" Someone was bullying Cami?

"He'd tell the boys I showed him my chest." By now her face was beet red and she wouldn't meet Kate's gaze.

"Honey, that's inappropriate. To inform the teacher isn't tattling. You're supposed to." She set her crocheting down and stooped in front of Cami. "Please tell me you let someone know."

Cami shook her head. "I did something else."

Now Kate worried. "What did you do?"

"I started a rumor about him. I wrote something on the bathroom wall. I said he's gotta sit like a girl to—"

"Catherine Amelia, that's… not right." Part of her wanted to laugh, though. Her granddaughter stood up for herself and put a bully in his place.

"There's more."

Now it wasn't funny. "What else?"

"They figured out the approximate time I wrote the rumor. All the girls seen in the area at the time gotta give a letter to their parents. Or you." She glanced up at that.

"Oh, so you're a suspect."

"Yeah, and they called us all into the principal's office, and gave us the letters, and wouldn't even let us talk. I don't want the others to get in trouble. They'll never like me then. But I don't want to get in trouble for making him stop picking on me." Cami uncrossed her arms and leaned forward, face to face with Kate.

"Let's look at the letter first."

Cami went to the kitchen and returned with an envelope before replopping in the chair.

The letter inside explained that because their student was seen in the vicinity of that restroom near the time the defacement happened, that parents were to speak with the child. Seems Arroyo Verde Middle School didn't have enough proof, though they had videos of who entered and exited the lavatory. They were concerned about punishing the wrong person. "This says nothing about a discipline. And you told me everything. They just want the problem stopped. However, Cam, the mature thing is to apologize to the principal for defacing the wall. Offer to wash the area where you wrote. You could say that you now understand your methods were misguided, but you were dealing with someone who bullied you. What do you say?"

Her face blanched. "Gram, you wouldn't make me do that, would you? That's so heinous! That's worse than what Kenny did."

"No honey. Doing right is always the better option."

"Gram!" She jumped to her feet.

"I can go with you. If you want. But you'll find more satisfaction in doing this yourself."

"What if I just write a letter? A confession like in the movies?"

Kate patted her shoulder. "If you are too afraid, I guess that would do. But shouldn't you face your fear, so you know who is stronger?"

Cami ran to her room and slammed the door.

Had Saundra slammed doors like that? A smile grew from the inside out as Kate recalled so many times that same bedroom door closed with a giant BAM. She'd give the girl time. But by dinner, she'd better be out to help.

Five o'clock on the dot, Cami wandered to the living room holding out a sheet of paper, her neat fourteen-year-old penmanship on display. "Here, tell me if this works."

Kate scanned the page.

Dear Ms. Fortuna,
    I am the one who wrote on the restroom wall.
    I don't want the other girls to suffer. I will wash the wall.
    I did it because I was being bullied. I am sorry.
    Sincerely,
    Cami Madison

"That says it all, kiddo. Except you might mention who bullied you so maybe they can do something." Kate handed it back. "Nice job, but are you sure you won't try in person? Sometimes that one-on-one is much better than when you send a note. Even when it's a good note."

Cami shook her head. "No, this is all I can handle. I'll put it in an envelope and stick it in my backpack. Then I'll help with dinner."

Kate held Cami's face long enough to kiss her forehead before releasing her to finish up. The girl grew taller every day. Once upon a time she bent to kiss the top of her head. In another year, her granddaughter might be as tall as she.

They returned to their usual evening, watching their shows, and enjoying their time before bed. Come morning Cami looked a little pale, but Kate could overhear her mumbling, "I am stronger than my fear." It would be okay. She'd send up a prayer or two, though, just in case.

This was her day to volunteer in the church office. Kate enjoyed doing that since she often was the first one to hear of a need. Sometimes she was able to do something to help, behind the scenes, something between her and God. Today she delivered groceries to a single mom with sick kids who wasn't feeling so great herself. She sent flowers to an elderly woman who'd fallen and broken her hip. And she ordered a Bible for a new believer who didn't have one. All in the church's name. No one needed to know she did it. Besides, her income was comfortable enough. It didn't hurt her one bit.

But by two o'clock she headed home, arriving at two forty after a few stops.

When she pulled into the drive, she could hear the phone inside ringing. She shoved the key in the lock, turned and ran to answer before her landline stopped. "Hello?"

"Gram? Where've you been? I've been calling forever!"

"Cami? Oh, I ran some errands. What's the matter?"

The sobs came through the speaker. "Gram, Ms. Fortuna said that since I confessed, I admitted to defacing the restroom. I'm suspended for a month. You gotta come get me."

Suspended? "On my way."

"Please hurry, Gram. I want to get out of here."

What did they do to her granddaughter? "I'm coming. Sit tight."

Kate pulled her keys from the door, then put them back in to lock up before tearing off for her car. Suspended? For a month? That's overkill. What was going on? A week's detention, maybe. But to embarrass her when she exhibited the courage to come forward? How did this woman's brain work?

A police cruiser sat parked at the edge of the AVMS lot. Good thing Kate spotted it before she sped into the school zone. She found a slot, locking the door before charging for the entrance. But then something slowed her, a niggle. What kind of example would she share by storming inside? She took a deep breath, changing her walk to purposeful yet not emotional.

Cami sat on a bench near the secretary. "Gram?"

Kate held out her hand, giving Cami a signal to wait a second, and approached the counter.

"May I help you?" The office manager was all business.

"Yes, I am here regarding my granddaughter, Cami Madison. I'd like to speak with someone to learn what happened."

"One moment, I'll let Ms. Fortuna know you are here. If you'll have a seat?"

"Thank you." Kate sat next to Cami while the clerk made a call.

"Gram, nothing worked like you said."

Kate winced. "I got that impression. I need to talk with the principal. This makes no sense."

"You won't like her. She looks all perfect, and talks as if she knows everything, but she never listens, and she doesn't care."

Kate hated to accept that. But the alternative was that Cami left out strategic information. The only plan was a discussion with Ms. Fortuna. And she'd better be willing to listen as well as talk.

MORGAN

Present day

Pastor Jeff opened the passenger door for Morgan and offered his hand.

"Thanks."

She was so groggy, and her stomach still roiled.

They'd been stuck at the surgical center an extra two hours because the anesthesia nauseated her.

"If you give me your keys, I'll open up for you."

A reflexive argument rose, but she hadn't the strength to get the words out. Instead, she unhooked them from her purse.

He accepted them, and then wrapped her arm about his and guided her to the front door. Once inside, he helped her sit on the couch. "Stay here and I'll get you situated before I call Nohemi."

It required her all to simply nod. Morgan tipped over, her head finding the pillow, and sleep overtook her.

Someone shook her shoulder. "Morgan, I'm putting this trash can next to you. And here's a frozen bag of peas for your head. Would you like a cup of tea?"

She tried to focus as the speaker morphed from three fuzzy blobs into one less fuzzy shape. Pastor Jeff. "Okay." Something flitted through her brain. She needed to remember...

But she couldn't make her mind function. All she wanted to do was sleep. Maybe tea would help. If she could wake enough to take a sip without dumping the contents of the mug.

"I called Nohemi, and she's bringing the kids back in an hour. I told her you were having a time with the anesthesia so she's giving you a chance to recoup." He called from another room, the kitchen most likely, so she only needed to listen while her eyes stayed closed.

But they popped open. The kids. She didn't want them to catch her like this. What could she do?

The shock of being discovered by her twins shot an adrenalin surge, enough to help her push up to sitting, the bag of peas still on her head. The world remained woozy. She blinked a few times. Her focus improved.

Pastor Jeff came in with a mug. "I'm guessing anything I add might mess with your stomach ailment. So plain chamomile. Is that okay?"

She cleared her throat. "Yes, thank you."

He handed it over. "I also put an ice cube in to cool things a little. That's how I do mine." He shrugged. The guy was a tea drinker. Who knew?

She sipped and nodded. "It's good." After a sigh and scanning the room, she remembered. "When will the kids be here?"

"In about forty-five minutes, give or take. I'll stay here until Nohemi arrives. Don't worry."

Morgan swallowed, trying to form her words. "I'm… not worried. To be alone. I can't let them find me like this." A tear slipped through. How pathetic could she get?

"Want me to assist you up the stairs? I won't go beyond the top. But if you can make it to your room, I'll help." So he was drawing the line between propriety and helpfulness. Funny how that popped in crystal clear.

"We've a bathroom. Down here. Help me to the door? I'll splash my face. Brush my hair."

He grinned, a dimple sprouting. No wonder Cami was taken with him. "Sure, that's a better plan."

She put the frozen peas on the coffee table, and he helped her stand, guiding her along to the downstairs facilities. Once past the doorway, she held tight to the countertop to keep steady. After a couple splashes of cold water, she felt a difference. More alert. She pulled the brush from the drawer and ran it through her tangles before pulling it into a ponytail. Addie owned more hair ties in that little container than Morgan owned her whole adolescence. Finding one wasn't hard. The getting her hair pulled through was the challenge.

Pastor Jeff waited outside the door, ready to help her back.

"Let me see if I can walk on my own. I'm doing better. Just be prepared in case I stumble."

He chuckled. "You aren't going down. Not on my watch. I'll stay close."

Security flowed in his voice and she hated herself for craving it. That was not the way to assert one's independence. The idea made her grimace.

"You hurting?"

She shook her head. "No, just mad at myself. I hate having to depend on others. Did they say when I need more pain medication? I can't remember the instructions." She'd reached the couch and dropped like a load of wet laundry.

"I have the pages. They prescribed nothing, said Tylenol or Ibuprofen would be enough. Do you have any on hand?" He handed her a folded packet.

She opened it to see all the notes. "In the bathroom medicine cabinet. Did they give information in front of you? Like any conclusions?"

He shook his head. "You know HIPAA laws. Maybe something's in the papers."

She noticed he never attempted to read them, but stayed back. If Cami didn't want the guy, she might. After trying to focus on the wavering print, she set the pages on the coffee table with the peas. "Do you recall them saying if someone would call with results?"

"Yes, that I do. Or rather, I heard them say you are to call them either today before four o'clock or tomorrow morning. The number is on the paper. I'm guessing to discuss the findings." He glanced at his watch. "Only three now. You've got time. I'll make myself scarce so you have privacy."

The guy was way too nice. "Thank you." She patted her pocket for her phone, then peeked up.

Her purse swung from his index finger as he brought the bag to her. "Everything should be in here." After he handed it over, he walked into the next room.

Morgan fished out her cell and called the surgeon's office. One automated choice was to hear findings from recent tests. She put in a code. Then received her message.

She listened to the words she'd dreaded. "The tumor is located at the far left of the liver, central to the body. It has attached itself to the bottom left edge of the liver, and is approximately six centimeters in diameter, though the shape is oblong. Pre-biopsy findings surmise it to be malignant. Chemotherapy treatment is advised to shrink the tumor to make it operable. Please make an appointment with our office at your earliest availability for more explanations and to schedule your treatment appointments. If you want to hear this message again, press—"

Morgan broke off the call. The worst outcome. Well, one was worse yet, inoperable. And she still might find that out.

Pastor Jeff peeked around the corner. "All done?"

She nodded, not trusting herself to speak.

He came closer, pushed the peas and papers to the side, and sat on the coffee table facing her. "Looks like you got some hard news. I won't pry, but I can listen if you ever need to talk."

This time she forced through a whisper. "Thanks." The temptation to pour everything out to him was strong, but she wasn't ready to speak the words aloud.

"Nohemi and the twins will be here in a bit. Would you like more tea?"

She shook no. It'd only mean another trip to the bathroom. Right now she didn't trust her legs.

He patted her knee and stood. "Okay, please let me know if I can do anything. I'll be in the chair." He motioned with his head, and then grinned at the silliness.

Morgan was starting to like his grin. But she'd liked Bruce's too. That made her cautious about trusting her grin instincts. She closed her eyes.

Car doors slammed, and running thuds sounded before the front door flew open. Aiden followed by Addie burst through the door. "Hi Mom."

She smiled at them, so full of life, so happy. To snatch that away was criminal. She held out her arms and they both gave her hugs.

Addie sat next to her. "Ms. Nona has two dogs. They're both small."

"Yeah, and one is a boy, and one is a girl, like us. She named them Jack and Jacqui. I like Jack best." Aidan remained standing in front of her.

"And I like Jacqui best. It's fun at Ms. Nona's house, Mom." Addie leaned against Morgan's arm, so she embraced the girl and pulled her close.

"How about I check on dinner? Kids, who wants to help?" Pied Piper Nohemi made it sound like a fun activity. They both cried "Me" and followed her to the kitchen.

Morgan stared at her palms until a quiet cough caught her attention. She looked up to see Pastor Jeff standing, the coffee table between them.

"I'm leaving you in expert hands. Call if you need anything. Or have Nohemi. I'm happy to help." He paused. "I'm still praying, Morgan. Remember your Abba loves you and cares about all this."

She blew out a breath and nodded. "Thanks." The notion

that she should walk him out passed through her mind, but she couldn't make herself rise.

Pastor Jeff flashed another grin and pulled open the door.

Someone stood at the threshold, fist raised to knock.

Bruce.

Cami

No chance at the promotion.

Did she hear him right?

Ray didn't stutter, and he definitely wasn't happy. Cami knew she should have talked to him and not tried handling things herself. Being a big girl carried its downfalls.

No matter how she finagled, the answer remained the same. To be honest, she was lucky he didn't fire her. She owed their friendship for that.

Ray let her have the afternoon off, knowing she needed privacy to regroup. Or maybe he grew tired of her pleading. Either way, Cami locked up and headed for her condo. She'd pulled into her space when her phone rang. Dericka.

"Hi, Cami. Hope I'm not bothering you."

She turned off the engine and climbed out while talking. "No, I'm taking a personal half day so just got home. What's up?"

The line grew quiet.

"Did I lose you?" Cami stuck her keys in the lock and opened her front door.

"No, well, I'd such a powerful impression to call you. Are you okay?"

Cami swallowed wrong and almost choked. "Oh? I've had one awful day. I've experienced worse, but not many. You've got a good impresser."

"Would you prefer to be alone? Or may I come over?"

That was a strange way to offer. But the girl's company was

gentle, easy. Might help her discover a streak of hope in this mess. "Sure, come on. I'd only be whining to myself. Maybe with someone here, I'll make myself look for some positives. Right now, though, I'm a tad lost where to start."

"I'll be by in ten minutes. I'm a safe listener."

Cami could well imagine that. "Good, see you in ten. And Dericka, thank you." She hung up and changed out of her work clothes into jeans and her favorite Beatles t-shirt. After a quick trip to her mailbox, and pouring herself a glass of iced tea, she sorted her mail—most of which was junk—and waited for Dericka's knock. Funny how she looked forward to her new friend's visit.

The girl arrived right on time, with her own travel cup. One of these days Cami should ask her what she drank. Maybe after-while. For now, sitting and crocheting with her seemed a soothing idea.

"Thanks for having me over again."

"You're welcome to stop by anytime. Did something happen?" Cami wondered if there's more to this visit.

Dericka reclaimed the spot on the couch from the last lesson.

Cami sat too.

"Oh, to me? No, everything is fine. I'm still working at setting up my website. I learn a little something, apply it, discover a question, and have to research and learn more. It's a cycle. One day, I'll get this. Gramma Opal is great with the kids and encouraging to me. They're on spring break, so they're bowling today."

"Oh, and you're not taking advantage of the quiet to do more applying?" Cami winked, hoping to make her comment more friendly.

"Well, that was the plan. But I got this notion I should visit you. One that grew stronger when you said you were having a bad day.'"

Cami searched the girl's face. She didn't look wacko. "What do you mean?"

"It's just an impression that I needed to talk with you. I'm not trying to pry, but you can tell me about your day. It won't go farther." Dericka's hands were folded in her lap, and she kept glancing between them and Cami.

"Well, I was… you sure you want to hear this?"

"Only if you want to tell me." Now she met Cami's gaze.

With a sigh, she started over. "I've been working on a special project—that I can't tell you about—but if it came through, I'd be a shoo-in for the promotion I've dreamed of since starting.

"My boss assigned me to work with another guy to help train him. That other guy, we'll call Moron, was a low-life. He broke into my office and stole things." Cami caught Dericka's eyes growing round at that, but she said nothing. "I realized what happened about the time I knew that our concept for the campaign was all wrong. I worked like crazy to put together a new one. But Moron figured he'd be the hero and land the account. Seems he fancied the vice-presidency too.

"Well, he scooped me using the old ad and offended the clients. On top of everything, he got himself fired—the only bright spot. My boss held on to me because he knew I wasn't to blame. But the promotion is off the table. The biggest client our company has ever handled, and because I kept my mouth shut wanting to see ol' Moron paint himself into a corner instead of standing up and delivering what would have worked, we lost them. I mean, it was almost gleeful to watch him fall on his face after what he put me through. But it backfired on us all. And now you've heard my sad story."

Dericka blinked, her face blanched. "That's what occurs in the corporate world?"

Cami chuckled. "My little part. Sleaze balls and stand-up people are everywhere. I want to be one of the stand-ups. But sometimes letting the sleaze balls catch it right between the baby blues feels…"

"Justified?"

Cami cocked her head and wondered for a second. "Yeah, justified. Not that I'm a caped crusader or anything, but something is satisfying about helping those like Moron get his."

"How about now?"

With a sigh, Cami could almost hear Gram in her head asking the same thing. "Not so good knowing this fiasco cost our company. And my boss trusted me. All I needed to do was talk to him first, or at least stop ol' Moron McSleaze before he tripped us all up. I held the antidote, but I waited too long to speak up."

Dericka took a breath, like she was drawing courage to say something. "Did you pray about any of this?"

Cami swallowed. "No. I'm not much of a pray-er. I started doing that while crocheting, it's a little easier to pray for someone else. But I'm not even sure I do it right or that God listens."

"Have you asked Him to forgive you and to be in charge of your life?"

She shook her head. The idea never crossed her mind.

"I'd like to show you something." Dericka pulled out her phone and opened an app. "Here's what the Bible says. In Ephesians 2:8 it tells us that we are saved by grace through faith in God. We only have to ask His forgiveness and accept His gift of freedom." She paused, rolling her lips in, and taking a breath. "Would you like me to pray with you?"

Cami watched as this shy young woman stepped beyond herself to offer help. This cost Dericka, but she accepted it as important enough to fight through. Maybe that made it important enough for Cami to try. "I guess. I shouldn't have done what I did. And I'm tired of trying to take charge of my life, though I don't trust anyone else to know what's best. Besides, adults shouldn't go blaming others for their own mistakes. But trusting Someone all-powerful sounds good about now."

"You know He loves you, right?"

"Who, God?"

"Yes, God, Jesus. John 3:16-17 tells us that He loves the world so much He sent Jesus to save us, not condemn us. To make it so we can live with Him forever. Gramma Opal told me that she prayed for you with your grandmother, for you and your cousin. She wanted you both to learn to love our Savior."

The unshed tears burned Cami's nose and eyes. "Gram did that?"

Dericka nodded. "Yes, she did. She loved you."

"And you'll pray with me?" Cami sniffed. She needed that love.

"I'd be honored. May I hold your hand?" Dericka reached out.

Cami grasped her friend's outstretched palm and stared at her lap. "I don't know what to do."

"Just repeat after me if you agree. Jesus, I am sorry for all the things I've done wrong. Even when I was sure my reasons made it acceptable."

Cami repeated the words, squeezing Dericka's fingers as she did.

"Your Word says that if I ask for forgiveness, You will forgive me, cleanse me from my sin, because you already paid for it."

She repeated those words too.

"Please come live in my heart and help me do things Your way."

Cami glanced up. This was what she wanted. She spoke those words too.

"Your Word says You love me. I choose to believe that."

Cami chose to, then and there.

"I love You too, Jesus. In Your name, Amen."

Cami didn't want to lie. But as she searched her heart, a warmth of love for the One Who loved her and died for her grew and permeated the broken parts she'd worked to keep hidden. To say she understood was way off. But she could, with honesty and sincerity, repeat the I love you. "Amen."

Dericka hugged her but pulled back fast. "This makes us sisters." She possessed a sweet smile.

"Guess it does. Thank you."

"Better?"

Cami pondered that. "Yeah, I'm lighter somehow."

"Whoo hoo. Paying attention to my impressions is a good thing."

Chapter Ten

MORGAN

All the air in the room vanished. Morgan's first instinct was elation at seeing the man she'd loved with everything in her being. Followed by an emotional flash flood of how he chose his job over her and the twins, She wanted to slam the stupid door in his handsome face.

Too late, the kids rushed past. "Daddy! Daddy!"

He stepped in, throwing a size'm up glance at Pastor Jeff, and caught the twins in a giant embrace as he dropped to his knees on their level. "Oh, I've missed you guys."

"We've missed you too, Daddy." The longing in Addie's voice pierced Morgan's heart.

"Yeah, Dad, we missed you. Come meet Ms. Nona. She's in the kitchen." Aidan grabbed Bruce's hand and dragged him to his feet.

Bruce glanced back at her, something unreadable, and then followed them through the dining room.

Morgan shook. What more would be heaped on her? How would she remain tough for her children? They needed her, but the pelting came from all sides—physically, emotionally, financially. She was about to lose her mind. Like the cherry on top of a strychnine sundae.

Jeff sat on the coffee table in front of her. "I better go. Though if you prefer me to stay I will. If I can help, I'm here, but I don't want to add any problems."

The tears broke their boundaries. "That's not possible, pastor. It's as awful as I can imagine."

He pulled a couple tissues from the box on the end table and handed them over. "Maybe we need to pray?"

She stared up at him, realizing prayer was the only suggestion she couldn't find fault with. After a nod, she bowed her head, her hands clasped in her lap.

Pastor Jeff touched her crown. "Lord, the load Morgan carries is heavy and bringing her to her knees. Thankfully, she's falling at your feet, Jesus. We ask you to lift this burden and replace it with Your peace that passes all human understanding and keeps our hearts and minds focused on You. If the wind and waves obey You, so can the cells of Morgan's body, and every other difficult situation she has calling for her attention. You are her Rock, her security, her protection, and her wisdom. Envelope her with Your love, and let her hear the steady lullaby of Your loving heart. In Jesus's Holy Name, we pray. Amen."

"Amen." She raised her face and ran the tissues under her eyes. "Thank you. To let go of control isn't easy for me. Every battle I tighten my grip."

He smiled. "I'll be praying that you relax your hold and rest in Jesus's arms. I'll head out now. Don't try getting up yet. Take your time and let Nohemi and your family care for you. It's humbling, but when you accept their assistance, you accept their love. It'll help you let go."

"I'll try. Won't be easy."

"I know. Someday I'll tell you about it." He patted her shoulder and left.

The door closing sound must've carried. Bruce came into the

living room followed by the twins. "Hey guys, would you let me talk with your mom a few minutes? I'll be back, I promise."

He shouldn't make those promises. Who knew if he'd keep them. Morgan winced. She needed to be more gracious, at least for the kids' sake. Bruce always was a good father.

"Your friend is gone?" He peered at her again, and she recognized his meaning. He was jealous.

That was a laugh. After he'd started dating already.

"That's my pastor. He's the one who brought Nohemi to us, and he took me to my procedure today while she watched the kids. Oh, and Cami is the one interested in him. I haven't time for that garbage." She wanted to be snarkier, but an argument in the first face-to-face conversation they'd attempted in a year wasn't a brilliant idea.

"I didn't know."

There's a lot you don't know, buddy, but I'm not in the mood to enlighten you.

"I heard you are sick. Want to tell me?" He sat in the chair across from her, making sure not to invade her space. Considerate or afraid of germs?

"I have a tumor. Looks like cancer, but we're waiting on the lab reports for certain. If it is, they'll start with chemo and radiation to shrink things. Makes operating easier." She took a breath and more exploded from her mouth. "And I have help in place, so I don't need you stealing my kids from me."

He leaned forward. "I'm not here to steal the kids. But I can make things easier by bringing them home with me until you are feeling better. Morgan, I still care. When I heard this was serious, I took a leave of absence so I could help. What does your schedule look like?"

"I don't have one yet."

His expression told Morgan he must equate her life with a schedule.

"That's gotta be disconcerting for you. I know how you

thrive on having your ducks in a row." At least he possessed the grace to be sympathetic.

But did she want his sympathy? Did she want him to care about her? How could she even handle him being in her house?

"Don't pity me."

He straightened. "Oh, we wouldn't want that. Morgan's too strong to accept empathy." After patting the arms of the chair, he pushed himself to his feet. "I'm not here to argue. Or make things difficult. Just figured I'd help. Should've known you wouldn't need any. I'll see to the kids."

Ouch. "Bruce, I'm sorry. Overwhelmed is waving at me in my rearview mirror, and someone's wired my accelerator to the floor. Let me get used to the idea of you being in the house and maybe I can hold my attitude at bay."

He nodded.

"And thank you for leaving your job to come. I don't know what to say."

Now she received a small grin from him. "Good. It's rare that I can shock you speechless."

Oh, that grin. "Go see the kids. Leave me to think."

He laughed and left the room. Just as she asked.

Except thinking wasn't what she wanted to do.

If she were honest, she craved to run into his arms.

But that would not happen.

She considered the living situation. If he came to help her, he must plan on staying somewhere. A snake of apprehension slithered up her back, making her brain envision all sorts of dangerous scenarios.

That man was not moving into her bedroom.

No way.

They were no longer married. He didn't have that right.

But where would he stay? She had no guest room. He might try the couches in the living room or family room. Aidan's room housed a set of bunk beds. Why didn't he spring for a hotel? What happened to that lucrative job he left her for? But then he said he took a leave of absence. Bet they were happy about that after only a year.

That didn't clear up the sleeping arrangements.

Maybe Aidan's room was best. The boy needed his dad. It broke Morgan's heart how her kids missed him so much. Truth was, she missed him too. But she couldn't get past the pain of betrayal, him choosing the job over her.

She pushed off the couch and started for the stairs. If he was sleeping in Aidan's room, she'd better make it ready. How would she even handle having him upstairs in her home? That stopped her progression up the steps.

Pastor Jeff's prayer came back to her. He'd prayed she would allow others to care for her and let them show their love. But if Bruce planned to show her love, and then return to his precious position when this was over, she'd rather suffer trying to do it all herself.

"Morgan? What are you doing?"

She spun around.

Bruce stood at the base of the stairway.

"Gonna get you set up to sleep in Aidan's room. If you are planning to stay awhile." She turned back and missed a step. Her arms flailed as her balance tripped away and a gasp escaped.

"I got you."

And once more she was in Bruce's arms. Secure like she used to be.

Safe.

Then she glanced into his face, those eyes that drew her. His lips assuring her it was all okay.

Like he did before he left.

She pushed off. "You know where the linens are. You make your bed."

His eyes bore into her back as she left him standing on the stairs.

Cami

That evening, Cami pulled up her laptop and jump drive to delete the work for the client.

Former client, she corrected herself.

Guilt over the complete mess again rose its ugly head. But then she heard Dericka in her brain, reminding her she'd given everything to Jesus, and He'd taken care of it. She had nothing to feel guilty about. She was forgiven.

But that didn't change what happened to Ray and Chukshon Advertising.

She scrolled through her work and realized it was rather good. Some of her best, for that matter.

Could she convince the client to look? Save the campaign?

Her first consideration would be for Ray to listen. Should she call him or maybe just send in one big zip file?

Zip file.

Perhaps to use as a springboard on another project.

She hit send and went to make a sandwich.

Five minutes later her phone dinged, letting her know she'd new email. From Ray.

Now you show me. It's excellent work, Cam. Sorry we can't use it. File for future reference. R

That's that. She bit and chewed her ham salad sandwich. Then an idea formed. What if she talked with Felicia? One on one. Show her what she didn't this morning.

How fast would they approach another agency? They were on a deadline, so pretty quick. They might have one waiting in the wings. For success, she'd better track the woman down. Now.

Was she local? Cami searched her notes. No, she lived in Redlands, California. So face to face was out. Zoom. She snapped her fingers. Yes! She'd contact her and set up a Zoom meeting.

But it's evening, she'd be home with her family. Tomorrow, for sure. One fortunate thing—at the moment they were all in the same time zone.

So, she'd established a plan. First thing in the morning she would call Felicia's office and set up… Why wait for morning? Send her an email tonight. If she doesn't respond, follow up with the call. Beside it would give her a chance to pray.

And she knew she must do that.

"Jesus, I gotta make things right. For Ray. For our company. And for the client. I know You forgave me, and I thank You for that. But can You please help me fix this? Give me the right words. Keep my motives pure too. This will be a harder selling job than any campaign I've done, so I know I can't do it without You. Please help. Amen."

She laced her fingers and stretched them out in front of her before starting her note. It needed a compelling opening line. What about honesty?

> *Dear Felicia,*
>
> *I owe you an apology. I let a personal situation color my actions and didn't speak up when I should have.*
>
> *Please find attached what was to be the nucleus of this morning's presentation.*
>
> *If you've any questions, contact me at your convenience.*
>
> *Again, I'm sorry.*
>
> *Sincerely,*
>
> *Cami Madison*

It might not get the client back, but there's the possibility she'd mend fences enough they would consider the company for upcoming projects. Maybe. Or at least they wouldn't badmouth them. She hoped.

But would Ray be happy she gave away the campaign? She didn't send the whole thing, just the central part. But Felicia might take things to a competitor now and give them everything on a silver platter. So much for future inspiration. If that happened, she'd made a massive oops.

Dear Jesus, please don't let this be a mistake.

She closed down, plopped on the couch, and pulled out the shawl. She'd binge watch some *Chesapeake Shores* while she added to that project. And it was still under deadline.

Laying out what she'd done, she realized this was doable, possible to complete in the time frame allowed. Of course, she recognized that the rows would become longer as the triangle grew, but slow and steady and all that. She'd do it.

So far, she'd added twelve rows, repeating the pattern three times. It got prettier each pass with all the variegated colors blending in and out. They almost striped the pattern. No, that wasn't it. More like waves, lapping over one another. Yeah, that's what it was. Waves of color. Gram showed good taste. It sort of reminded her of that phoenix rising painting in Morgan's bedroom.

By nine thirty she put crocheting away. Dericka had showed her that YouBible app on her phone, and Cami downloaded it. Now she possessed a Bible to read before bed.

When she'd asked where to start, Dericka suggested Luke, using The Message version. So, Luke. She got herself ready, plugged her phone in to charge (the long cord allowed use in bed), and snuggled in to begin her first reading of the Bible.

In Sunday School as a kid, she'd looked things up. They called it Sword Drills. Cami enjoyed the competition, but paid no attention to the words. But tonight was different. No one challenged her. This was her own choice. And it's those words, that's what she wanted to read.

She figured how to work the app and chose The Message as the translation. Dericka called it conversational, but a little poetic. Gave her a fresh view.

The first chapter of Luke started off like someone telling a story to a friend. She became so involved, she read through the first three chapters before she knew it. Dericka was right, this was wonderful.

But morning would come early, and with it she prayed for resolution for everyone's benefit.

The buzz from her phone woke her fifteen minutes before her alarm would've gone off. This better be good.

Ray. And she knew. It wasn't good.

"Hey, awful early. Don't you sleep?"

"Not when I'm trying to save the company. What did you do?"

She'd not heard that edgy voice. Ever. Not even when he fired Moron… Monty.

"If you'd give me a reference, I might be able to tell you. What are you talking about?" Though she had an inkling this concerned last night's email.

"I got a text from Felicia today. She wants to talk. Did you go behind my back?"

She blew out a breath. "I emailed an apology. Figured it might be points in our favor for the future."

His turn to blow out a breath. "Okay, I don't like getting blindsided. But an apology wasn't a bad idea. Maybe she's changed her mind about you needing to be fired."

"She's the one who wanted me fired?" The guys, she kind of expected that, but Felicia? Cami thought they'd made a connection.

"Yeah, she was the most adamant. I never agreed to fire you, though. Okay, maybe I can save this. We've got a Zoom meeting at ten. Can you be here?"

"Of course." She paused. Maybe she'd better let him know about the attachment. "Um, Ray, something more."

Did he growl? "What?"

"I attached something."

"Don't tell me. The campaign file?"

"No, not the whole thing. Just a teaser. In case. Figured if it caught her attention, she might give us a second try." Her heart pounded in her ears.

"When are you going to start running things by me? Catherine Amelia Madison, if this goes south, you've given away proprietary property. I'll have to fire you."

"Fire?" She not only regretted telling him her full name, now she regretted her actions.

But her intentions were honorable.

Wasn't firing overkill?

"No choice. I'll have to sue to get the property back." No growl now. Just sadness.

"I'll be there in half an hour. We'll have time to go over everything together." She unplugged her phone and threw the covers back as she spoke, heading for her closet.

"Make it twenty minutes." He disconnected.

Panic started up her throat. This wasn't supposed to happen. What did she do? What could she do? Dericka's face floated through her mind. *Pray.*

That she would do. But it might help to get others praying, as well. After stopping to say a *Help Me* prayer of her own, she sent a text to Dericka, and then to Jeff. Both said the same thing.

Please pray. Important.

She needed all those prayers.

Now to dress and face whatever awaited. Made her wonder about the Christians walking into the arena before the lions were released. At least she'd walk back out. But at what time? And what would she be carrying?

Kate

Fourteen years ago

"Ms. Fortuna, thank you for seeing me." Kate held out her hand, but the other woman ignored her.

"I told my secretary I'd give you five minutes. How can I help you?"

No wonder Cami was upset. "I'm here regarding my granddaughter, Cami Madison. I understand you've suspended her for one month. Perhaps we might discuss the situation. This seems a bit harsh—"

"She defaced school property, and wrote statements to incite bullying of another student." She interrupted as though her word were gospel. Kate could tell this conversation was over before it started. The woman refused to make eye contact while citing her edict.

"I don't deny that. In fact, I encouraged her to come speak with you, hoping you would understand her remorse and hear the rest of the story."

"The one about her being bullied? They always say that. It's the big excuse for everything. But we've got proof that she was involved in bullying, and our school has a zero tolerance for that type of behavior." She shoved in a drawer with enough force to make plaster crack.

Kate took a breath, working to keep her temper under control. "So, what you are stating is that if she'd not taken the initiative to be responsible for her actions, nothing would've happened. And that bullying little pipsqueak would've been silenced. But since she behaved with maturity, she is subjected to punitive punishment? And he gets to bully again? I can agree to having her scrub the wall, or paint over if need be. A day or two of suspension or a week of after school detention, perhaps, but a solid month of suspension when she was more wronged than… than that weasel…"

"Mrs. Hanson, you must control yourself or I'll have you removed."

If she'd slapped Kate, she wouldn't have stunned her any more.

"No need. I will accept Cami's withdrawal papers as soon as you can get them ready. This is not the institution I envisioned it to be, and I'll not allow her to suffer one more day under your less than stellar supervision." She turned to leave the office before the ice queen could make another foolish statement.

By the time she'd reached the front desk, the secretary was hanging up the phone. "I'll have the paperwork ready for you tomorrow at nine. You can pick it up then."

"Not acceptable. I will send someone else to get it. Neither my granddaughter nor I will step foot in here ever again." She turned to Cami. "Let's go." With her chin tipped a little more than she should, Kate headed for the front door and tripped on the rubber mat. She caught herself in time before becoming a spectacle. But the shame of her actions flamed as bright as the heat of her embarrassment.

Cami followed her to the car.

Once in, she cranked up the AC. If she didn't know that menopause was long past, she'd have sworn she was living through her worst hot flash. She shouldn't have lost her temper, but no way would she let that witch inflict any influence on her granddaughter. The woman wreaked enough damage, and Kate could only imagine what she'd said to Cami. "Are you okay?"

"About to ask you the same thing. What was all that paperwork talk about?"

"I'm withdrawing you. I had no idea how awful it was, sweetie, and I'm sorry. You are so strong to endure all this. I will find you a school where you are safe." Kate reached over to the passenger side and pulled Cami into an embrace.

"Gram, how could you do that?"

"What?"

"You're pulling me away from my friends and my favorite teacher! You didn't even ask me."

Kate was shocked. Cami didn't want to leave this house of horror? "Honey, this school isn't for you. If you want, I'll let your friends' parents know when I find you something better. Maybe they're hoping for a better school too."

"Gram, the school isn't bad, just the principal and she's new.

I can suffer through. I promise I won't get into any more trouble. Please don't make me leave."

Kate started the car and put it into reverse. "Let me work on it. I want what is best for you, and I'll protect you with everything in me. This place doesn't seem safe, but you've given me something to consider. Will you give me time, please? Whatever we decide, you can't go back before month is up, anyway."

"Yeah, I'll give you time. Wait! Oh, no! That means I can't be part of the field trip to ASU. We're supposed to visit their Visual Arts department." Cami slammed her head back against the seat rest. "I am so stupid! I shoulda just kept my mouth shut and none of this would have happened."

Kate pulled into the drive and parked. "No, you did the right thing. The mature thing. It's your principal who's in the wrong." Notions and niggles morphed into something fuzzy. "Maybe there's another solution. Not sure, and it's only a slim chance, but I've got an idea. Let me see what I can do."

"Tell me, Gram." Cami bounced in her seat, eyes pleading.

"No, don't want to get your hopes up. Go in, change your clothes. I'll work on it."

They both headed for the house and to their respective bedrooms. Kate sat on her bed and pulled her phone to her along with her phone book. Somewhere she had the district's number. If she requested an appointment with the superintendent, and added tons of prayer for safe measure, maybe things might improve.

Ten minutes later, she headed for the front door. "Cam, hon, stay inside. I'll be back as soon as I can."

"Where are you going?" She turned the TV to mute.

"A little crazy. But that's a good thing. Bye!" She hurried out so Cami wouldn't follow and catch up. By the time she was in her car, Cami stood in the doorway with questions all over her face.

Better than hopeful excitement followed by disappointment.

Kate arrived at the district office, signed in, and was directed to a waiting room. Another secretary greeted her. She looked familiar. Wasn't she the girl Kate visited at the hospital a couple months ago?

"Mrs. Hanson, I wondered if that's you. From church, right?"

She remembered. "Yes. Stacy, is it? How are you feeling?"

"Much better. Thank you so much for visiting me. A burst appendix isn't fun. How can I help you? Oh, I just added you in for an appointment with Dr. Dugdale. He's about ready for you. Let me go check."

Kate smiled and studied a piece of student artwork lining the walls.

"He'll see you now." As Kate walked past, the girl gave her a quick hug. No way she knew how that helped.

A tall, distinguished man in his late forties to early fifties stood and ushered her into the office before closing the door. He held out his hand. "Nice to meet you Mrs. Hanson. I'm Dr. Dugdale. I got the impression this was urgent. How can I help you?"

Kate sighed. "I'll confess to seeing myself as a bit of a schoolgirl tattletale, but I'm looking for help to get a situation resolved. I made an attempt on my own earlier and lost my temper."

He chuckled. "I can't picture that. But go on."

"My granddaughter attends Arroyo Verde Middle School. She was being bullied, but rather than ask for help, she took matters into her own hands, writing something inappropriate on the girls' bathroom wall. All girls seen in the vicinity near the time it happened were given letters to take home. My granddaughter didn't want her friends to get into trouble, so she wrote a letter of confession and offered to clean up what she'd defaced."

He leaned back and crossed his arms. "That sounds rather mature. Not the graffiti part, but the taking responsibility part."

At last, someone who agrees. "That was my thought. She was

willing to take the consequences. But the principal wants to make an example of her and gave her a month suspension."

Though he said nothing, he sat a little straighter.

"This is where I made my part of the mess. Cami called for me to pick her up. When I did, I asked to speak with the principal. We didn't see eye to eye, and I pulled Cami out of the school. Only now, my granddaughter is upset. She says that though the principal isn't her favorite person, she doesn't want to leave her friends and some excellent teachers on site. Ms. Fortuna and I didn't get off to the best of starts, and it's unlikely we could sit and work this out. But if you might join us, perhaps we could come to an agreement? I'm not asking you to override her, just be part of the conversation."

Dr. Dugdale sighed and stood, walking around the desk to sit on the corner. "As a rule I don't interfere. It tends to cut the legs out from under my principals. But based on what I've heard, and what you've requested, let me see what I can do. I'll have a discussion with Ms. Fortuna, and perhaps we can set up something. What does your week look like?"

Chapter Eleven

CAMI

Present day

Cami pulled into her parking space with two minutes to spare, though Ray would count from the moment she stepped into her office. Oh, please let the elevator be fast today.

Ray paced in the upstairs lobby. Once he knew he caught her gaze, he tapped his watch and headed for his office.

Guess she was to follow.

"We'll work in here, set up at the table."

At least he handed her a cup of java at the door. Not enough Stevia packets in the world would fool her into imagining this bitter brew was actual, palatable coffee. She tried to keep her wince away from his view, powered up her MacBook, and plugged in the jump drive. The action made her heart skip. "You know, Monty stole my original thumb drive with the first ideas on it. He might still have it, could've slipped it into his pocket. Though it wasn't right for this client, there's stuff saved that could be used elsewhere."

Ray nodded. "Figured that. I asked the guards to make him dump his pockets before he left. I've got the drive. It's work that belongs to the company, and since he didn't even purchase it, he's outta luck."

One more good thing. Something about Monty made her sure he'd enjoy sharing his misery where he could. But this fiasco offered little he could do without putting himself in jeopardy. He must know that to give Ray as a reference, he'd be asking for trouble. Ray would have no qualms telling a new employer everything the man did.

"I combed through your files while I waited. You did good stuff, Cam, and if we save the account, all the better. Tell me how you moved from 'I'm stronger than my fear' to 'Your strength lives inside you.'"

"I'd started with the I'm stronger because I spotted the initial comment in the first book, and Gram used to say that to me, more times than I can count. But I've been learning stuff about her through her writing. So I re-listened to several of the audio versions. Did you know my grandmother was the voice artist?"

Ray shook his head.

"It was a little unsettling to hear her. But as I listened, I heard the full message. It's of faith, strong faith that lives inside and conquers fear. I figure that's what Gram was trying to tell me all along."

"Okay, then let's run with that. How do you visualize it?"

They talked for two solid hours without a break, Ray asking, Cami answering by following where the threads took her. She showed what she had done, tweaking with his comments. When they came up for air, they stared at the best campaign pitch they'd ever put together, separate or as a collaboration.

"Will this do it?" Cami's stomach grew more knots with each tick of the antique clock Ray kept on his credenza. He had an old heart. Probably one he stole from some elderly curmudgeon.

"Yeah, it'll do. We make a great team, Cam. Don't know if the client will buy it, but yeah, we'll get a foot in the door. I'm pretty sure. Just need to establish what her mood is, whether she's up to listening or is steamed." He drained his third cup of the bitter brew as the number on his clock flicked to 9:48.

Cami needed to use the restroom before this started. Her nerves wouldn't give her another choice. "I'll be back in five. I promise."

Ray didn't look like he trusted her, but he'd never follow her to the ladies' room.

Once inside, she took a second to check her texts. Dericka sent a praying hands emoji. Jeff wrote: *Got you covered. C U tomorrow.*

Peace settled over her and she remembered the words she'd centered in the campaign. *Your strength lives inside you.* Dericka told her that the Holy Spirit came to live in her heart when she asked Jesus to take control of her life. She believed that, clung to the faith that it was true. The Holy Spirit was the strength living inside her. It was stronger than her fear, and the peace relaxing her stomach muscles attested to the fact.

She returned to Ray's office, noting the wash of relief flooding his expression. Though he tried to hide it, he harbored feelings, just like everyone else.

He motioned her behind his desk.

She leaned against the credenza while he connected to the Zoom meeting. A minute later Felicia's face filled his screen.

"Hello, Felicia. What can we do for you?" Ray wanted her to make the first move since she asked for the meet.

"Good morning, Ray. I see you've got Cami with you. Fine. I am intrigued by the attachment I received last evening. But first, tell me what happened. Cami, you said you owed me an apology for not speaking up?"

"Yes, ma'am." She was back in school, using her best manners. But if it returned the client to the table, no problem. Without a lot of detail, Cami explained how she'd allowed Monty to fail as payback when she should have been considering the others, and then apologized for doing so.

"I understand. Being a female in a competitive field can

tempt you to harsher tactics. Don't let the pressure force you into becoming someone you can't respect." A bit of a smile from the woman lit a tiny glow of confidence in Cami.

"You mentioned that you're intrigued by the attachment. What would you like to know?" Ray would keep her focused on this point of business.

"Yes, the attachment. If we choose to not come back, I will return it. I haven't spoken with Vince or Doug. I realize you went out on a limb, Cami. But I looked it over. It is more in line with what I envisioned. And with what the author hoped. You see, Cami, I knew Kate Hanson. No, I didn't know about you, ours was a business relationship. But she was a woman of integrity. I learned who she was, that she wrote under a pen name. My first contact was to thank her for what she was doing. I watched all these young girls become stronger women from reading and interacting with the books. I was grateful. But as we spoke, the idea of making this bigger, maybe even global, well, I couldn't get away from it. I lost a friend when your grandmother died."

Cami ran a finger under her eye, but the tears still flowed.

"That's why I was so dumbfounded that her own granddaughter missed the central theme of the series. But looks like you didn't."

That brought a smile, but Cami remained too choked to speak.

Ray stepped up. "I'd be happy to share any details with you, Felicia."

"No, Cami should make the presentation. She can do it. Let me speak with Vince and Doug, check on our schedules. Monday should work. Can you be ready with the full presentation then? It would put us ahead of schedule."

Ray didn't wait for Cami's nod. "Yes, you name the time, we'll be ready."

"Good, I'll text you with our itinerary. I'm glad we got this worked out. This will be something your grandmother would've appreciated."

That tiny light of confidence bloomed into a blaze. Cami nodded her head. "Thank you, Felicia. I know she'd be happy we're working together."

"Me too. See you Monday. Goodbye." Felicia exited the Zoom room.

"Monday. We're in good shape, but Cami girl, we've got a ton of work to do to be ready. We'll camp out in my office until we've divvied up sections, and then work solo through today. Tomorrow let's start early, I'll meet you here at seven. With a lot of luck, we will wow her out of her mind."

Tomorrow? "Um, tomorrow's Saturday."

"Yeah, what about it? The biggest presentation of your life is on Monday. You can't plow through the weekend?"

"I've got plans."

"Cancel them."

"Ray." He didn't know what he was asking, rather demanding. Of course, he wouldn't have the same feeling about Jeff either. But would Jeff understand?

The man didn't even look up. It was settled as far as he was concerned.

"Fine, but I need to make a phone call. I'll be back."

"Don't take too long."

She scooped up her cell and locked herself in her office. No walking in on this conversation. She pressed Jeff's number, praying he was available.

He answered on the second ring. "Hey, are you all right?"

Oh, his voice. How could he cause her stomach to flutter and send her to her happy place with a simple word? "Yes, prayer worked. Yesterday we'd lost the client, but today we got them back. Only one hitch. I have to work tomorrow."

Cami held her breath, waiting for his response.

"That happens. Hey, I'm not on schedule to speak Sunday,

our youth pastor is sharing about the spring break retreat, so I could slip away and come down then if it works for you?"

Did he say that? This guy is too perfect. "I'll tell Ray we have to work until we're done tomorrow because he can't have Sunday."

Jeff laughed. "Hey, we could make the second service at my buddy's church. Mount Lemmon's Shadow Community, isn't that where you said you go?"

Oh. "I'm in a group there, yes." And she'd aimed to start attending this weekend. She just never realized it would be with Jeff. Good thing he didn't catch her wince. When they could discuss it in person, she'd explain everything.

"Great, I'll be at your place by ten. Text me your address. Planned to call you in a bit for that, anyway." Man, she melted at his grin she sensed beaming through the cyberspace.

"I will. Thank you for understanding. I'll see you then." And hope my heart doesn't thunder out of my chest.

"See you. Bye."

She disconnected, still in a daze. That guy was magical. When he talked, a bunch of Monarch butterflies took off on their odyssey in her gut. When he laughed, she was sure her skin rippled from all the tingling. If he ever held her hand, she'd fall into a million pieces at his feet.

Oh boy, this was bad.

Back at Ray's office, she informed her boss he could count on her for Saturday until the presentation was complete. But Sunday was off limits. No amount of begging, pressuring, cajoling or guilt would change her mind.

He looked at her as if she'd lost hers, but said nothing other than to analyze where they were so far. Two hours later, Cami stopped at the break room for a salad, and then holed up in her cave, working on her part of the deal until six, at which time she returned to Ray's office. He'd ordered dinner in, and they ate while sharing what they'd accomplished. By ten they had it pretty well locked down and Ray was agreeable to going home.

Cami wasn't sure she'd keep her eyes open all the way to her condo, but with her AC cranked to the max, and *Sgt. Pepper* blaring, she stayed awake. Long enough to step inside, undress for bed, and do a face-plant with her pillow. She wanted to read more in her Bible, but she was too exhausted, so promised herself and God that she would read first thing in the morning.

Which she did. Only getting up to use the facilities, brew a cup of coffee, and grab a breakfast bar before she snuggled back in and started Luke chapter four.

After chapter six, she glanced at the time. Whoa, she needed to get moving. Ray would be waiting. She braced herself for another long day and crawled into bed that night, sure they'd done everything possible.

She fell asleep in seconds and dreamed of her family, Mom, Dad, and Gram all laughing and picnicking on Piestewa Peak. Someone held her hand. Jeff. She introduced him to everyone, and they were all so happy together. She woke with a smile and set up for a few more chapters of Luke before racing to the shower.

After doing her makeup, she stood in front of her wardrobe, staring at her choices. What if he expected her to wear a dress? She hadn't one in her closet since she never wore dresses. Not with her legs.

Oh, for Pete's sake, if her outfit was appropriate for professional attire, shouldn't it be acceptable for church? Man, she hoped so. She grabbed her navy linen dress slacks and her blue and green swirl chiffon top that she paired with a navy tank beneath. With her favorite statement necklace and earring set added, she felt… passable. Maybe even presentable. If only Jeff agreed.

She added a barrette to hold the sides of her hair back when she heard the knock. A glance at her phone told her he was five minutes early. Since he'd just driven two hours to be with her, she ought to forgive him. When she opened her front door and spotted him standing on her welcome mat dressed in his teal polo and khakis, she knew. He was forgiven. Whoa.

"You look pretty. I love your hair like that." His dimples were deep enough to hold diamonds, and his eyes twinkled as if they did.

"Why thank you, sir. You look sharp yourself."

"Got a sports coat in the car if I need it. We're pretty casual up at Desert Bloom, but I haven't attended one of Caleb's services."

Cami's face heated as she swallowed. How would she know what was acceptable? "You're fine. I wouldn't worry about the sport coat. Too hot anyway." She flashed a smile she hoped changed the subject.

It did. He asked about her day yesterday. She started to tell him how they got into the fix, but that would mean telling him she'd just become a Christian, and might lead to her confessing that she'd never attended a church service at Mount Lemon. All stuff she'd rather steer clear of until they could sit and chat, if even then.

At least she was able to direct him to the campus. Points in her favor. She patted herself on the back for remembering the way after only one visit.

He parked, and as they walked in, he slipped her fingers between his. It was like shaking hands with electricity. Her heart skipped with erratic beats. And she loved it.

Once in the lobby, she heard her name.

Dericka waved.

Cami led Jeff over and they made introductions.

"I'm so glad to see you this morning, Cami." Gramma Opal came over with a big hug.

"Glad to see you too, Opal. This is my friend, Jeff."

He gave her hand a little squeeze before shaking hands with Dericka's family. Maybe he appreciated that she held back the Pastor label. He could be just one more person here today.

After some small talk, they went in where Dericka encouraged them all to sit together. Gramma Opal whispered at Cami's ear. "You're good for her."

That filled Cami with a warmth she wanted to embrace. The truth was, Dericka was the one good for Cami. If she could return the favor, that was pure pleasure.

Somewhere during the announcements, Pastor Caleb must've spotted Jeff because when the congregation was instructed to greet one another, he made a beeline to them. The guys shook hands, pounding each other's backs. "Hey so who is this? Don't tell me someone finally caught your attention."

Jeff grew a funny expression. "This is my friend Cami Madison. She attends Mount Lemon. I drove down for the day. We're kicking things off here."

"Nice to meet you, Cami. I'm sorry we haven't met sooner. But hey, you're with the right crowd. How's the Raiden family today?" He shook hands with Dericka's husband, Thomas, and then Gramma Opal and Dericka.

With all the pleasantries out of the way, Pastor Caleb returned to the front to finish announcements, but Cami caught the glance Jeff flashed her way. That talk would come sooner than she preferred.

Her luck held out though since neither Pastor Caleb when they left, nor Jeff once they were in the car brought it up.

Instead, Jeff asked where they should grab a bite.

Cami directed to a little mom and pop Mexican food place in a strip mall close to the church. Migi's.

Though the setup was similar to Chipotle, it possessed something a chain restaurant couldn't—that special personality and one-on-one friendliness.

Plus, the food was amazing.

They got through the line and chose a small table against the rear wall. Once seated, Jeff offered to give thanks.

Cami just nodded.

Afterward, they tucked in. It was better than last time. And that said something. A bite of carnitas with the perfect amount of spice melted on her tongue when Jeff cleared his throat.

"So, tell me again, how long have you been attending Mount Lemon?"

That perfect bite bit back and she choked. Jeff stood, ready to do… something. She didn't know what. Her hand reached for her Diet Coke as she tried to gain control. "That was my first service."

"I thought you said that's where you go." At least he didn't sound judgmental, more curious.

"No, I've attended a group that meets on site. That's how I met Dericka and Opal. They're part of the group. They suggested I come. I'd planned to start today. When you said you were coming, it seemed like a fun idea to go together." She shoveled in another bite before she made a bigger fool of herself.

"Oh." He wiped his mouth with his napkin. "I'm not pushing, Cami, but I told you I've a rule about dating people who aren't believers. I don't want to become attached when it can't go anywhere. We'd both get hurt."

"I get that."

"So…" He cocked his head to the side, waiting.

"So?" She shrugged, needing more of a clue, though her gut told her what he asked.

"So, are you a believer in Jesus Christ as your Savior and Lord?"

"Yes." Yes, she was. That was the truth. Still he might have his doubts if he knew how long she'd been a believer.

He opened his mouth, but glanced past her and said nothing.

Cami turned and peeked over her shoulder.

In time to lock gazes with Monty.

She turned back and put her hand next to her face, hoping he wasn't coming her way.

Oh, but he was.

A moment later, Monty stood next to the table. "Now that's perfect. Abso-freakin' perfect. My two favorite people. Not."

Two? He knew Jeff?

"Hello, Monty. How are you doing?" Jeff knew Monty?

"Oh, she must not have told you. Your little friend here got me fired."

Jeff glanced at her. She read the question in his eyes. But she couldn't explain, not this second.

"That's okay. My job was only the most important thing to me. Since my older brother's gone."

Now Jeff stared at his plate.

"Oh, he didn't tell you either. You two need to talk more. Jeff, meet Cami, the princess who stole my job. And Cami, meet Jeff, the guy who killed my brother."

Kate

Fourteen years ago

A day passed after Kate met with Dr. Dugdale without a word. A part of her wanted to quote "no news is good news." But with things taking so long, she bet Ms. Fortuna was not pleased. It wasn't as if she asked the superintendent to charge in on a white horse and fix everything. She simply requested a rational discussion. Cami did something wrong. But she attempted to make amends. Why be vindictive?

Maybe if the principal had shown a modicum of interest, they could've discussed the situation.

But Kate couldn't figure the reason for the woman's attitude.

Something soured it before she entered the office.

Cami stayed home with her, not knowing what went on behind the scene. Better that way. For now. But if that phone didn't ring soon, the child would ask why her grandmother climbed the walls.

But around 3:30 it rang. Dr. Dugdale called direct. "Mrs.

Hanson, I apologize for the delay. The schedule mesh took a little finagling. Could you come tomorrow at ten?"

As relieved as Kate was that something moved forward, her heart still pounded at what lay ahead. "Yes, of course. I appreciate you doing this."

He paused. "You might not want to thank me yet. Ms. Fortuna's quite adamant that the matter remain closed."

"Oh, well, that's my fault for losing my temper." This'll be unpleasant. She could tell already.

"I convinced her that a discussion might be in everyone's best interest, that perhaps we could uncover pertinent details. I also suggested that Cami be in attendance. She was mature enough to confess. She's mature enough to sit in on at least part of the conversation. If you or I conclude this is not a good place for her, I'll ask her to wait in the lobby." He sounded pretty firm. Perhaps he wanted facts from everyone.

Kate wasn't sure about Cami being in attendance, but since he'd allow her to leave the room if necessary, she didn't argue the point. "Will we meet at the school or your office?"

"At the district. We've conference rooms there, we'll use one. A more neutral ground." She could feel his diplomacy through the telephone lines, causing her to wonder about his conversation with Ms. Fortuna.

"Cami and I will see you at ten tomorrow at the district office. Thank you, Dr. Dugdale. Thank you for your help."

She heard him pause a moment before speaking. "My secretary told me what you did for her when her appendix ruptured and she ended up in the hospital. She said you are a believer and the type of person to serve others in need. She wanted me to tell you it's your turn to receive a little help, and that she'll be praying for you."

Kate didn't know what to say. Her mouth dried. Like the Sonoran desert. Arid. "Ah, thank her for me."

"Until tomorrow. Bye." He sounded hopeful as he disconnected.

Kate hung up and plopped into the nearest chair. She knew beyond a shadow of a doubt that he stood up for her. Of course that didn't mean things would go her way, nor did it presuppose he wouldn't back his principal. As he should. But his eyes were open. She sent up a thank you prayer before filling Cami in.

The next morning, they piled into her Sentra at 9:45, giving plenty of time to reach their destination. Cami never mentioned a word about the meeting after Kate told her. Glancing at her now, the child's face had paled. She's afraid.

"How about some *Rubber Soul?*" Kate popped in her CD before she responded.

Cami's gaze remained straight ahead, and her lips moved without sound. No matter. Kate knew what she said.

Once parked, they entered the building and signed in at the desk. The receptionist directed them to the waiting area outside the conference room.

A strident voice carried through the closed doors. "That's poor policy to override my decisions." Ms. Fortuna's dislike could put dog whistles out of business.

The answer remained undetectable. But a moment later Dr. Dugdale stepped out and greeted them. "Hello, Mrs. Hanson, Cami, thank you for coming. We'll meet in here." He held the door while Kate nudged Cami to keep moving in front of her. They took seats on one side of an oval table. Dr. Dugdale sat at the head, and Ms. Fortuna glared across from Kate.

"Let me get things started. As Mrs. Hanson requested, we are having a discussion hoping to find an acceptable decision. Perhaps we can start with the facts of what happened. Cami, please share with us how this all began."

Kate glanced over.

The girl twisted her fingers together and stared at her hands.

"Go on, Cam. I know you can tell them. You told me." Kate patted Cami's forearm, wanting her to understand she wasn't alone.

Cami raised her gaze, still quite pale. "Um, Kenny Blackstrom sits in back of me in fourth hour math. He likes to poke me with his pencil. I told him to quit, or I'd ask the teacher to move me. He said he'd stop if I would give him my homework. When I said no and to leave me alone, he said if I didn't he'd tell everyone I..." Her voice dropped to a whisper. "Showed him my chest."

She glanced up that the adults. "But I didn't. I don't do that. But I couldn't think how to make him stop. Then I figured out if he got embarrassed, got a taste of his own medicine, maybe he'd stop picking on me. So I wrote on the girls' bathroom wall that he has to sit when he... you know..."

Cami returned to staring at her hands. "No one saw me. But several girls came in. After I finished, but before I returned to class. They read what I wrote and started laughing. Pretty soon they told others. And then a bunch of us got called into the office together. Ms. Fortuna said that since she didn't know who did it, we all needed to take these letters home to parents.

"I gave mine to Gram and explained what happened. She wanted me to talk with Ms. Fortuna. I was too scared. But doing the right thing's important. The other girls shouldn't get in trouble. So I wrote the letter instead and gave it to her. Then she called me to the office and said she suspended me for one month for defacing school property. That's everything."

Kate slipped her hand over to Cami, who grabbed it like a life preserver.

Dr. Dugdale inhaled, seeming to mull over Cami's words. "Ms. Fortuna, do you have the letter Cami wrote you?"

The principal shoved a file toward him.

He cut her a glance and then opened it.

Kate recognized Cami's precise penmanship.

After he read the page, he asked Ms. Fortuna for her side of the situation.

"It's obvious. The girl wanted out of trouble. So she manu-factured that accusation about a classmate. I know the boy's parents. He wouldn't do what she claims. I even asked him, and he denied the entire issue."

Dr. Dugdale cleared his throat. "Let me understand. You have a personal acquaintance with the parents of the boy in question?"

Something flitted through the principal's eyes. Was it fear? "We attend church together."

"Uh huh. So, because you attend worship services with his parents, he couldn't be guilty or lie to you?"

Her face flushed. "I've been an educator and administrator for many years. I know when a child is lying."

Everything in Kate's power came to bear to keep her mouth closed.

Cami's grip grew lethal.

"So you say Miss Madison lied?"

"Of course she did! Look at her."

Dr. Dugdale leaned back in his chair, his elbows resting on the armrests, and his fingers steepled. "I did. I paid close attention while she struggled to share something quite difficult for her. And for your information, if you are basing someone's honesty on if they attend a place of worship, you'd be remiss as both Mrs. Hanson and her granddaughter do. With my secretary. Not that church attendance makes one perfect, or in this case honest. But given what we have here, I tend to believe Miss Madison."

Kate wondered if the woman's face would end up the same cherry red as her suit.

"So you are saying that I'm not allowed to make the decisions for my own school?"

Dr. Dugdale rose. "Miss Madison, Mrs. Hanson, I want to thank you both for coming. I'll phone you this afternoon to let you know of our decision."

Kate stood, thanked him, and got Cami out before the explosion. But she knew, as sure as Vanna would spin those letters at six tonight, there'd be fallout. Without a doubt.

Chapter Twelve

CAMI

Present day

Somewhere in Cami's brain she knew she stared at Jeff with her mouth open. Could she have been so wrong in reading this guy? How does one kill someone and become a pastor? Wouldn't he be behind bars if he did what Monty said?

And Monty, dropping that bombshell and strolling into the sunset, or out the restaurant door. Must've been satisfying to kick her one more time.

She shoved her meal away.

"Cami, I'll tell you everything, but not here. I'd planned to today, anyway." Pain clouded his eyes. Something of Monty's words spoke truth.

"He stole from me, Jeff. He got caught. Now wants to get even. That's all. Right?" Her gaze pleaded with him to agree.

"I didn't know you two were acquainted. My guess is that I'm the one he wanted to hurt, and you are bonus. I'm not hungry either. Let's go somewhere and talk." He gathered their remains to the trash.

It gave her a moment to pull her thoughts together. Did she

care to hear what he might say? Was he merely a con man with a great story?

Listen.

She blew out a breath. Listening wasn't her plan. It's too easy to be deceived. Plus, she was still smitten enough to be fooled. That was a given.

He returned to the table and held her chair for her before taking her hand and leading her to the car. "Would you rather talk while I drive or go to your place? Or we can find another spot for a private conversation."

"My condo is fine." That way, if it's too much, she'd chase him out without worrying about how she'd get home.

They arrived ten minutes later. She let him in, and they sat on her couch, though she needed to keep some distance between them.

He took a deep breath. "When Monty says I killed his brother, he's talking out of pain. We had an accident. But there's more to the story. His brother's name was Freddie. We'd been best friends since second grade."

"Wait, you said you were raised in Phoenix." She'd fact check every part. He'd not slip something over her.

"I did. Freddie and Monty grew up around Maryvale. But after the accident, his family moved to Tucson for a fresh start. Monty always wanted to attend U of A anyway."

"I see. Go on."

He rubbed his pant legs. "Well, Freddie and I didn't always make the best decisions. By the time we hit high school, we were drinking and partying with the seniors. I'd just gotten my driver's license…"

No. Oh, no. Not a drunk driver. Not like the person who killed her parents. And sent her to the hospital for six weeks. Please, no.

"… I drank a couple of beers. But Freddie, who drove that night, drank so much I carried him to his parents' station wagon. I figured the trip was only about a mile. I could handle that. But I couldn't. I missed a turn and plowed into a six-foot block wall. No airbags. The crash threw Freddie from the car, and he broke his neck when he landed."

Cami swallowed, wincing as she experienced the impact all over again.

She must know. "What happened?"

"I spent the next couple months in the hospital, and then, after I'd recuperated enough, I was on probation as a juvenile offender. At eighteen, they expunged my record."

"Recuperated enough?"

"The steering wheel crashed into my chest, and I ended up with organ damage. Lost my spleen." He paused and held her gaze. "Ask me anything you want. I won't lie, and I won't hold back."

Cami stared. Who was this guy? "How'd you go from delinquent to pastor?"

He smiled at that. She didn't try to get him to smile, but maybe he'd hoped she'd ask that question. "Those months after the accident were dark. Not the pain of healing, but knowing my best friend was dead. I blamed myself. I should've called someone, not tried driving on my own."

Ouch. But she'd never caused a death by being Miss Independent.

"About six months afterward, Freddie's parents came by the house. They told me they forgave me. That did me in. How could they forgive me? Then they shared the gospel. This is Monty's biggest problem. He never understood forgiving me. Plus, he grew jealous of the time they spent with me, discipling me in my new faith. That's the primary reason they moved to Tucson, to give Monty a fresh start. But sounds like that didn't happen. Any other questions?"

He should know why she struggled. She studied her folded hands. "I know I mentioned the crash. But there's more. When I was thirteen, my parents and I were going out to celebrate after a band concert. I'd played a solo that as a rule went to an eighth grader. Kind of a big deal." She stood and paced the room, nervous energy flashing through her veins.

"On the way to the restaurant we collided with a drunk driver. Her passenger died at the scene. So did both my parents. I was in a coma and hospitalized for over a month with broken legs, a shattered elbow, and head trauma. Gram stayed with me and took me home with her to Phoenix. She became my lifeline and helped me learn to be independent, maybe a little too independent at times. But Jeff, this is hard." She stopped in front of him. "I've got floods of painful memories bombarding me."

"I'm sorry, Cami. You are one more reason I wish I could change that night. I can't. But I can give it all to Jesus. That's what I did. He called me to be a pastor. It's the best way I know to show my gratitude for what He's done in my life." His eyes were so earnest and open. And blue. Though without the fun twinkles now.

"I'm sorry too, Jeff. I like you. A lot. I've gotta think about this. To be fair, I'd better share something else." As long as they were being honest, and if getting around his past became impossible, maybe telling him would help him walk away. She sat back on the couch. "I have not lied to you. When you asked where I attended, I said I was part of a group. That is true. The group is one I looked up on-line to remind me how to crochet the shawl so I can finish Gram's project. Thursday when we were to give our presentation, Monty tried to scoop me. He'd already stolen a thumb drive from my office, but I realized ahead of time because I needed to fix some things. So, I built an alternate plan, got everything ready. But then Monty dove for the limelight. He couldn't tell he'd sunk. The client hated the whole thing. I could've jumped in and saved him, the better plan lay right in front of me, but I wanted to see him fail. For stealing from me."

She glanced at him, but he never moved. Just kept watching.

"When he finished, and realized the client's unhappy expression, he blamed the project on me, and outed me as the author's granddaughter before I could tell them. They told my boss to fire us both, but because he understood what happened, and already knew of the connection, he didn't fire me. Just took away my chance at promotion."

Cami leaned forward and stared at her shoes. "That evening Dericka called. She said she got an impression that I needed to talk with her. Was she ever on the money. I invited her over. In the process, I prayed to ask Jesus into my heart. I've only been a believer since Thursday. Figured you've the right to know." When she glanced in his direction, he met her gaze, his expression unreadable. Was he angry? Did he feel betrayed? Was he processing her confession?

After the longest moment of Cami's life, he blew out a breath. "Looks like we both needed to share some important things. I'm glad you made your decision, Cami. It's the best one you will ever make. But we'd better digest all that's been said. And do some serious praying. It'd be so simple right now to tell you everything is fine. So easy." He smiled, but sadness dimmed his twinkles. "I've learned the hard way, Cami. I can't decide those things without taking them to God first. Do you understand?"

She nodded. "I agree. I'm attracted to you Jeff. But if every time I see you I'm reminded of my parents' death, I don't know. Praying sounds like an excellent idea. Just one question."

"What's that?"

"Better make it two questions. How will I know God's answer? And what happens if you get a different one?"

MORGAN

"Addie, Aidan, come set the table." Morgan heard Bruce's call to the kids.

"I'll get the plates."

"I'll get the silverware."

"And you both do the drinks. Work together on that." He'd

kept the twins busy, sticking to their routine but adding in plenty of time with them.

Though grateful, he was the last person to whom she wanted to owe a debt of gratitude. In fact, it galled her that he was doing so well. Considering she wasn't.

Morgan grew weaker by the day. Moments of dizziness were the norm. Her body, like everything else, betrayed her. The doctor informed her on Friday that her tumor was indeed malignant. Now she waited for the scheduling of her chemo treatments to begin. They were to call. Any time. In fact, she'd expected to hear today, but that hadn't happened.

Instead, Bruce hovered, just out of throwing range, checking on her condition. Did he hope she'd croak, and he'd get the kids to himself?

What an awful thing to imagine. After all he'd done.

Morgan's emotions were out of control. One minute she couldn't fathom that he'd returned to be such a help, the next she wanted him to take her in his arms and tell her it'd been a gigantic mistake and he was back for good. But the usual emotion was deep, guttural, and beyond her labeling. She'd be happy to see him horsewhipped, drawn and quartered, head on a pike. Yeah, she was losing her mind.

"Want a hand to the table, Morgan?" He stood just out of reach, somehow knowing when he was in the safety zone.

"I can manage." She stood from the couch and wavered.

He was at her side before she could sit again. Maybe he liked to live a little dangerous. "Let me help you. For the kids."

Like nothing happened. She finished that thought. Aidan and Addie both wanted them back together. Even for the kids, she wasn't sure she'd ever look at him without seeing that night he walked out. But, for the sake of tonight's dinner with the twins, she would stuff her pride and pain, and let him help her to the table.

"Can we say grace like we used to at Gram's house?" Addie

enjoyed Sunday School and church yesterday. Maybe attending stirred up good memories for her.

"Sure, honey." Bruce glanced her way as he answered. He attended with them while Morgan slept in.

The strength needed to get down the stairs winded her. To dress up and go somewhere? Made her nervous about her chemo treatments.

"How about you pray?"

"Okay, Daddy. Come Lord Jesus, be our guest, and let these gifts to us be blessed. Amen."

Morgan, Bruce, and Aidan echoed a chorus of "amen."

Morgan glanced about the table. Bruce barbecued, roasted some potatoes, and opened a can of baked beans. Not too bad. She remembered barbecue was in his wheelhouse.

The kids passed the serving dishes like troupers.

Morgan's phone buzzed. "I'll get it." Bruce excused himself, returning with her cell. "One minute, please." He handed it to her.

"Yes, this is Morgan Pembroke."

"Mrs. Pembroke, this is Dr. Newton's office. We've got your first chemo session ordered."

Morgan's blood chilled. "I see. When do I start?"

"You need to check in Wednesday at ten. We'll give you a tour of the facility, and insert your port. Your schedule will be Monday, Wednesday, and Friday for six weeks. Then we'll begin the radiation treatments about a month after that. The clinic will call you tomorrow for more information and to let you know what to bring, etc. Doctor has called in a script for you for ondansetron to help with nausea and a mix of lidocaine and Mylanta for your mouth—we call it Miracle Mouthwash. Please drink plenty of water, keep yourself hydrated during this time. If drinking water causes vomiting, then keep a bottle or tumbler close for sipping. This is important. The first round often goes pretty well. It's after the second or third round that the nausea can sneak up on you."

"What about…" Morgan swallowed and wished she possessed the energy to stand and walk from the table. All eyes were glued to her. "What about my hair?"

"That tends to happen after the third treatment. At your tour they will give you the information on contacting *Wigged Out.* They are wonderful about helping get wigs and soft caps and advising what to do. This is a lot to take in. Give yourself a moment. Then please call us if you have questions. Anything else I can do?"

How about take the treatments for me? Just because something flitted through her brain didn't mean she should say it. "No, not at this time. Thank you. Good night."

Morgan disconnected, knowing her family wanted to know. This wasn't how she'd planned to tell the twins. But maybe Bruce would make things easier. For their children.

"Well, guys, I've not been myself for a while. So, the doctors ran tests. Guess I've got cancer and need chemotherapy to get better." She hoped they heard the get better part.

"Cancer?" Addie's eyes filled with tears.

Aidan grew pale.

Bruce covered her hand with his, and for the time being, she let him. "Mom is a fighter. She'll be okay. But she's gotta take the medicine to get well."

"I'm to take a tour, and get my port on Wednesday at ten while you guys are at school. Then chemo starts on Monday." Addie's lip quivered. "We're going to be all right." If only she could convince herself.

"Why did you ask about your hair? Do you need to get a haircut?" Addie would catch that part.

"Sometimes when people have chemotherapy, they can lose their hair."

"You mean you're going to get bald, Mom?" Aidan seemed more shocked that Addie.

"That very well could happen, son. But hair grows back. What's more, hair's not what makes a person who they are.

Nothing in the chemo treatment will change the fact that your mother is who she is. Do you understand?" Bruce squeezed her hand, and she hated how she took comfort in that. But he'd made the best reply to their kids, and she couldn't help but love him a little again for it.

"I better lie down. I'm not all that hungry. Please excuse me." She pushed away from the table.

Bruce stood and guided her out of the room. "Want to go upstairs? Or to the couch?"

"Thank you, upstairs." Where she could be alone with her thoughts.

He never pressed, but continued to be kind. Why? Why couldn't he fight fair? She needed her anger to give her strength and endurance through this, and all he did was quietly, gently erode every block of protection she'd erected.

"Here ya go. Can you get to the bed?" He stopped at the doorway, never crossing that boundary.

She nodded, not trusting her voice. But something insisted on pushing through. "I hate relying on you."

"I know. Morgan, you aren't strong enough for us to talk. But we need to. We've left too much unsaid."

Some of that strengthening anger rose in her. "Like what?"

"Like that I… care." He turned and left her standing in the doorway. Still not fighting fair.

She sat on the edge of her bed and peeled out of her clothes. If she didn't get strength back, she'd be in a fix. No way she could shower and dress herself. And she wouldn't ask Bruce.

This was more than she could bear. If her mother could see her now, she would tell her to buck up, don't let anyone catch her falling apart. The worse you feel, the better you dress. Slap a smile on your face. Always look your best. First impressions last. Perception is everything.

Well, Mother dear, you are wrong. There's more to life than appearance. And she'd better adjust since it looked like she'd be spending a portion of the future vomiting, breaking out in mouth sores, and going bald. Talk about a first impression.

She'd just crawled under the covers when she heard a knock at her door, which stood open.

Bruce stayed at the threshold. "I brought you some tea. Figured it might soothe." He held a tray with a cup, a teapot, and a honey bear container. "May I come in?"

She nodded and swallowed her pride.

He set the tray on her nightstand and turned to leave.

"Bruce, thank you. I… care too. I don't want to. But I do."

He blinked a couple times. "I know." Then he left.

He didn't fight fair.

Cami

Monday's presentation to the clients, part *deux*, occupied the biggest portion of Cami's thought processes.

She figured if she kept her mind on that, it would not only help her do her job to the best of her ability, but it would also keep images of a handsome man with dark blond hair and robin egg blue eyes from floating through her brain and distracting her.

She arrived early to the conference room and set up with the proper handouts, tested the remote with her iPad, and made sure water and chocolates were available on the table. Of course, Ray's secretary could have handled most of the setup, but it fed her independence to know things were done her way. Once ready, she surveyed her handiwork, everything in place as far as she could tell. What else did she need?

Prayer. Cami heard the word in her head as if someone whispered in her ear. She pulled out a chair and folded her hands.

God, I don't know what Your agenda is, but I figure Your way is better than mine. So I'm giving my plans to You and hope You will tweak them to be what You want. Take out anything that's not right. Add in whatever I've missed. I need You to hang on to me too, God, because I'm a little scared. I'm not bigger than my fear. But You are. I'll step out of the way and You handle things. Okay? Thanks for all You've done for me. Amen.

When she looked up, Ray entered with a funny expression. "Didn't know you prayed."

"Figured we need all the help we can get." She flashed a smile, hoping he wouldn't go delving too deep. This prayer thing was still new, personal.

"You're right. Cam, I've never been this nervous about a presentation. Scratch that. I'm just a little rattled. They'll arrive, you'll be in your zone, and all will be perfection." Funny, but he did look rattled, like he said.

"Deep breath, Ray. We've done this before. This is what we're good at. Simply one more day at the office."

This time he returned her smile. After a glance around the room, he pronounced them ready and went to meet Felicia, Vince, and Doug downstairs.

Cami grabbed a last trip to the restroom. As she checked her makeup, her phone dinged.

Jeff: *praying for you.*

She grabbed the counter to keep from sinking to the floor. When she pulled herself together, she answered.

Cami: *Thanks. Need it. Praying for you too.*

And she did. She'd not only prayed to forgive him—which felt strange as he had nothing to do with her accident, but she figured that might help her get past the problem—but she'd also prayed that they would have understanding for each other, and that God would guide them to reach the same conclusion.

If only she understood God's plan with Jeff.

But not at this moment—it was show time. Bob Fosse's jazz hands flashed through her brain.

She returned as Ray led the group into the room.

Cami greeted them all with a handshake, but caught a glance from Felicia. Did she root for her?

Ray gave an opening welcome before Cami came to the front and began. Then something wonderful happened. She never once needed to look at her notes. It crossed her mind that she might have skipped an item, but it didn't matter. And once a new key point popped out of her mouth that she'd never considered, let alone processed before. And it was brilliant.

As she closed, she knew the clients were in agreement and loved the proposal. She asked for questions. Felicia asked two. "Can you be ready to launch in five weeks?"

Before she could answer, Ray broke in. "Yes.

"And Cami, where are you regarding your inheritance? Will continuing with us be a conflict of interest?"

She met Felicia's gaze. "Right now, no conflict. I haven't been notified of any inheritance. My grandmother left a project for me to fulfill. Unless I complete it within a given timeframe, a charity will be her only beneficiary. But if I finish the task on time, then I'll inherit something. I've no clue what, though. Should a conflict arise, I'll inform all of you."

Felicia smiled and nodded. "That's fair. Thank you, Cami. Now, if you wouldn't mind. We should be able to give you an answer if you'll allow us this room to discuss it a moment."

Ray stood with Cami. "Of course. Text me when you want us to return."

They stepped out and walked to Ray's office. He closed the door and turned to her, his expression cryptic. Then he grinned. "We did it, Cam! You did it. Where did you get that extra stuff? I mean, we made such a thorough outline, and you winged it to perfection!"

For a moment she feared he might grab her and spin her around. The terror must have registered on her face as he became less animated.

"Sorry, got carried away. But wow, Cam, just wow."

"You saw me pray. I..." She peeked at him, worried he'd make fun. "I requested God to take out what He didn't want and include what He did. Guess He did that."

Ray cocked his head and stared. "Serious?"

She nodded and chewed her lip.

"Well, keep on doing that because it worked."

His phone buzzed, notifying him of a text. He checked. "They've made their decision. Come on."

Cami followed him to the conference room where he charged ahead of her. She took her seat, but she could tell excitement kept Ray from anything but standing.

Felicia stood too. "This presentation gleamed the polar opposite of the previous. I'm glad you reached out, Cami. And your honesty is refreshing. Vince, Doug, and I are in agreement. We want you. We'll hand over our time-line to you and let you run with it. The most imperative thing you must do is discover our Stinkerella. She is the key. Please keep us apprised. But I'm more confident now that you'll recognize her." She held out her palm to Cami. "You did a fantastic job. Your grandmother would be proud."

Cami blinked back the moisture threatening her vision, stood, and shook the woman's hand. "Thank you. That's the best feedback you could have given."

"We'll leave, let you two get busy."

Vince and Doug, those silent partners who Cami figured out were just around to open doors of opportunity for Felicia, who was the real one in charge, rose.

"I'll walk you down." Ray held the door. Once the clients passed through, he tossed her a wink before going with them.

Cami collapsed into the nearest chair, a deflated balloon that lost its air while zipping all around the room and landing depleted. A nap about now would be fantastic. She knew Ray would charge back, though, energized, and ready to tackle the world. Her phone dinged. A text.

Dericka: *Been praying for you this morning. Still on for this evening?*

She started to reply yes, but would Ray call a late night tonight? No, she could say she needed to process and start fresh in the morning. All true. Just because Ray figured everything out by out-loud self-talk didn't mean everyone did. Quiet time at home to mull and follow idea threads, that was her method. He understood her well enough to figure that. Shouldn't be a problem. She texted yes and anticipated a chance to share yesterday with her friend. If Dericka was so sensitive to hear God and check on her, she should be able to help her answer her burning questions.

Ray returned, elated. When she told him she needed time to process, he didn't blink. Gave her the rest of the day. To focus on planning. He even hugged her, but that seemed to surprise them both, and he mumbled an excuse before running to his office.

Cami took him at his word and packed up. Once home she texted Dericka to give her a heads up that she had some serious questions to discuss. Only fair she didn't blindside her.

When the knock sounded at her condo that night, Dericka wasn't alone. Gramma Opal came too.

Cami held the door, welcoming them inside.

But Gramma Opal enveloped her in an embrace.

"Cami, dear heart, we will pray together and find some answers. Let's get busy."

Chapter Thirteen

CAMI

Cami blew out a breath and started the next row. She had made progress, but with the campaign going into high gear come Monday morning, she would have to make the best of her weekend toward completing the shawl. It wouldn't be so bad if she could stop finding her mistakes after starting a new row. The stitches wouldn't line up and she pulled out a row and a half, sometimes more, to fix things. Wasted time when she had precious little to begin with.

The schedule she'd made for herself of working on the campaign for a couple hours and then the shawl for a bit once home might not happen if required to stay late at the office.

She hoped Ray wouldn't pull the extra-long day card until closer to deadline. That way she could arrive at her condo at a reasonable hour and get this done. Maybe.

Or she could bring the shawl to work, crochet at lunch. Locked in her office, who would know? And it wasn't as if she was working on the company clock, this was her break. She could do what she wanted then. Right?

Great, she'd missed a stitch, more ripping. Take it a day at a time. Do her best. That's all she could do.

Her best better be good enough.

She set the project aside and grabbed a glass of water. Plus something to munch. She needed to order more groceries.

Truth was, she was doing everything to keep herself from ruminating about all the praying she did this evening with Dericka and Opal. They were so understanding about her feelings. Which was amazing since they left her confused. How could she, with her background, be this attracted to a guy who was a drunk driver and killed someone? All right, maybe helped cause his death.

But that wasn't who initiated those flutters in her heart. It was Pastor Jeff, the kind, funny, handsome, witty, caring… if she kept going, she'd have herself convinced without God's wisdom.

Her phone buzzed. New text. A fleeting notion made her imagine it was Jeff. Other than the one that said he was praying, he'd been silent. But he'd remembered, so hope sprang eternal.

Not him.

Morgan: *Cam, I hate to ask, but can you come watch the kids Friday while I have chemo? Turns out it's a half day at school and Nohemi has an appointment. I've a ride to and from. But I've no one to pick up the twins. Please?*

Cami: *Let me check with Ray. Will get back to you ASAP.*

Morgan: *Thx*

Now how did she tell Ray? If she must be in Phoenix by noon, she could put in a couple hours extra early and leave about nine, just in case she faced traffic. And Morgan said nothing about her staying overnight. So she could return to the office as soon as Morgan got home.

Home from chemo. Cami blinked and blew out a breath. That was rough. As much as her cousin made her life crazy, she'd wish nothing like this on her. She must be terrified.

She bowed her head and prayed for Morgan right then.

Afterward she let Ray know. She explained she needed to cut out in the middle of Friday but would return to the office and work late.

He wasn't pleased, but even he couldn't argue with chemo and cancer.

She texted Morgan and returned to her crocheting.

At ten she packed it away and headed for bed, starting a routine that ran all week—crocheting in her locked office at lunch, working until seven, crocheting until bedtime and starting over the next day.

All the way to Friday.

At which time she put in a few early hours of work before hopping in her car, praying that God would remind her that He lives inside her and is bigger than her fear, and pulling out toward Phoenix with "Yellow Submarine" pouring from her speakers.

She experienced the calmest drive she'd ever made between the cities.

Morgan texted the dismissal time, so Cami drove straight to the twins' school. With golden timing, she arrived ten minutes before the bell rang. Kids poured from the building, and teachers checked to ensure they were picked up.

Aidan saw her first. "Cami!" He tugged on Addie, who let their teacher know.

Cami waved back, and they ran to the car, hopping in the backseat and buckling in.

"So how was school today, guys?" She signaled and pulled out into traffic.

"Okay. We're s'posed to have Art today, but because of early dismissal we don't get to go. Art's my favorite subject." Addie could wrench a heart when she wanted to.

"Art was always one of my faves too. I learned how to do cool stuff on the computer. Do you ever do art on the computers at school?" Hm, could she show them anything?

"No, that would be awesome. Is that what you do?"

"One thing I do. I make mock ups for projects, like a sample or a test. If it works, then we hire the special graphic designers, professionals who know more than I do. But the mock-ups are fun. Maybe when we're home, I can show you."

"Yay!"

"I don't want to do that. I want to play catch with Dad." What did Aidan mean?

"I thought your dad moved away and that you'd go visit maybe over the summer."

"No, he's here. He's with Mom. She has to take a special medicine to get rid of her cancer." Aidan knew more than Cami realized. And the whole Bruce being at their house was new.

"Well, I'm glad you get to see your dad. And that he's helping your mom. She might be feeling pretty puny when she gets home. That medicine can make you sicker before helping sometimes." Cami pulled into the drive and parked.

"That's what Daddy said. I'm glad he's back. Mom's been so sick. I want her to get well fast."

Aidan unpinned the key from inside his backpack and unlocked the door.

Inspiration struck while Cami hauled her tech bag in out of the heat. Why not help the kids use Canva to make get-well cards for their mom?

She shared the idea, and even Aidan was on board.

After setting up her computer, and giving them a short tutorial, she allowed them to design to their hearts' content. She'd just stepped away when a knock sounded at the front door.

Cami opened to Jeff. Her heart bounced from her stomach to her throat.

"Hi, what are you doing here?" Guess she surprised him too.

She held the door, stepping away to let him enter. "About to ask you the same thing. Nohemi had an appointment, and school got out early, so Morgan asked me to come pick up the twins."

"Oh, I see. Well, I learned from Nohemi that this was Morgan's third treatment. Realized that's when stuff can get rough. So wanted to check on her. Where is she?" Jeff stood too close.

Cami moved further into the room, adding space, and gaining breath. "She and Bruce haven't gotten back yet."

"Cami, I'm done." Addie went first.

"Okay, coming. I'll be right back, Jeff." Thankful for the break, she checked the girl's work. A pretty picture of flowers and wavy colors, though the handsome man in the living room filled her mind too much to notice more. "I can't print your card out, but I can email it to your mom and she can. How's that?"

That garnered a big grin. Addie gave her a quick hug and ran off to play elsewhere.

Aidan took her place and got started on his design. Bolder colors, stronger lines. Very much his personality.

Once he was involved, she slipped back to the living room. "Sorry. The kids are making cards for their mom on my computer." Just looking at him gave her heart butterfly wings. And no bad feelings rose. Good sign, right?

"No worries. I'll go. Please let Morgan know I'm praying for her." He was leaving. Which was a good thing. She presumed. But it still hurt.

It really hurt. Like eye watering pain. She blinked. "I will. Or you could stay until she gets here." *Please say yes.*

"No, she'll want her rest. I'm glad you're here for her."

Her heart beat faster. "You are?"

"Of course." He paused, as if trying to decide. "Cami, I'm still praying."

"Me too. I want to run ahead, but I am praying and reading and journaling and listening. Dericka and Opal showed me about that, and check on me each day. I'm learning a lot, but what I need is to hear what God has to say."

He smiled and opened his mouth like he was going to add something, but turned away. Then, his fingers on the knob, he turned back. "You're growing in faith. That's good. But make sure your roots anchor deep. Do you know what I mean?"

She nodded. "I do. This isn't a passing thing with me, Jeff. Not a hobby or fad. I'm learning to take everything to God. I am growing, like you said. But I've a lot to learn."

"Yeah, you're right." He brushed a few strands of her hair behind her ear.

Her insides trembled at his touch. "Jeff, you will tell me, won't you? Whatever, you'll let me know?"

His eyes grew misty and he nodded before going out the door.

Kate

Fourteen years ago

Kate picked up the phone on the second ring. Dr. Dugdale.

"Cami may return to school on Monday."

Tears pushed past their boundaries. "Thank you so much. I know that wasn't a pleasant experience for you."

"Nor you and Cami. I'm new enough to my position, having come from another state, and I'm getting acquainted with my administrators. I hadn't spent enough time with Ms. Fortuna before yesterday, so as painful as things were, and I'm so sorry about that, it was informative for me. Thank you for bringing the situation to my attention."

Kate pushed her hair behind her ear and switched sides with the phone. "Won't say it was my pleasure, but I'm glad some good is happening."

"Cami's been home now for two days. We'll call that her suspension, and consider the discipline complete. Please let me know of any repercussions from anyone in this matter. She may make up all work."

Kate blew out a breath. Cami's grades were always at the top, putting her into the junior Honor Society. "Thank you. I will. We appreciate all you've done for us, Dr. Dugdale."

They said their goodbyes, and Kate went to find Cami and deliver the good news.

A smile streaked the child's face. "I go back Monday? Yay!" How many kids loved going to school, Kate wondered. Of course, at six thirty in the morning when she was attempting to get Cami out of bed so she would arrive at school on time, it wouldn't be such a celebration. School was fun, getting up early before the sun to attend wasn't. Kate understood.

Monday, she sent Cami off with a hug and a prayer. If things were normal, she'd volunteer at the church again, but out of caution—she refused to label it fear—she stayed home.

No calls, so by the time she'd tuned in to hearing Cami pop through the kitchen door, she dared hope things had returned to normal.

She waited for the door's whoosh and the sound of a backpack plopped on the counter. The intensity of sound would reveal Cami's level of good in the day.

No slam, no thud. In fact, too much quiet. "Hey sweetie, I'm in the Arizona room."

If an eighth-grade girl ever resembled one of those waifs with the enormous eyes, it was Cami. *Oh, no.*

"Come here, lovey." She held her arms wide, offering an embrace.

Cami ran to her. "Oh, Gram." Her granddaughter sobbed so hard.

Kate longed to know the reason, but knew Cami wouldn't be able to talk yet. So she gave her time and guided Cami to the old sofa, stroking her head, kissing her temple.

The child pulled back and worked to catch her breath. "I'm kicked out of Honor Society."

"What? How?"

Kate realized who stood behind this trauma. But how did she orchestrate it?

"Because I've got a suspension on my record, I have broken the rules, and can't be a member anymore. Mrs. Alvarez, our adviser, was real upset but said she couldn't do anything. It's not fair. Is this gonna follow me forever? Will it be on my high school records or keep me out of college?" Tears raced her cheeks, but the sobbing didn't return.

"No, this won't be a problem in high school. Or college. It's one thing taken from you. But you still have the best. No one can take your integrity. Hold your head up. You have nothing to be ashamed of." Someone else has, but Kate would leave that in God's hands. This was only a skirmish after they'd won the war. An enemy who didn't want to admit defeat. Jesus said to pray for our enemies. So she would. But moving those prayers from raining fiery coals on a certain person's head to petitions for her welfare might take some extra effort.

Cami wiped the tears from her cheeks. "I'm sorry, Gram, to be such a messed up mess."

Kate placed her hands on either side of Cami's sweet face. "You are a jewel, my love. A rare gem and a gift. I love you so much and wouldn't trade you for the most perfect kid in the world."

Cami embraced her tight. "Oh, Gram, I'm so glad I have you."

That brought a knot to Kate's windpipe. She cleared her throat. "How about a treat? Let's go out to eat tonight. Or would you rather we get take out and come back to watch our shows?"

"Serious?" Cami's eyes danced, and then she sobered but smiled. "Let's get take out so we can watch your shows."

"My shows? Aren't they our shows?"

"Aw, Gram, you know I have fun watching with you." The following grin was worth everything.

The week passed. At church, the pastor preached a sermon on loving the unlovable. Guess God wanted to emphasize His point.

Come Monday, Cami left for school. Kate took the chance

and returned to volunteering. She arrived home a little before Cami, who stormed in, slamming with fervor.

"What happened, Cams?"

The girl stood Peter Pan style in front of her, anger blazing from her eyes. "That woman's a witch. With a capital B."

"CATHERINE AMELIA!"

"I'm sorry Gram, but she is. Guess what she tried to do?"

Kate shook her head. "I'd appreciate you telling me and not making me guess."

Cami blew her bangs off her forehead and plopped on the couch next to Kate. "I got called into the office today. Seems another person wrote on the bathroom wall, so she insisted on blaming me. But a teacher was my witness. I was with Mrs. Alvarez giving her the secretary stuff for Honor Society. Someone else has gotta do my job, so I was going over everything with her. I told Ms. Fart-tuna," she spit out the new nickname "and she wouldn't believe me. I called for Mrs. Alvarez to back me up and she did. Gram, she's out to get me. What am I gonna do?"

That was a good question. Another: What's wrong with that woman? And how did she get so twisted?

You don't need to know. Keep praying.

Kate realized the nudge came from God. It didn't make her feel any better, but at least she knew what He expected. Prayer. For her enemy. For the unlovely. Not fun.

"You're going to continue being the good, kind, sweet girl I know you are. Please, please PLEASE do not try to fix this yourself. I need you to trust me. Continue to do your best in class, be respectful, and above all, never go into the restroom without a witness. Can you do that? We've only a few months left. Spring break is around the corner, and then the home stretch."

"Oh, Gram. That's a lot to ask."

"You're right. But it's not forever. You can do this. I'm praying for you." Kate patted Cami's knee.

"I'll try. But maybe I'll devise a plan I can enjoy in the

privacy of my room. One where Ms. Fart-tuna gets hers in front of everyone, and Dr. Dugdale fires her."

"That's not a good idea. What if you slip and share that with someone and word gets back? Remember how fast things traveled when you wrote on the wall?" Though to be honest, Kate understood. She knew Cami's great imagination would figure out something. "Don't worry about retribution. That's tied to unforgiveness. When we can't forgive, that's like drinking poison and waiting for the other person to die. Don't let her chain you to that."

Cami tipped her head and peered at her, as if studying each cone in her iris. "I don't know how you can forgive like that. Some things are just unforgivable, Gram."

"If I head down that path, then I have to figure out what I've done that is unforgivable. It runs both ways. Do you want to be considered unforgivable?"

Now she stared at her hands. "No. But that is so hard. Too hard. I mean, what about that woman who killed Mom and Daddy? Can you forgive her? I can't."

Kate wouldn't lie to the girl. But the truth was, she still dealt with that situation. She knew what God expected, and she knew what His Word said. That drunken woman stole her daughter, son-in-law, and came close to stealing Cami from her. She had irreparably altered lives and walked away with bruises. Not fair, so she still cried out to God. "I'm working on it, Cam. I'm working on it."

Cami

Present day

As she turned from the door, something inside Cami clenched. She recognized fear. Fear Jeff would say they couldn't work. Fear she'd convince herself she could do this only to have the memories taint everything. And the fear

God would tell her one thing when her heart cried for the other.

If she meant what she said about this not being a passing fancy, then she'd better resign herself to submit to whatever God planned and trust Him to make all okay. Like Gramma Opal said. Yeah, that's what she ought to do. Easy to say…

Aidan finished his card and Cami saved it too. Their parents walked in as she hit send on the email to their mom.

Bruce guided Morgan, almost holding her up as she took tentative steps. But when Morgan heard Aidan and Addie come running from the kitchen, she straightened her back. Cami watched as she inhaled and smiled. Did the twins make her feel better? Or did she do this for them?

"Glad you're back, Morgan. Kids were great, and no hitches about getting them."

Morgan gave the children quick hugs while Bruce shooed them to the other room with a promise of ice cream. "Thanks." She dropped onto the couch.

"Jeff stopped by to see how you're doing, but decided not to wait." He didn't want to be near her. *Stop*. Way too easy to build a pity party.

"Okay." Morgan leaned her head back and closed her eyes.

"Anything else you need?" Any reason to remain?

"You don't have to run if you want to avoid traffic. Bruce will fix dinner. Eat with the family. I'm not eating." She never opened her eyes or moved her head.

Cami sat next to her, not too close in case the movement bothered. "Are you okay with…?"

"With Bruce being here? No. But he's been a help. Always was a great dad." Sounded almost rehearsed, as if she'd been saying the line over to herself.

"Do you need me to stay?" Cami wanted to get home, but Morgan was right about traffic. And maybe she could be a buffer? She shook her head. Too late for buffers. Bruce had been here a few days. Wonder where he stayed?

Bruce showed up with a trash can and a cold rag. "Can I get you anything else, Morgan?"

Funny, Cami remembered hearing him call his wife honey all the time. It seemed strange for him to use her name.

"No, I just need the quiet. Thanks." When he left the room, Morgan cracked open an eye, glanced over at Cami, and dropped her voice. "He hovers. The worse I feel, the more he does. He said he still cares. But I can't take the hovering." Then she leaned her head back again and put the cold compress on her forehead.

"A lot has gone on since my last trip, for sure. Oh, wanted to tell you, unless something goes wrong, I should finish the project on time. The inheritance should happen."

A tear streaked Morgan's makeup free cheek. "Thanks."

If nothing else, that told her she needed to push to finish the shawl. Which meant she'd better leave for Tucson. And pray for a safe, uneventful drive. "I'll text when I get home. When you are up to it, check your email. And it's okay to give Bruce my number to keep me posted."

Morgan nodded.

For some inexplicable reason, Cami leaned over and kissed her cousin's cheek.

Another tear slipped free.

Cami needed to escape.

The trip home proved exactly what she'd asked for—no fear, no trauma, not even something funny. An uneventful and little-trafficked trip with great Beatles music. On a Friday afternoon. Now that must be a miracle. Maybe God listened to her prayers. And if He did, maybe He had an answer for her concerning her heart and Jeff. But would she recognize it?

She pulled into the company's parking lot a few minutes before four. After checking in with Ray (who didn't get ticked, another prayer answered), she spent two hours with the *Stinkerella* account, and one prepping the last of her other projects to hand off to a colleague. She hated not seeing them to the end, but Ray told her to do this, so she'd be focused on her primary job.

As she closed up, he peeked in. "Headed home?"

"Yeah. Why?"

"Oh, wondered if you'd like to get a bite."

Since she'd not eaten since her breakfast bar at four-thirty this morning, Ray's idea sounded great. Her tummy growled in agreement. "Sure. I can meet you downstairs in five."

He smiled—on anyone else they'd call it a grimace—and nodded before heading for the elevators.

Cami got her tech bag loaded, and her purse slung over her shoulder, locked up and got to the lobby with thirty seconds to spare.

After an awkward, "what sounds good to you?" round, they agreed on Italian. Ray said he knew a little place and gave her the address so she could follow in her car.

Her idea. He'd glanced at her funny when she suggested it, and she told herself that she'd misread him. Yet at the restaurant, he was… attentive.

Weird.

He held the door, which for Ray was a stretch. But she chalked up the novelty to being a fluke. Right? Then he held her chair for her. It was so out of character she caught herself staring.

"What?" He stared back.

"That's my question. Where is Ray and what have you done to him?"

He smiled/grimaced again. "Am I that uncouth? I do have manners, you know."

She started to make a smart comeback, but worried if she'd hurt his feelings. Ray? "I'm sure you do. We've been friends too long, so I've seen your unvarnished side a lot more, I guess."

He chuckled at that. "Nice, Cams. But you're right. I just wanted to say thank you for all your hard work. Especially with the other stuff dumped on you. You're a good friend, Cami. You don't pull punches, but you go the extra mile."

Her face heated. This was so not Ray.

The waiter took their order. Good thing. She needed that moment. After ordering the angel hair primavera and a salad, she returned to normal, sort of.

"Thank you, Ray. Great idea." She smiled and slid her napkin onto her lap before swiping a bread stick.

"I figured I owed you. I've kept you hopping. How's Morgan doing, by the way?"

She filled him in on bits and pieces. Only things she knew Morgan wouldn't mind her sharing.

"And your project for your grandmother? I figured you gotta be burning your candle at both ends between work and that. How's it coming?" Ray was born to advertise, he knew more clichés and jingles than anyone else.

She smiled. "It's coming. If I keep going, I'll be done on time. Maybe. Did I tell you what I'm doing?"

"No."

"I'm crocheting a prayer shawl." She waited for his sarcasm. From him, she'd take it. They'd bantered for too many years.

"A prayer shawl? I've never heard of that. Was your grandmother religious?"

She swallowed. He was too interested. "I wouldn't have said so. But looking back, I think her faith was just part of her. I learned she helped tons of people without fanfare. Maybe that's why I didn't realize. Just accepted. We always prayed before a meal. I walked in on her once, praying beside her bed. I slipped out, I'm sure she never knew. But I'd forgotten that until this moment. Hm."

"And crocheting, that's something. Never knew you could do that." He propped his head with his fist, his elbow anchored to the table. Why did he probe like this?

"Lots about me you don't know, Ray. But guess there's more you do. We've been friends forever."

His eyes got misty. "Yeah, that's true."

"Anyway, I gotta finish the shawl. And give it to someone in need before the deadline. Then report back to the lawyer that all's been accomplished, or no one but a charity gets the inheritance."

"Nothing like a little pressure, huh? But you've always worked well under pressure. You'll make it."

"The hard part now is deciding who gets the shawl."

"Why not Morgan?"

Cami tipped her head. Why hadn't that occurred to her? "You're brilliant, Ray. That's what I need to do. Can't believe I never thought of that."

"I have my moments. We make a great team, Cam."

The food arrived. Not a moment too soon. Something about the way he said great team started an uncomfortable churn inside. The farther removed from it, the better off she'd be.

Talk slowed while they ate. Too tired for dessert, Cami only wanted to head home, put in another row, and read one more chapter of her Bible.

Ray picked up the check, refusing to split it with her. "Nope, my treat. I owed you that."

"That's the second time you've said you owe me. Why?"

"You've worked hard for the company. We wouldn't have this new account but for your efforts." He paused, like he searched for words. "I took the promotion off the table when Monty blew things, so I went to George Whitman—"

"The CEO?"

He nodded. "Told him you'd gotten it back and that you are perfect for the job of VP." Ray glanced away, and then captured her gaze. "He said no. Turns out he's had his eye on someone else outside the company the whole time. Bringing him in next week. I'm sorry, Cam."

Chapter Fourteen

CAMI

Present day

She got home. Cami had no idea how she arrived at her condo. From the moment Ray dropped his bombshell, she'd been numb.

Truth? She never allowed herself to hope for the promotion. She'd wanted to make things right. But hope is a funny thing. Even when not focused on hoping, it hides just under the surface. Like that old Sandra Bullock movie, *Hope Floats*. A bar of Ivory soap. You can push that little white chunk under, but it still pops to the surface.

Unless you take the soap out of the bathtub.

Then no more hope to float anywhere.

She plopped on the sofa and pulled her crochet bag to her. What would this mean for her job? What if this new vice-president didn't like her? Would she ever find another chance for an administrative position?

Too hard to concentrate on crocheting, no matter how important.

"Alexa, play *Rubber Soul*." The music started, and Cami

headed to her room to change into her pajamas. As she pulled her hair back into a braid, her phone dinged. A text.

Her hand shook as she reached for it, thoughts pouring in before she checked. Jeff? Morgan? Was it about Morgan? Was Ray checking on her, worried she'd not handled his confession? Now fear kept her from looking.

But she was more afraid not to. She unlocked her screen.

Jeff: *We need to talk. All right to call?*

Cami: (with her fingers shaking so much she corrected the one word's spelling four times) *Yes.*

She sunk onto her bed. Could she take another hit?

The phone rang and she answered. "Hey." Before he spoke, she'd curled into a fetal position. She realized this hit would wound. *Please Lord, no more hits tonight.*

"Hey. Hoped I'd catch you. Did you drive back already?" He groped for things to say and she wanted to yell, "Spit it out!"

"Yeah, they didn't need me in the way. Plus got a lot happening with the presentation."

"You're able to save your project?" That's right, he'd said he'd pray. She never told him what happened. But she'd tried to keep her distance.

"Um huh, and the client liked the changes. Next week we put out a casting call, and the following week we start auditions." Things would get crazy by that point.

"Yeah. So you're pretty well set down in Tucson?"

What did he mean by that?

"That's where I live." What's he talking about?

"Cam, I've been praying about this. The only thing standing in our way, from my end, is location. I want to see where this goes. If you're ready. But if things develop, like I hope, I gotta know. Any chance you might move to Phoenix? I'm not sure about a long distance romance."

Romance? He said romance. She sat up. "I've never considered leaving Tucson. Never had a reason. Before. And I've been praying hard too. I hoped God would give me a verse that said *goforit* or stop. But that didn't happen. Instead, when I think of you, the accident or drunk driving doesn't cloud my mind. God's given me peace about you. I don't see the old you, I see you now."

She heard his sigh through the phone. "Thank you. I needed to hear that."

So he'd been nervous about her decision?

"Since you mentioned long distance, can we learn about each other before I move? You might decide you don't want to know more, and I'd be stuck in Phoenix without my job." *A job that might not want her in the near future.* Where did that notion come from?

"I'm good with that. Let's try a bit of the long distance. I can come see you tomorrow, but I'll have to be back home by nine. Gotta make sure I'm ready for Sunday. Are you game?"

The wash of warmth that flowed through her caught her by surprise. "I like that idea. If you get here early enough, I'll fix, no, grr. I'm out of groceries. Oh, I know a great omelet place."

He laughed and her world became perfect. As long as he remained her primary focus. "I'll text before I pull out of the drive."

"Can't wait."

The next song from the album started. "In My Life." The words highlighted her emotions. She couldn't say she loved him more. Not yet. But that's the direction her heart steered, in case anyone asked.

Now tons of adrenaline flowed, making her too keyed up for bed. So she put in a couple hours of crocheting and told Alexa to read the last couple chapters of the book of Luke. Dericka told her when she finished to start the book of Acts. Listening to the Bible read aloud while she crocheted relaxed her so much she came close to falling asleep on the sofa. But she called it a night after realizing she'd only one skein of yarn left. The end was in sight.

Come morning, she got up, dressed, and ready for company

early, though she tried on four outfits before deciding what to wear. Her jeans and a sleeveless white baby doll top with lots of cotton lace ended up the winner. Only because it was the least wrong. As she brushed her hair, she remembered his comment and only pulled the sides into a ponytail and let the rest hang long. She'd just slipped into her sandals when a knock made her heart stop. And then race. Why did her nerves have to run amok?

He stood on her doorstep, no white charger, no armor, but she knew exactly how those Disney princesses felt the moment he flashed his grin. "Hey you."

She drew the door wide, and as he stepped in. He pulled her into an embrace. Tingles curled her toes and shot sparks out her ears. It must have happened because her face heated faster than the desert at noon in mid-July making her ears burn. Security and excitement melded in his arms. She had no idea how they coexisted, but they did for a fact.

"I've needed to do that. For a while." He grinned.

She loved that grin. And his dimples. She loved them too. She needed to quit saying love so much. Even in her head. Even if true. "I've wanted you to. For a while."

"Glad to oblige. Are you ready?"

She stumbled away to get her purse. Okay, maybe she walked just fine. But she'd bet even money the floor of her condo up and rolled like a wave on the beach. "Ready."

Cami directed him to a local cafe. The breakfast crowd was in full swing, but they found seats right away, and the waitress brought fresh coffee before she took their orders.

She was so stinking happy to be with him. Moments ticked by before she caught the shadow passing through his gaze. "What's wrong? Aren't we good."

"We are. But I've got one more thing to tell you."

More? He's got more? That clenching in her gut returned. "What?"

"Remember when we met, and I told you I've been through lots of MRIs?"

She nodded.

"I have a condition with my heart. Left over from the accident. I'm super healthy for someone who deals with what I've got. But you won't find me in a pickup basketball game or backyard football. I love the games, don't get me wrong, but one wrong clobber and the pacemaker…"

"You have a pacemaker?"

He nodded.

"What about getting excited? Is that safe for you?"

That's when he busted out the dimples again. "I wouldn't have called otherwise. I get all kinds of excited in your company. Thought you'd figured that out."

And she breathed again. "Jeff, you are going to give me a heart attack. I don't know if I can take more confessions. So, I guess that game of volley ball I lined up this afternoon is out."

Now he laughed. "Never good at spiking, anyway."

Things got comfortable from that point on. They toured old town before grabbing some lunch. She invited him back to her place for a movie since the weather had grown too hot to do outdoor stuff.

He agreed.

She popped microwave popcorn for him—the last bag in the cabinet—and poured them both iced tea while he picked something from Netflix. After taking the glasses out to him, she noticed he'd cruised into the classic section. Did he like older music too? Hm. She returned for the bowl of popcorn and set it between them.

He grinned as if sharing a secret. "You're about to view one of the all-time greatest movies ever made. *The African Queen.*"

Cami snorted, and her tea went up her nose.

"Are you okay?" He'd set the popcorn on the floor and pulled her to him, rubbing her back.

She nodded against his chest. He smelled good. She'd love to keep her head there and just breathe in his scent forever—kind of a citrus-y, sandalwood scent that made her pulse pound in her ears. With a sigh, she sat up and nodded. "You said *The African Queen*. That's one of Gram's favorites."

"Oh, you've seen it." He sounded so disappointed.

"Been awhile, but yeah. First time I watched was with Gram. I figured Humphrey Bogart was nothing to look at. But as I got older, I grew to love his character. Charley. Great movie and I'd love to watch it with you. I'm just tickled you like old movies too." She hoped her smile told him she meant what she said.

"Okay. But for the record, what other old movie faves do you enjoy?"

She paused, recalling all the ones she and Gram binged. "Of course, *Casablanca*. Then *The Philadelphia Story*. Oh, can't forget *Angel on His Shoulder*, *It Happened One Night*, *Adam's Rib*. Gram loved the older ones. Oh, and we liked *The Sting*, *Young Frankenstein*, and some musicals—all the old Rogers and Hammerstein's, plus *Singing in the Rain*, *Band Wagon*—"

He laughed. "And I wanted to introduce you to the classics. But I'm glad you like them too. Should I pick something else?"

"No, *The African Queen*. Please."

Twenty minutes into the movie, the popcorn disappeared. Jeff moved the empty bowl to the floor and draped his arm over her shoulders. Somehow they both scooted closer until her head leaned against his chest. She liked that. Oh, she liked that.

When the film ended, she sat up but didn't pull away. Her bottom lip rolled over her teeth as she held her breath. She knew what she wanted to do. But things were different, so much had changed. Did pastors kiss? Should she kiss him? Would he question her faith if she kissed him?

And then his lips found hers. Soft. Gentle. Making every one of those crazy ideas vanish. In slow motion, he drew away, blinked, and ran his finger down the side of her cheek. "I've needed to do that too. But I'd better hit the road." He stood and pulled her to her feet.

She walked him to his car.

He reached out the window and caressed her face. "This long distance stuff is gonna be tough."

He'd just read her mind.

MORGAN

It'd been a grueling three weeks. Morgan wasn't sure she could get out of bed. As it was, Bruce carried her up last evening before they all sat down to dinner. She was out of energy and fight.

You're dying.

The notion popped into her brain and stole what little breath she possessed. Was she? Dying? Was she ready? What would happen to her kids?

Those sweet babies. Not so baby anymore, but she longed to watch them grow. They were just getting started. They had sports and gymnastics and grade cards and best friends and first loves and high school and college and so much more ahead. Marriage and grandbabies. She wanted grandbabies. A thunderbolt of fear drove deep in her gut and she cried out from the pain.

"Morgan, are you all right?" Bruce was there. Still. Why?

"No." She couldn't hold it together one more second. "No, I'm dying, and I'm scared, and I don't want to and—"

He sat on the bed and pulled her into his arms. "You aren't dying, but I'm guessing it feels that way. This is serious. But you won't die."

She shoved back. "How can you say that? How can you know?"

"I don't. But I love you too much to let this second chance escape. You aren't allowed to die. I need you. The kids need you. Don't leave us, Morgan. Don't give up."

She swiped her hand over her face, a practiced habit that missed her absent hair. "You love me?"

"I always have. My pride got in the way."

Her voice wavered. "But I'm… bald. And ugly."

He kissed her head. "I didn't fall in love with your hair, though I'll admit, yours is pretty spectacular. I fell in love with a determined woman who works hard to do the best possible. You're still doing that, whether or not you recognize it. I see how you protect the kids."

"No choice. A mother has to. Bruce, I'm so scared."

"I know, sweetie, I know." He pulled her to him again and she could hear his heart beneath her ear. "We'll get through this. I promise."

She wanted to tell him not to make promises he couldn't keep. He did that sometimes. No, she wouldn't play the divorce card. If she pulled through, maybe they'd work through this. But for now, she'd pretend like she believed him.

She woke to him laying her back onto the pillows and kissing her forehead. Rather than respond, she let him figure she still slept. Perhaps it'd make him feel better. Besides, his strength helped. Some. She kept her eyes closed and drifted.

Soon sounds stirred her, and she cracked her eyelids to spot Nohemi bringing a tray of tea and Jell-O to her. "I stopped to check on you in case you needed anything. I know it's not a regular day, but Bruce said you had a rough morning."

"What day is it? Without a calendar, I've a hard time remembering." Days were either chemo days or ordinary days. Nohemi picked the kids up on Sundays for church but Bruce stayed with her. She only left home for her treatments and Bruce got her ready for those.

"It's Saturday. I'll take the kids, get them out of the house." She began straightening the bedroom while she spoke, pouring humiliation over Morgan's head. Her perfect sanctum was less than immaculate, and each misplaced item the woman fixed pointed out the imperfections.

"Please, don't clean." She had another idea. "Would you sit and talk with me?"

"Of course." Nohemi pulled up the chair Bruce brought into the room for visitors. "What would you like to talk about?"

"Dying."

The woman's eyes enlarged a bit before returning to normal. "What about dying? Is it on your mind?"

Morgan nodded. "Yeah. I'm scared. This has come so fast. I buried my grandmother seven weeks ago and considered myself perfectly healthy except for maybe an ulcer. Now this."

"It doesn't fit your plans, does it?"

Morgan realized that was it and gave a half-hearted smile. "I do tend to plan."

"Yes, you do. But my greater concern is about your heart. We all die, it's a part of life. But what happens afterward, that's much bigger."

"You're talking about heaven, right? And God? I've tried hard to do the right thing. Everything I know to do." She scrunched up the sheets in her fists.

"And you aren't sure it's enough. Let me tell you, it isn't."

Morgan gasped. This wasn't the comfort she wanted.

Nohemi sat on the bed's edge and patted her hand. "Honey, it's impossible to be good enough. None of us are. But God fixed that. He sent Jesus. When you surrender your will to His, ask Him to take away your sins, and come live in your heart, that's enough. The Bible tells us to believe in Jesus and be saved, that it is by faith in God's grace that we are. Not by what we do. Does that make sense?"

For the first time, it did. Do your best was her mantra. But then her best wasn't enough? What should she do? Surrender. She could surrender. She nodded.

"Would you like me to pray with you?"

Morgan cleared her throat. "Please."

"If you agree, then repeat after me." Nohemi prayed.

Morgan repeated every word, meaning each phrase. She

confessed her need for Jesus and asked him into her heart. When done, something was different. Something returned that had been lost. Hope. She'd found her hope. Tears poured and she didn't stop them.

Nohemi pulled her close and rocked her back and forth, just like a mother. Like she'd rocked her babies. Like she wanted to be comforted.

A knock sounded at the door.

Morgan drew away to find Cami in the doorway. "Hi, I don't want to interrupt."

Nohemi helped her back to the pillows. "I'll step out so you two can chat. Good to see you again." She patted Cami's arm as she passed by her and out of the room.

"Nice lady." Cami glanced over her shoulder at Nohemi's exit before coming into the room. "Wanted to catch you up on some stuff. Up to talking a minute?"

Morgan pasted on her best smile. Funny how she'd grown closer to Cami now after all these years and didn't want her cousin to worry. "Sure, sit." She scooted up a little.

Cami sat in the chair. "I've got news. I finished the project."

A tingle of hope shot through Morgan, giving her more strength than she'd known seconds before. "You did? What was it? Can you tell me now?"

Cami grinned and put a gift bag on the bed. Morgan never noticed her carry it in, and by the size of it, she should've. "Go ahead, open it."

Beneath crumpled tissue paper was a printed sheet. Morgan pulled that free and read it.

This is a prayer shawl.
Aptly named because you were prayed for
while it was made.
If you are cold, may you feel God's warmth.
If you are sick, may you feel His healing.
If you are overwhelmed, may you feel His peace.

May God's grace be upon this shawl,
Warming, comforting, enfolding and embracing.
May this mantel be a safe haven,
A sacred place where you feel
the intimacy of the Father,
Sustaining and embracing in good times
as well as difficult ones.
May you be cradled in hope,
Kept in joy,
Graced with peace,
Wrapped in love.

As Morgan put her hand inside, tears pushed through her barriers, and her hand made contact with the softest yarned fabric she'd ever touched. She pulled it free and it unfurled into a large triangular shawl full of clusters and fans. "You made this?" She sniffed, running her pajama sleeve over her face.

"This is what Gram had me do. She knew I hadn't been able to pick up a crochet hook since the accident. So she boxed me into a position. If it had been only me, I might've walked away. But I couldn't let you down. Now I'm doing the last part of Gram's instructions. I'm to give it to someone who needs it. I'm giving it to you."

Morgan tore her gaze from the beautiful shawl to notice Cami's wet pink cheeks. "For me?"

Cami nodded.

"And you prayed? For me?"

She nodded again.

"I kinda want to hug you, Cami."

"I kinda want you to." She stood and embraced Morgan.

Another knock sounded. It was Bruce. "Nohemi came down and mentioned you're warmer than you should be. I phoned the doctor, and he wants me to take you to the ER. Sorry, honey, but we need to get you there."

Cami pulled back. "I'll keep praying. And I'll meet with

Gram's lawyer as soon as he'll see me. No worries. It's going to be fine."

Morgan grabbed hold of Cami's hand. If she was going to die, at least she'd mended some fences and got right with God.

She still didn't want to die, though.

Cami

Nohemi agreed to stay with the kids, so Cami followed Bruce and Morgan to the hospital. Once inside, she called Jeff. She planned to meet him after giving Morgan the shawl. And she promised Ray the trip would be short as he wanted her working. She'd promised to be back by four, so she needed to call him too. He'd understand. Maybe.

Funny thing about Ray, he'd been more… human, for lack of a better word, lately. Asking about Morgan, and if she'd finished the shawl. That kind of stuff. Maybe he's concerned about when she'd get her head back in the game—only the normal Ray would just shout, "Get your head back in the game."

She got him on the line and explained, and could've sworn she heard him bite his tongue. Maybe. But then he said something thoughtful, and that he'd see her when he saw her.

Was missing the old Ray weird?

She needed to discover why he acted this way.

They admitted Morgan. Her doctor called ahead, so they took her from the ER straight to admitting and to her room.

Jeff showed up a few minutes after. Turns out he flashed his pastor's ID and by-passed the waiting.

Cami thought, *Thank God*, meaning every word.

He sat beside her as she waited in the hall while the nurses got Morgan situated. When his fingers intertwined with hers, tiny sparks raced up her arm. "Want to pray?"

"That's all I've been doing. Except for letting you and Ray

know. I kinda want my crochet hook to keep my fingers busy." She glanced at their clasped hands. "But I sort of like your idea too." She grinned.

So did he. Those dimples would drive her out of her mind.

"This isn't where I wanted to spend our time today. But perhaps this is good. I often get called to the hospital. It's a big part of my life."

"Guess I never considered that, but I get it. Maybe if I work at making prayer shawls, I can go with you sometimes and bring one for who you visit." A spontaneous idea, but one she liked.

"That's wonderful. But I don't make too many hospital calls in Tucson."

She sighed. "I know. There's gotta be a solution. But until this campaign's wrapped up, at least for me, we can't make plans."

"What do you mean?"

"I need to contact Gram's lawyer. I finished the shawl and gave it away, as instructed. Now I must let Mr. Jones know so he'll send the will to probate and the heirs can learn about their inheritance." She shrugged.

"Why would that end your campaign?"

"If I'm an heir, then that's a conflict of interest, even if Felicia wants me on the project. I'd be technically part of hiring myself and paying myself twice. As long as I'm not listed as an heir, no problem. And Gram might not leave me any money. I received a good settlement from the trust fund my parents left for me when I graduated. I don't need the money as long as I am working. But I realized Morgan did. And I've no clue who else is effected. But if I receive money that's tied to this campaign in any way, I'll have to withdraw from the project. It's the right thing to do."

"If you withdraw, could you change jobs? Maybe move up here?" He looked so hopeful.

She didn't want to raise his hopes. "I don't know. To land a job in Phoenix like I've got in Tucson would be tough. I rose pretty fast up the ranks, but I've only worked the one place. I don't have a long resume, so either they'd only have lower level openings and say I'm over qualified, or not have anything for me. A friend of mine tried last year in Oklahoma City. Took her nine months before she landed a position. In the meantime, she worked at Burger King."

"Oh." His hopes deflated anyway.

"Who knows what might happen? Right now, I'm just concerned for Morgan."

He squeezed her hand. "I understand. We'll take this as it comes. Want some coffee?"

She shook her head. "I'd rather you just hold my hand, unless you need some?"

He chuckled. "I hate hospital coffee. Just wanted to do something for you."

"You're doing something right now." She squeezed back.

The nurse came out from Morgan's room, followed by Bruce, who motioned them in. Morgan's face, without her frame of black hair, blended into the white pillowcase. The soft baby blue head wrap did nothing but make her look paler.

"So what did they say? Any ideas yet?" Cami felt Jeff's hand signaling. She shouldn't pepper them with questions. She knew that. But she also needed to know.

Bruce tucked Morgan's covers about her and she understood the hovering. "They've only made her comfortable until the doctor arrives. Should be soon, they said." He spoke over his shoulder while making sure she had water and tissues at hand.

The ever-present yet always absent They. They say this. They advise that. Who is this they? Why can't they come and explain?

Morgan drifted, and the two guys chatted Diamondbacks baseball in hushed tones.

Cami sat beside her cousin's bed, fingering the shawl she'd draped about her shoulders. Morgan insisted on bringing the new wrap. The only thing besides her cap and slippers. Bruce carried her down the stairs and into the hospital until they brought a wheelchair for her, so she didn't need slippers, anyway. But Morgan kept the shawl wrapped tight about her.

When Bruce had picked her up, Cami realized how much weight Morgan had lost. The reality sent a shock wave through her.

Now when she gazed at her sleeping cousin, she viewed a sister. Someone she loved and didn't want to lose. This is what Gram wanted, what she'd tried to make happen. Well, she succeeded, even if after she… Cami refused to acknowledge that word. She'd lost too many people in her life. *Please, Lord, not Morgan too. I'm selfish in my prayer. I don't want that pain, and I don't want Bruce or the kids to know that pain.* A tear dropped onto the bed.

Morgan opened her eyes. "Don't cry. I have hope. I don't know what'll happen, but I found hope, Cam. You got to hang onto it with me."

Cami took hold of Morgan's hand and nodded. "Yes, I'll hope with you. And pray for you."

A smile spread across Morgan's face for a moment, then her eyes closed.

The doctor came in, checking the chart. "Do you want everyone to wait in the hall while I check you Mrs. Pembroke?"

Morgan shook her head, her eyes still closed. "They can stay. I know they want to hear too."

The doctor slipped his glasses up to his forehead. "Very well. From the chart I notice your temperature has risen. That can mean you've contracted an infection or you're having a reaction to the chemo. We're going to keep you here and see if we can get it down."

"How long?" Morgan's voice rose almost above a whisper.

"For what? Your stay or until you start back on chemo?" At least he walked closer to Morgan's bedside.

"How long do I have to live?"

Cami gasped and held tighter to Morgan's hand as if she'd hold her here no matter what.

"We're not to that point, Mrs. Pembroke. At least that's my opinion. This is serious, and I don't want you to imagine otherwise. But we've already seen your tumor shrink. A little more and we'll be able to operate. I guess we could try now if necessary, but safer would be if we could make that sucker smaller first." He smiled at that, and Cami knew he hoped to get Morgan to smile.

She did. "Thank you. I needed to hear that. What is our next step?"

"Our next step is to wait. We're running tests to learn if you have an infection. If we don't find one, then you're off the chemo for the next couple treatments while we reassess. Can you hang in there for that?"

Morgan nodded. "Thank you, doctor."

Cami let out the breath she'd held. At least he didn't crush her hope, in fact, he gave her more. It made her want to give hope of her own.

The best way to do that was by letting Mr. Jones know the task was complete.

But today was Saturday. Maybe he took calls on the weekend?

"Excuse me, Morgan, I'll be right back." She'd get through. One way or another. Even if just to leave a message. Cami would bring Morgan the hope she needed and push Mr. Jones to get the inheritance checks sent right away.

Then Cami remembered.

Morgan was the executrix.

And she was in no condition to handle Gram's estate.

Now what would they do?

Chapter Fifteen

Monday morning found Cami ready to strike early at the day. She'd tossed throughout the night, too excited to get started.

Today she and her team would interview the final picks for the character of Stinkerella. They'd narrowed it to seven little girls, and any of them could play the part. But her job was to weed the choices to three, and be ready to present them on Thursday. Felicia and her group would view those video interviews and make their decision. Friday, they'd launch *Stinkerella*, and the project, to the world. Everything would be a go—beginning with a grand reveal party on *Good Morning America*.

One more reason she must know if Mr. Jones got her text. She needed that all settled before she stepped into Thursday's meeting. Cami had emailed asking for an appointment via Zoom, as each day grew more Looney Tunes, and a trip to Phoenix would have to be postponed until the next week.

And that was past the deadline. She completed the project on time. Still, she wasn't sure how Mr. Jones the Stickler would interpret the letter of the law in this instance.

So she sent up a prayer for the Zoom choice.

With her phone always at the ready, Cami prepped waiting rooms for the little girls and their chaperons.

Her team would explain the plan to the adults once everyone arrived and the girls got settled into their own room.

Parents and guardians could keep an eye on everything through a two-way mirror, but it was important to see the children without adult interference.

Then, given various playthings and craft ideas, the girls were encouraged to have fun.

Cameras videoed how they interacted with each other and the supplies.

Cami prepared a checklist of qualities she wanted to see, and whether the child emerged as a follower or a leader.

The second part was to invite each girl to answer a few questions one-on-one. Some "suppose you…" type queries. They would be videoed as well. With all this in mind, and a tick sheet of the traits of the books' heroine as a guide, her team would spend the next two days whittling the choices to the final three.

It sounded so perfect on paper.

These seven made the cut from over two hundred possible unknowns and showed the best acting abilities.

They also gave points for following directions and improvisation.

So summing up, Cami's job was to find the one child most naturally like Stinkerella.

And since Cami had been the model—yeah, Gram stole a lot of ideas and characterization from her, and it was a little weird since the character was tons nicer, and things ended up better for her. But she couldn't help but figure that the girl with whom she experienced the most affinity might be the better choice. But she knew to give the data a chance to prove her gut right.

Her gut was wrong.

Cami viewed as Sara, a cute little blonde who could be a Mini Me and a shoo-in, became a bit of a bully in the group room. The child was bossy, even ostracizing one little redhead.

But what grabbed Cami's attention most was how that redheaded child, Emma, didn't let it faze her. She found something else that interested her. When others caught on to what she was doing and checked, she welcomed them with kindness.

Before long, Sara was alone and, while Emma interacted with the other five, she invited her bully to join them and have fun. No pressure. No retaliation. She issued the invite and kept doing what she was doing. Sara later came around and the group created a mural together.

That's how a true Stinkerella would behave. Independent and inclusive.

Just as the girls put on the last touches, Cami's phone buzzed. An email from Mr. Jones. He had an afternoon opening for a Zoom meeting. Could she be available at two?

Cami raced to Ray's office and filled him in.

He promised to cover for her so she could take the call and she breathed for the first time that morning.

Five minutes early, she pulled up the Zoom invitation and entered the conference room. Her heart thudded on her rib cage. She'd fulfilled her part, but now what happened?

Mr. Jones popped in and they made their greetings. "So, Miss Madison, you say you finished the project? Can you tell me about it?"

"I learned to crochet all over again, but I completed the prayer shawl last week. Did you get my photo?" Nowhere did she find anything to say what proof she should show. She hoped that was enough.

"I did. To whom did you give it?"

She blew out a breath. "My cousin, Morgan, is dealing with some major health issues. I felt, after a lot of..." would he understand if she explained how she arrived at her decision? "A lot of prayer that she should receive it. Much healing has gone on between us. I guess that's what Gram wanted all along."

"I agree. She confided that her one regret is that she didn't know how to bring you two together. Looks like she succeeded."

"She did. So where do we go from here?" She tried to look as calm as possible, as if it were an everyday occurrence to talk about wills with Gram's lawyer.

"I'll send to probate right away. Your cousin is the executor, though there's little for her to do. As I was your grandmother's attorney, with her instructions Social Security was notified to stop payments until further notice. All her accounts are up to date and she is debt free. The will has only three beneficiaries, yourself, your cousin, and your uncle. His is nominal as your grandmother said he wasn't interested in the money, and was by far more concerned about his career. She wanted an account set for him that he can use if he retires. The rest is equally split between you and Mrs. Pembroke. The only things to contend with are the selling of her house, and dealing with the royalties from her books."

She took a deep breath and plunged in with the news. "I'm glad to hear it is easy, though at this point, I doubt Morgan can do any of it. She's in the hospital. Can you advise on this? I know she'd like to get things dispersed." Cami hoped that didn't sound like she was a mercenary trying to take Morgan's job.

"If she can't handle it, have her ask the probate court to excuse her. She'll find forms on line, and anyone can help her fill them out. Then she can suggest someone else or leave it for the court to appoint." He paused. "I hope she is not too ill and will recover fast."

"Thank you, sir. That's our prayer. I'll let her know. She or her husband may be in contact with you soon. I appreciate you meeting me via Zoom. This is Crazy Week here in Tucson."

"Not a problem. Give your cousin my best and tell her I'm available to answer all her questions now."

They signed off and Cami hunted down Ray to let him know she was back.

"Hey, that little Emma is something. You'll want to watch her video." He grinned. For such a curmudgeon, he sure had a soft spot for kids.

"Yeah, she stood out to me, as well. Too bad her hair isn't the right color. But she'd be so good."

"How'd it go with the lawyer?"

"Looks like I'm an heir and will be receiving royalty payments. So I need to recuse myself when we meet Thursday."

Ray scrunched his face. "You aren't receiving anything yet. Why not hold off? Don't leave the project before you have to. We need you on this."

"Why put it off? Besides, Morgan needs the income, so she'll be pushing to get this handled as soon as possible."

He peered at her. "But who's to know? You won't do anything underhanded. Cam, you're honest to a fault. So why stop working on something where you do great stuff and make your gram proud to boot? You think Felicia would care about it? She loves you, and your personal touch to make sure things are right for your grandmother's memory. Stay on the team, Cam." He reached for her hand.

She shook her head. "The reasons you state are the ones that require me to tell the client. I need to be upfront with them. Besides, Felicia already knows about the possibility. It's only a matter of time."

"Please, at least think about it. This is too important to just fall on your sword." He gave her hand a little squeeze and walked away.

Cami turned and followed with her gaze. Fall on her sword? That was a strange thing to say. What in the world did he mean?

Kate

Eleven years ago

Kate checked her watch. Cami would come home from her after-school club in about ten minutes. It was hard to believe she was a sophomore now. Unless you looked at her legs, she showed no outward signs of the accident, though Kate knew she'd always be scarred.

She was a good girl, a sweet kid, even more she seemed to enjoy time with her old grandmother. It was one thing when the child came to visit a couple times a year. It was different when you lived together. Kate ran her finger over the clipped school photo hanging on her refrigerator. They'd developed a friendship that Kate cherished.

The phone rang, the high school's number showed on the caller ID. "Hello?"

"Is this Mrs. Hanson, Cami's grandmother?"

An icy chill shot up her spine. Almost the exact words as when the hospital called her four years ago. "What happened to Cami?"

"Oh, she's fine. No, I'm calling about something good. I'm sorry I frightened you. This is Mrs. Moss. I teach math and have Cami in my advanced algebra class. Are you okay?" The woman sounded worried. And with her name, Kate could picture her looking concerned. They'd met at Meet the Teacher Night.

Kate exhaled. "Yes, sorry. It…well…go on. You said it's a good thing?"

The woman's smile transmitted through the lines with her voice. "Yes. She's doing great in my class, but that's not why I'm calling. Did you know she's started a club on campus?"

"No, she didn't mention it to me. What sort of club?" Kate pulled out a kitchen chair and sat.

"At Saguaro Trail Crest High, we encourage students to try out ideas rather than turn them over to an adult. She developed an idea for a club and asked if I'd be the sponsor. Paperwork needs to show the student has put intention into the plan. Next they discuss it with a sponsor for a little guidance, but it's still on their shoulders to follow through. Once they've met that criteria, they must find other students interested in joining. They need a minimum of seven with an additional five more before the end of the school year in order for it to continue.

Plans are designed so that the club continues after the student is graduated."

"Cami did all that?" And never said a word?

"Yes. In fact, she has the fastest growing club on campus. She spotted a need and stepped up. Not only helping one student but to crafting it so many could be on the receiving end. Her club is the Kindness Project."

Kate was glad she was sitting. Not that Cami was unkind. But that she'd done all that and never uttered a word. Not one word. That independent streak was growing. "I'm so grateful you told me, Mrs. Moss. What a wonderful thing to share."

"Well, that's not all. We have a school-wide convocation after Spring Break where all the students active in a club can be honored. It helps showcase the diversity and community spirit of our campus. What you might not know is that the staff and students all vote for various awards for clubs. It's a write-in thing, not a multiple choice. The Kindness Project won hands down, voted the most influential, and most beneficial, and club of the year. We'd like you to surprise Cami as she receives her award."

Kate couldn't get a word out. Her Stinkerella won this from her peers and teachers. She swallowed hard and forced a sound. "Yes, yes. Thanks. Yes."

"I knew you'd be pleased. This will be two weeks from today. I'll call again after we return from break. Please mention nothing to Cami. We want her to be surprised."

"I understand—"

The back door opened, and Cami plopped her backpack on the kitchen table. "Hey, Gram." That sweet girl dropped a kiss on Kate's cheek, kicked her shoes off in the corner, and padded to the family room.

"I can't talk any longer. Cami is home from school now." She blinked away her tears.

"That's fine. We'll connect after break. Thank you for your help with this, I know it will be great."

"Yes, thank you. Goodbye." Kate didn't even listen to hear if Mrs. Moss disconnected before hanging up the phone. A second later she hoped that in her daze she'd not hung up on the woman. But wow, her Cami doing something so wonderful…

And now she must keep it a secret for two weeks. Ouch.

But she did. Even through Spring Break with Cami home all day. Well, some of the days. When she heard Morgan was coming for a short visit, she made arrangements to stay with a friend saying her parents invited her to take a quick trip with them.

Kate didn't want to imagine Cami finagled an invitation for herself to get away from her cousin. But it was lovely to spend time with her other granddaughter. And to be honest, she didn't miss the fighting.

After an eternity of keeping the secret, the special convocation day arrived. Kate waited until Cami was out of the house before getting ready and heading for the school. She went straight to the office and prayed Cami wouldn't stop by and catch her. When she checked in, the secretary buzzed into Mrs. Moss's class asking her to come. It was her prep period, so no kids were in the room.

Mrs. Moss showed up and took Kate back to the classroom. "She won't be in before the convocation. We'll be meeting on the football field so everyone can attend. I need to get a couple things together, and then I'll walk you over to where you'll be ready to pop out and surprise her."

As the teacher gathered items, she explained the plan. "Save your surprise for the last announcement. For Club of the Year. We won't be calling everyone up, just Cami at the end. So, are you ready?"

Kate nodded, too excited to talk. She was busting with pride for the girl.

They walked to the staging area, and Kate found a seat in the wings of the stage. She could watch but not be seen.

Soon a cacophony of teen sounds filled the football field as students came and sat in groups. Looked like they sat with their club mates. Kate wondered what happened when someone belonged to more than one, but that was something she could ask Cami when they were both home.

The assistant principal grabbed attention by speaking into the mic and doing a roll call for each of the clubs. When the particular one was named, the members stood and made a cheer. He made a brief speech about how STC High could boast the best and most inclusive clubs of any school. And then he asked for quiet so he could read the award winners.

With each presentation, Kate's pulse quickened.

When her granddaughter's club received two awards in a row —most beneficial and most influential—she forced herself from jumping to her feet with applause.

And then came the last announcement. The students did a make-shift drum roll on their laps.

The assistant principal held up his hand and most stopped. A few needed the teacher sponsors to help quiet the groups. When he'd everyone's attention, he read from the paper in front of him. "The last award for Club of the Year goes to The Kindness Project, Cami Madison president. Please come to the stage, Cami."

The applause rang out as Kate's granddaughter stood and glanced about. Mrs. Moss, her club's sponsor, motioned for her to move forward. Pink rose in Cami's cheeks as she mounted the steps.

Funny, but she never looked Kate's way. Instead, she kept her eyes down as she moved to the front of the stage where the assistant principal waited with the trophy. "Miss Madison, we award this prize to you and your Kindness Project. I understand you're the one who started the club. Would you say a few words?"

Cami's eyes got wide, and Kate saw her swallow hard before she accepted the mic. "Thank you, everyone who voted for The Kindness Project. But I gotta tell you I'm not the one who came up with it. My friend, Nora, and I were talking over lunch and she wondered what it would be like if we had such a club. But she was too nervous to start it. She moved away during Christmas. But it was her idea. She said I could try, but she's the one who should be honored. We've all benefited from her idea. I wanted you all to know. Thank you."

Kate stepped out from the wings, tears streaming down her cheeks. Her granddaughter was a young woman of integrity and growing up so fast.

Cami glanced her way just then and her mouth dropped open. "Gram?"

Kate smiled from her heart, so proud. "Good job, Stinkerella." She mouthed the words so only Cami would know. And then Kate was wrapped in a giant hug. "I'm proud of you."

"Really?"

"Yup. If you can do this, you'll succeed at anything. You'll do great."

Cami

Cami promised Ray she would consider not letting the client know she was an heir. And she did, for about two minutes. Even the idea made her feel dirty, underhanded. To the point she got a little resentful with Ray, at least in her mind.

Monday night she called Morgan. Bruce answered and said she was still feeling puny but put her on speaker so they could chat.

"I conferenced with Mr. Jones today. He sent the will to probate this afternoon. Now you've access to things." She wouldn't volunteer the rest unless asked.

"I don't have the energy, Cam. What do I do? I can't take care of Gram's estate." Cami didn't need to be present to realize Morgan had started to cry.

Okay. She'd been asked. "I wondered about that. He said

you can refuse to be the executrix, you aren't forced. Just inform the probate court. You can suggest a trusted person, Bruce, for instance, or allow the court to appoint someone." The last thing Cami wanted involved Morgan imagining she wanted to steal that position.

She heard a pause. "I can name anyone?"

"Yeah. The law gives options because things happen. Sometimes the named executor isn't available, or he doesn't want to handle things. Might be too grief stricken or something."

"I pick you."

Cami sucked in a breath. Had she heard right? "Me?"

"I trust you, Cami. Maybe Bruce can check out the court, get the paperwork. Perhaps stuff's on-line. Anyway, he can help me put you as the new executrix so you can get this all cleared up." Another pause. "Are you okay with that?"

Was she? Mr. Jones said the job was pretty straightforward. And if she no longer worked on the *Stinkerella* project, time no longer became a problem. Her thoughts wandered at that point and she resigned to reign them back. Too soon to follow that path.

"Yes, that's fine. In fact, I'm honored, Morgan. Thanks for trusting me." Just saying the words made her tear up.

"You're the one. You'll do what's best for all involved. I trust you, Cam. We'll see if Bruce can find anything online first. If not, he can go downtown to probate court tomorrow and see what he can learn. We'll let you know… once done… though they'll notify…"

Cami couldn't hold back her grin. This was Gram's dream for them. "So, tell me the latest on you. Got an ETA on getting home?"

The line grew quiet, and then Bruce's voice came through. The sound told her she was no longer on speaker. "She's so tired all the time. They said maybe by next week if she gains some strength, but just that conversation with you wore her out. I'm here in the hall now, she's asleep."

"Thanks for letting me know, Bruce. Anything I can do?" She hated to zap Morgan's minuscule energy.

"She's been requesting lots of prayer, from anyone who comes in. Guess she and the kids were going to church with Nohemi. A few people from the congregation stopped by. Even her pastor—"

"Jeff?" Oops, she didn't need to cut him off. But he said Jeff's name.

"Yeah, that guy. Are you seeing him or something?"

She chuckled. "Or something. Kind of an experiment, sort of. We'll see where it goes, but things would be easier with us in the same city."

"I get that." He got quiet for a moment. "Cam, can I ask you a question? I'm not after Morgan's money. That's not what this is about. But I can't quit my job while she's sick. My insurance is paying her bills—it's a part of the divorce decree. So I can't move back home until we've got money to get her through this, and my leave of absence is going to run out soon. I could start with my old job again, but there'd be a span of her without coverage until things worked out. She can't be without coverage, Cami. Besides, the cut in pay from my changing wouldn't cover the cost of her copay. I must decide. Will she receive enough income from the inheritance to help?"

How did she answer that? "Bruce, all I can do is guess, but knowing what I know, I'd say you've a strong possibility."

He blew out a breath, and she could hear the smile in his voice. "Thanks, Cami. That's what I hoped. Gotta go now. We'll talk later."

She said goodbye and disconnected.

This entire day screamed crazy.

The next two weren't much better. She knew if she made Ray aware of her decision, he'd hound her until she broke. So when he'd ask, she just told him she was still thinking. And she was. But not about that.

Instead, she focused on the seven little darlings who needed to be pruned to three. Cami figured one for and one against due to what she'd observed. But of the five left, she needed to pick two and that proved harder than anticipated.

In truth, none of them cried Stinkerella to her. Only little Emma did that. But she also knew that the fact she possessed red hair while the character was a blonde made some overlook her. But Cami's gut told her Emma needed to be the face of this new franchise. She'd do for *Stinkerella* what Daniel Radcliffe did for *Harry Potter*. No doubt.

On Wednesday Cami asked her assistants to each pick their favorite, with Sara and Emma out of the mix, and finally got things narrowed. Now they must introduce three little girls to the client.

Thursday morning Cami set up the room and laid out folders containing head shots and bios of each pint-sized nominee. She caught her hands shaking as she placed them on the table at the places where the clients always sat. No wonder her insides quivered like Jell-O.

Ray peeked in. "Are you ready?"

She nodded, not trusting her voice.

"Are you going to—"

Ray's secretary tapped his shoulder.

He spun around.

"Sorry to interrupt but the clients are downstairs."

He nodded and left for the lobby.

Cami swiped her bangs off her forehead. Too close. She didn't want to blindside him. He'd been a good friend and deserved her transparency. But he pressed too hard. She knew right from wrong. If he'd gotten the question out, it would've forced her to answer him and the meeting would be tense. This way was better.

She kept telling herself that.

Once everyone got seated, Cami guided them through their packets while she introduced each girl, discussing the pros and cons. Once complete, she shared their video interviews and studied Felicia's face. Would she fall for Emma too?

Something special about that child sang to her. She carried herself as someone older.

After the clients viewed the videos, Cami brought up the lights. "So, any thoughts?"

Felicia cleared her throat. "How many girls did you look at?"

"We put out the call, heard from 217, selected 130. Then we took them through some brief scenes using a rating system to check for ability to memorize, emote, follow directions, and insert improvisation. The top seven ratings got called back, and we allowed them interaction with each other, unaware we viewed them—parents also watched. Then we interviewed all seven, like the three you saw. After which we narrowed to these three." Cami hoped that her method came across as precise and clear. But what if she missed a cue?

"Of these three, have you a favorite?" Felicia captured her gaze and wouldn't let go.

"Yes, I do. But I'd rather not influence you if you have someone in mind." Cami gnawed her lip. Why was her mouth so dry?

Felicia sighed. "I'd like to know. I've a favorite too, and want to know if we're running along the same lines."

"Emma Hartlyn, in my opinion, is who would do the best for you. I know her hair color isn't right, but everything else is. I've watched her in action, and you'll get a solid performance from her." Well, Felicia asked. And she refused to lie.

"Then we are of the same mind. The world's got plenty of wigs. Her hair color is no problem. We'll make her a strawberry blonde and her skin tone and features will stay in the right category. Great job, Cami. Ray. We'll be announcing this tomorrow. Do they know why they auditioned?"

Ray spoke up. "No, we kept things nebulous and made it sound like a possible local commercial."

That response brought a smile to Felicia. "Good, then we'll

contact Emma's family right away. Are they willing to start work immediately?"

"Yes, they signed documents stating that if chosen, work would begin straight off." Ray stood, signaling the end.

Felicia rose as well.

Almost as an afterthought, she turned back. Cami caught Ray's glance and knew what he hoped.

"Oh, Cami, have you learned any more about your grandmother's estate?"

The question removed all options from all their hands. Decision or no, she knew Ray would never want her to outright lie to a client, giving them reason to break a contract. "Yes, I will be an heir. In fact, because the executor cannot handle the estate, I'm to be named the new executrix. Guess it's time to make this formal. I need to recuse myself from this campaign. I've everything ready to pass on to whoever takes over. I'll give the file to Ray this afternoon. I know he'll smooth the transition."

Felicia came to her, hand outstretched. "Cami, I hate to lose you. You have been a Godsend, and I know your grandmother would be proud. But you're right. Too much conflict of interest for you to continue heading this campaign. However, since you are the executor, you'll still be part of the process, working on your grandmother's behalf. And I look forward to your input as we build this franchise." Instead of shaking hands, Felicia pulled her into a hug and whispered at her ear. "God bless you, Cami."

When Cami drew back, she noted a sheen in the woman's eyes. "Thank you. I'm honored to have been part of this and appreciate the opportunity."

As soon as Ray walked them out, she headed to her office to gather what she needed to take to him. Including the letter she typed last night. After prayer and discussion with Dericka and Opal, she found peace. It's what God called her to do. But it didn't stop her from sending up one more prayer for Ray to understand.

Before she could head for his office, though, he peeked into hers. "I sure wish she hadn't asked you."

"I know. But I couldn't have held it back. Even for you. If the client can't see us with integrity, they won't stay. You realize that." Her finger slid along the envelope on her desk.

"Yeah. You did a whale of a job, though, kiddo, and they are pleased."

"Thanks." She picked up the envelope and handed it to him. "I need to give you this."

"What is it?" He glanced at her as he pulled the letter from the envelope. "Your letter of resignation? You're quitting?" She couldn't tell if his shock mingled with anger or hurt."

"Ray, I need to move to Phoenix. I've thought this through, and with having to settle the estate and all, it'll be easier if I'm not trying to juggle a job and trips back and forth. Besides, you just allowed me to work on the best campaign I'll ever have a shot at. Nothing will come close. We both know it. We experienced that one in a million and I'm grateful. Thank you."

His hands hung at his sides, the letter dangling from his fist. "Cami…"

She walked over and gave him a hug. "It's going to be okay, Ray. You're a friend for life. And Phoenix isn't that far away."

"Great. Now what'll I do? You're the only person here who even considers me human."

She laughed. "I still have my doubts too. That found-under-a-rock theory has validity."

"Oh, cut that out." He blinked hard. "Let's get out of here. I'll treat to lunch. I don't have to show this letter around yet. And maybe I can talk you out of it."

A smiling face with deep dimples and twinkling blue eyes passed through her brain. "You can try, but don't hold your breath."

But then she realized that face didn't know about her decision either. Maybe he wouldn't agree it's all that smart.

Chapter Sixteen

MORGAN

Funny how being picked the executor of Gram's estate seemed like such a big deal only a few months ago.

And today she'd hand over the responsibility, with a smile and blessing, to the one person she'd never trusted. Only now, she wanted to live and build a relationship with Cami.

But since that responsibility flew off her shoulders, she'd focus on getting healthy. For her kids. And for a second opportunity with Bruce. If he'd agree to that.

She figured he would. Maybe. He'd said he loved her, but he still had never asked why. How she let it all come to this moment. Did he not want to know? And if he didn't care to understand, even if her reasoning proved wrong, would a chance remain for them? Or would they mess up again?

She sighed and used the remote to raise the head of her bed. Her muscles ached from lying around so much. Common sense said she'd have to go slow, but something inside wanted her to move. Try.

"Do you need help?" Bruce still hovered, but she'd started to enjoy his being at her side.

"Needed a new position. Any water?" Her mouth grew

parched.

"Sure." He poured her a half cup. "Let me know if you want more."

She shook her head. "A little's fine." How long since she'd eaten? "I'm sort of hungry. Would you find some saltines please?"

You'd have thought she said Santa left him a gift. His face lit and his eyes grew. "I'm sure I can scrounge some. Be back." He raced out the door.

Morgan yawned and even desired having a stretch. Was she getting better? The doctor said she'd picked up an infection, and they'd attacked with all sorts of antibiotics. Parts of her stay she remembered, but parts all blurred together into a hospital fog. When did she last speak with the twins?

Bruce returned with the crackers followed by a nurse in tow rolling a stat machine.

"I hear you have a little appetite. Before you snack, let me get your temp. Might be your fever broke." The nurse, Andrea, shoved that digital thermometer in Morgan's mouth before she responded. "Well now, that's good. You're back under a hundred."

"Not normal?" Bruce beat her to the question.

"Below 100 is fine for now. That's considered low grade. Normal is better, but low-grade sure beats the numbers you've been putting out." Andrea removed the thermometer's used cover, dropped it in the trash, and wheeled her computerized baseline checker out the door.

"Guess that's why some of my memory is blurry. How long has it been since I talked with the kids?"

"Yesterday morning." Bruce came close and enveloped her hand in his. "Today is Friday. In case that's your next question."

She smiled. "Thanks." He knew her too well, and it still scared her. "Will they let them come up? For a brief visit? I feel ready. "

He traced little circles on her palm with his thumb. "They

need it as much as you. Plus, I've a couple things to take care of."

"You didn't get in touch with the probate court?" She remembered Cami calling and that they planned to handle everything. Didn't he do that yet?

"Yes, I went online, and it's all finished. Cami should receive the notice from the probate court today or Monday at the latest. It's something else, nothing for you to worry about." He wouldn't meet her glance.

And that started a churning inside. They'd not talked about anything yet. Maybe he waited for her to start. "Do you need to contact your new girlfriend?" She tried to sound nonchalant.

"New girlfriend? What are you talking about?"

"Bruce, we're divorced. No problem, even if I'm not fond of the idea. I understand, we're both adults."

He dropped her hand but captured her gaze. "Where'd you get a cockeyed notion like that?"

"Our mothers keep in touch and mine couldn't wait to tell me." She blinked hard. Not going to be tears. No, sir. They'd discuss this as grownups.

"My mother shared that you're dating some Honeywell engineer."

That stunned her. Where in her jam-packed schedule would she have penciled in a date? "She said what?" Morgan shook her head. This was too crazy. "You realize what has been going on, right? I don't know what those two conniving old grannies plotted, but they've lied to us."

Bruce laughed until tears streamed down his face. After wiping them away with his sleeve, he sat on the bed's edge and pulled her close. "Morgan there's never been another since you. I came back to fight for us and found you sick. It wrecked me. I wanted to beg you to take me back. I'd quit my job and move home."

Bruce was coming back to her. Came back to her. Planned to fight for her. She let the stupid tears flow.

He let her lay back on her pillow before he stood and paced. "But with you so ill, I didn't dare quit. You'd lose your insurance. And because the firm here is small and privately-owned, they can require a lead-in time before they'd pick up your policy. I didn't know what to do."

Great. She gets him back but can't keep him. Her body betrayed her yet again.

"But honey. Even if I've gotta work at that company until you're well, I still want to be married to you. If we've gotta do the long distance thing, we'll do it. To ensure we've enough to cover everything. I only want you."

She swiped tissues from the little box on her stand and wiped her face. "You never asked why I wouldn't go with you. And I don't know that I could've explained it before." She folded and unfolded the edge of sheet that lay smooth across the hospital blanket. "You gotta understand, my parents dragged me from one army post to another until they divorced. Mom would find a boyfriend and we'd go live with him until they either married or split up. I didn't have any real friends until college. Still not many. Since I've never learned how to make a friend." She hadn't ever shared this with him, she never allowed him to discover the chinks in her armor.

After a third tissue swipe and a hiccup, she continued. "The idea of our babies suffering through that, well, that's why. I couldn't. I grew terrified of messing up the twins. Like me. And then when we split, pride kept me from telling you. But I messed them up anyway, ripping our home apart." She couldn't speak another word, but at least she'd gotten that out. She grabbed the sheet, holding it to her face, too afraid to see the disappointment on his face.

He said nothing. Did he leave her? An invisible python squeezed the breath from her lungs until it forced her to raise her eyes.

Bruce stood by the bed. He placed his hands on her cheeks, drawing close. First, he removed her little blue cancer cap and kissed her bald head. Next he kissed her forehead and each eyelid, the tip of her nose, and then he kissed her trembling lips that hungered for him. A kiss that awakened the passion she had forced to go dormant.

With every fiber of her being, she longed to live just to call this man her husband once more.

"Morgan." He whispered her name, making it sound like music. "Marry me. Again."

"Yes, let me get well and I will marry you. We'll be a family once more."

He pulled back. "I don't want to wait. Let's call Jeff to do it here. Nohemi will bring the kids, and Cami can drive up to be a witness. Let's do this tomorrow."

Tomorrow? "Don't we need a license and stuff?"

He grinned. "I downloaded the license last night when I got home with the twins. Jeff signs as the minister, Nohemi and Cami can be the witnesses, and then we send it back. All done." He stood next to the bed and grasped her hand. "Morgan Hanson Pembroke, will you marry me? Tomorrow? I'd kneel, but I'd be too low and you—"

"Yes! Yes, I'll marry you tomorrow. With our kids." She reached for him and pulled him close. "Bruce Pembroke, I love you so very much."

"Morgan Pembroke, I love you too. Let's call the twins and let them know. Their mom and dad got their act together."

She laughed as he pulled out his cell phone. For the first time in a C. S. Lewis-length winter of the soul, life bloomed.

Cami

The shop opened at ten and Cami was their first customer. If Morgan was getting married today, she'd want to look her best. A new cap should help. Cami chose one that picked up the colors in the prayer shawl. Maybe a new nightgown too, so even if she were stuck in bed, she'd feel pretty. Cami spotted a perfect creation—white with delicate lacey details—and added her gift to the purchase. Now she could head north.

Though she popped in *Abbey Road,* Cami didn't go through her mantra.

Instead she held a conversation with God the entire trip, sometimes listening for the whispered impressions and enlightenments.

And sometimes she just shared her heart.

Her trips between the cities had grown to be second nature, so easy and peaceful. She arrived before one, allowing her a chance to see Morgan, and shoo Bruce away before the three o'clock ceremony.

But up in Morgan's room, Bruce took more convincing to leave. He finally agreed after Morgan assured him she wanted him to.

Cami stepped into the hall with him and suggested he return with some flowers. That gave him more of a mission state of mind.

"So are you ready to get dolled up?" Cami winked as she came back to Morgan and pulled out her supplies.

"What do you have planned?" Morgan seemed a little hesitant. That control thing again.

"I figure you want to feel pretty today, so I have some things to help with that. First, a night gown—your something new." She laid the delicate negligee across the bed where Morgan could finger the silk. "And of course, you've gotta have something blue, so here's a new cap. I figured you might want to wear the shawl and this one goes with."

"Oh, yes, that's perfect." Morgan's breathy voice told Cami she was onboard with the plan.

"The something old is also something borrowed. This is a locket that belonged to my mother. If you'd like to wear it?" The simple necklace wasn't Morgan's style, too understated for that, but she hoped the offer told her cousin that she loved her.

"Oh, Cami, I remember Aunt Saundra wearing this." She agreed, her eyes filled with moisture.

"Okay, then. We just need to get you cleaned up, into your new stuff, and I'll do your makeup. If you want." Cami hesitated, not wanting to come off pushy.

"The nurse helped me shower this morning. I loved being out of bed, but slept for an hour after. That little bit wore me out. So let's do this. I'll need to rest before everyone arrives." Morgan's smile lit her face in a way Cami had never seen. For the first time since she'd received news of Morgan's illness, she experienced a peace that God would heal her cousin.

They started by changing into the gown, which required Nurse Andrea to unhook and reattach the IV cords. Once that was complete, Cami drew the sheet up to Morgan's neck to keep her wedding clothes clean from the makeup she was about to apply. With a few swipes, Morgan appeared more like herself. Only better. Still beautiful, but glowing. "You are gorgeous." Cami put the lipstick brush back in her kit. "Now for your cap and shawl."

Once those were added, Cami pulled back the sheet and held out a hand mirror.

Morgan peered at the face staring back as tears threatened her makeup. "Oh."

"Remember the mascara!"

They both cracked up at that.

Morgan handed the mirror back. "Cami, I can't thank you enough. Why did we allow so many years to get between us?"

"I don't know. I never thought I'd rank good enough in your eyes. Figured maybe you saw me as a pain in the butt." Cami grinned, hoping to take away some sting.

"I was jealous. Gram loved you and was always pushing us together. She was the only stable person in my life, and I didn't want to share her. Then when you moved in, I understood why, but wished I could've lived with Gram instead. Not that I wanted my parents dead, but I wasn't much on their radar. Gram was the one who cared." Morgan smoothed out the sheet folded over the top edge of the blanket.

"I guess I didn't understand since my parents weren't like that. I'm sorry."

Morgan reached for Cami's hand and clasped on. "Me too. But we're past that. I've learned you are an amazing, capable woman. I'm proud of you."

Now Cami blinked hard to keep her mascara from running. "Oh, I can tell you now. The project at work? Only the biggest our company ever had. And it was Gram's."

"What?"

Cami nodded. "Yep, her *Stinkerella* books were getting so popular that a media firm bought the entire publishing house to get the rights. They're going to make a series of movies, and I just helped pick the little girl to play the lead. This'll be put together like the Harry Potter franchise."

"You're kidding! Oh, Bruce turned the TV on yesterday and I caught a glimpse on *Good Morning America*. That's what you were working on?"

"Um hm. But here's the hard part. I recused myself from the project after Thursday's meeting because of the conflict of inter-est. Since we're heirs, we'll be receiving royalties from all this. By the way, the potential is multi-million, easy."

Morgan gasped.

"So, I gave two weeks' notice. I'm moving to Phoenix and I have a little plan. Still working things through. I'll tell you when I've got everything together. But for now, I'll live in Gram's house until my condo sells. I can buy something without rush-ing." She sat in the chair and brushed a speck of lint from her slacks.

"Multi-million? Bruce can move home then. We can be a proper family and not a long-distance one. Oh, Cami, you knew all this when I begged you to give up the project."

Cami nodded but couldn't look up. "I wasn't allowed to explain."

"How can I thank you? I'm so sorry I didn't trust you at first." Morgan reached for a tissue and blotted her eyes.

That statement brought a chuckle. "I didn't know any of this when I accepted the project. I said yes to prove you wrong."

They both laughed. And they were still giggling when the rest of the wedding party and guests arrived.

Bruce brought a bouquet of star lilies and blue hyacinths, making Morgan fight another battle to save her mascara.

Nohemi dressed the twins in cute outfits and they hugged their mom.

Jeff arrived looking spectacular in a navy three-piece suit. Cami inhaled and couldn't let her breath out until he grinned and laced her fingers with his. Then all was right with the world.

She leaned her head against his shoulder and whispered at his ear. "We need to talk after."

He shot her a glance, two vertical lines forming between his brows.

"All good, I promise." *I hope you'll agree.*

The guests took their places. Morgan sat on the edge of her bed, Bruce beside her, his arm protective around her shoulders.

The service was short, Jeff only mentioning a couple sentences on love and forgiveness, and the couple stating their vows. Then, once pronounced man and wife, the kids ran to hug them while Nohemi pulled out her phone to take photos. So like Nohemi, so thoughtful.

Nurse Andrea brought in a tray of cookies—she'd baked them herself after working a ten-hour day yesterday.

Once the marriage license was signed by the participants and witnesses, Jeff put it in an envelope and gave it to Bruce.

That was Cami's cue. Since he'd completed his official duties, she motioned out toward the hall, and they went for a walk.

"So what's your news?"

Now that the juncture was here, a spark of panic attempted to ignite fear in her gut. But she had wrestled with the fear monster too long. It wouldn't steal this moment. He who was in her was stronger than her fear. "We finished the project. Did you see the announcement on TV yesterday?"

"I did. Though I couldn't tell a soul, I wanted to shout how proud I was of my girlfriend." He squeezed her hand.

"Your girlfriend?"

"You're my girl, aren't you?" He gave her that same questioning look.

"Yeah, I just like hearing it." She grinned. "But I have more news. The shawl project is finished. In time too. And before the campaign. So. I told the client about the conflict of interest and walked away. That got me wondering and praying. I consulted with Opal and Dericka, and they prayed, and we reached the same conclusion."

"What's that?"

"I gave my two weeks' notice because I'm moving to Phoenix."

He stopped and turned her around to stare into her eyes. "You're serious? You are moving here? Oh, Cami, I'd never ask you to do that. I only prayed God would figure this out."

"I know you never asked. But everything lined up exactly right with my inheritance. I might start my own agency. Maybe. But as for the move, I believe God's saying it's time. So, what do you think?"

He caressed her face and drew her to him with tenderness, placing his lips on hers.

She wrapped her arms around him, holding on as tingles ran up and down her spine, making her toes curl and her fingers dance on his back.

He pulled away in slow motion. "That's what I think. So, the question is, Cami Madison, what do you think?"

"I'm not sure. I need help to decide."

He cocked his head to the side.

"Do it again and help me make up my mind."

He grinned and obliged.

Epilogue

CAMI

The satiny folds of white slipped over Cami's head and down her body, sending delightful shivers over her skin. This was the first dress she'd donned since before the accident. Even at prom, she'd worn a jumpsuit rather than something fluffy. But today? Today was different.

Today she would marry her best friend. The man who believed in her, who supported her. Convinced her she could open her own ad agency. Tallis Inc.

Dericka held her hair out of the way while Opal hooked up the back.

Someone knocked on the door, holding it ajar. "Okay to come in?" That graveled male voice brought a smile.

"Yes, I'm decent. Get in here, Ray."

"Just checking. In case you want to back out, kid, I've got your six." His wink told her he was joking, at least a little.

"That rock of yours needs to teach you more manners. I'm not about to back out. I've waited too long for today."

"Now cut that out! I was *not* born under a rock. I even have a mother to prove it." He grinned, letting her know he wasn't upset.

She sighed in anticipation. Ever since Jeff asked her, and slipped the engagement ring on her finger, her mind became preoccupied with this moment. And their future.

"Keep this shut. No telling who'll walk by and wander in." Morgan arrived and closed the door behind her, throwing a wink at Ray. "Addie is excited to be your junior bridesmaid and Bruce is hanging on to the rings until the last second so Aidan can't lose them." She strolled around Cami, glancing up and down, arranging a fold here and there. "You look lovely, Cami. If Jeff can't get any words out, no worries. He's going to be so gaga over you that could happen."

"Oh, I don't know whether to hope you're right or not." She giggled, her nerves wanting to take control. She glanced at her cousin.

Morgan not only finished all her treatments with a successful surgery, she was getting back to her old self—the good parts of her old self. Maybe a new and improved old self. Whatever you called it, the result was Cami found the sister she'd always wanted. And though her hair wasn't like before, it was growing, and she now sported a spiky look that fit her personality.

"Ray, did you see Felicia? I want her to sit with Opal in the mother's row." Without Mom or Gram, she'd felt a hole until she realized those two women stepped up and deserved those places of honor.

"Felicia's in the lobby. Should I bring her back?"

"Yes, please. Then Thomas can seat them together before we start."

Jeff had no brothers, but during the times he'd visited Cami before her move, he'd gotten to know Thomas a little better and the two became great friends. Now Thomas would stand up as a groomsman, Bruce as best man, while his friend and her former pastor Caleb arrived from Tucson to perform the ceremony. Morgan was the matron of honor and Dericka the bridesmaid. The little wedding party was complete with Ray walking her down the aisle.

Jan Berghouse from the church peeked in. "Almost time to head for the narthex. Five minutes, okay?"

Cami's hand went to her heart that couldn't decide whether to pound like crazy or just stop mid-beat, and then without warning start again.

Morgan handed her the bouquet of calla lilies. "I have something here. I know you did the old, new, borrowed, blue thing. But what if you wear the shawl today? I brought it with me. Consider it a hug from Gram."

Cami started blinking. Hard.

"Remember the mascara!" Morgan winked and they both giggled as Morgan draped the shawl around her. Rather than over her shoulders, at her elbows hanging loose across her back.

"Borrowed and blue. I have Mom's old locket and my new dress. I guess I'm set." But her body quaked with her nerves going crazy. "Oh, my veil, can you help, Morgan?"

"Of course." Her cousin made sure each fold of the netting was perfect.

Felicia stepped in for a quick hug before Jan escorted her and Opal to Thomas.

They lined up and she linked arms with Ray, who gave a low whistle. "You clean up pretty good, Madison."

"Thanks." From him, that was a compliment.

They gathered in front of the sanctuary doors. Jan opened them when they were ready and let each person know when to start down the aisle as guitar music set the pace for their gait.

When Cami and Ray stepped to the doorway, the guitarist changed the song.

She froze. That's not what she'd planned. Did someone mess up? On her wedding day?

Then she recognized the tune, and no matter how she tried to save her mascara, tears streamed. Jeff turned to capture her gaze as Lennon and McCartney's "In My Life" carried her down the aisle. He did that for her. How perfect.

This place was filled with people she loved, representing

places and stages of her life. Some attended in spirit. Some she only saw on special occasions. But she loved them all.

Yet that man at the front? That incredible guy with the deepest dimples and bluest eyes? Yeah, that man. In her life, she'd love him more.

Acknowledgments

Abba Father, this story touches my heart—thank you for whispering it to me.

To my fabulous group of croknitting friends and supporters at Needles of Hope—especially April Earl who came up with two characters—well thought out and described in detail for me—who ended up being essential to the story. Dericka and Opal. Yep, they are from April's fertile imagination. Thank you my friend!

Again my wonderful P.I.T. crew who prays me through each story kept me accountable and on task. Annie, Deb, Lori D., Julie, and Dorothy—you ladies are the best! Thank you!

Thank you to my cover artist, London Montgomery, and the great cover he put together.

Thank you to my specialty readers who checked my medical and pastor life scenarios to keep me accurate—Lori Doe and Andrea Cullinan, and AnnaMarie Norris.

My Beta Readers and Street Team, you are such a huge support. Thank you!

Thank you to my Pencildancer friends—Jennifer Crosswhite, Diana Brandmeyer, Liz Tolsma, and Angela Breidenbach. You encourage, support, suggest, and pray for me. Love you!

And speaking of Jennifer Crosswhite, my editor and friend. We're getting good at this. Thank you!

Speaking of encouragement, I must again thank my friend and mentor Esther Bailey. Love you to Jesus and back. And I miss you.

As always, my love and thanks go to my extraordinary family —Phil, Jaime, Jonathan, Alyssa, Juan, Natalia, Meg, Mat, Owen, my Stinkerella Kami with a K, Mom, Amy, Rick, Rusty, and all my extended loved ones.

And, as always, E.B. I still miss you.

Author's Note

Every story has a nucleus. This one is no different.

I wanted to do a story that celebrated the wonderful ladies I've worked with for about ten years. As the countless numbers of prayer shawls crafted and gifted from those talented hands grew, I knew I needed to honor them.

We talked about it a few times, but I couldn't get a handle on the story. I'd even asked the girls if they wanted to suggest some characters.

My friend April was the only one who came back with anything, but what she had was amazing. I think it was one of the catalysts to get this story rolling. Until that point I thought it would be a multi-point of view about a group of women. Then somehow the opening scene played out in my head, and I couldn't write it fast enough.

Prayer shawls are a very personal thing. I've made them, prayed over them, and never knew who would receive them. But sometimes things align, and I get to find out after the fact. It always humbles me and brings me to tears at how perfectly God can orchestrate things.

So I am including a special pattern for anyone interested.

This pattern is supplied with permission by the designer's granddaughter, Cece Costa.

Oh, one last thing; my next project is another trilogy titled *The Weather Girls*. We'll be going back to Kokomo, Indiana, in 1970. I've included the first chapter in case you are interested. Look for the first book, *Sunny*, to release sometime this summer or fall.

Until then,

Jenny

Before you go, would you please leave a review? It can be a simple "I loved it!"

Lacy Shawl in Crochet by Della Mae Christmas Johnson

This shawl takes **four 40-gram balls** (about 6 ounces) of 4-ply yarn.

Use **size K crochet hook** or size needed for gauge. It is necessary to crochet very loose for the lacy pattern.

Abbreviations
ch (chain)
sc (single crochet)
dc (double crochet)
tr (treble)
st (stitch)
sk (skip)
sp (space)
lp (loop)

Gauge: 6 dc = 2 inches

Shawl: Ch 4 to begin.
Row 1: 3 dc in 4th st from hook.

NOTE: Always count turning chain as first stitch.

Row 2: Ch 4, turn, sk 2 dc, 8tr between 2nd and 3rd dc—9 tr

Row 3: Ch 3, turn, dc in each st—9 dc

Row 4: Ch 4, turn, 8 tr in 1st st (shell), sk 4 dc, dc between 2 dc, sk 3 dc, 9 tr (shell) in top of turning ch.

Row 5: Ch 3, turn, dc in each st and top of turning ch —19 dc,

Row 6 and all even rows: Ch 4, turn, 8 tr in 1st st, sk 4 dc, dc in next sp, sk 5 dc, shell in next sp, sk 4 dc, dc in next sp, sk 4 dc, shell in top of turning ch.

Row 7 and all uneven rows: Ch 3, turn, dc in each st and top of turning ch.

Continue to work in this manner, having one more shell each end of every other row until 17 rows of shells have been completed. Fasten off.

Finishing – Row 1: Working around shaped edge of shawl and with right side facing, join yarn in st at end of last row, * ch 5, sc in top of tr, ch 5, sc in top of next dc, repeat from * around.

Row 2: Ch 5, turn, scin 3rd st of ch of previous row, repeat from * around, ending ch 5, sc in st at edge of shawl, fasten off.

Fringe: Cut strands of yarn 12 inches long. Knot 4 strands in every 5 ch lp around shaped edges of shawl. Trim ends.

(This pattern was written in the early 1960s. The yarn it suggests may not be available today but I will list it here: Bernat Yarn Company's Dorlaine Yarn, a fashion glitter yarn—79.5% acrylic, 14% wool, 6.5% polyester. Also, the final direction is to lightly steam. I'm not sure that is needed with today's yarn but felt full disclosure important. If you make this shawl, please send a photo of the completed project to jenniferlynncary@gmail.com Enjoy!)

About the Author

Jennifer Lynn Cary likes to say you can take the girl out of Indiana, but you can't take the Hoosier out of the girl. Author of The Crockett Chronicles trilogy, she makes her home in Arizona with her husband of forty years where she enjoys sharing her tales of Kokomo with her grandkids.

You can find her at www.jenniferlynncary.com

facebook.com/authorjenniferlynncary

instagram.com/jenny.cary_author

Sneak Peek of Sunny: The Weather Girls
Book 1

Prologue

May 20, 1947
  Los Angeles, California

Aaron Day scooped up the pink bundle and cooed at the scrunched face staring back while he gently bounce-stepped to the window. A glance back at Cheryl, his wife, told him she followed his every move.

This was their first child, a tiny, exquisite little girl. But she needed a name.

And then, as he turned to gaze out the window on the beautiful Southern California spring morning, the perfect name for their perfect child bloomed in his head. Inspired by the azure sky, he knew exactly what he'd christen his first born.

Aaron drew the receiving blanket back more and pointed the vista out to his daughter. "See the beautiful clean sky, sweetie? I know you don't understand yet about the glorious weather and the golden rays shining in through this glass, but you will. One day you're going to embody all the promise this day holds." His fingertips skimmed over her feathery blonde hair before he leaned in and kissed her wrinkle-free forehead, her eyes continuing to bore into him all the while. "I name you after this day of your birth. You are Sunny May. You will be a light in our house, filling each room with laughter and joy."

"Aaron, her last name is Day. Do you really want to do that to her? Sunny May Day? Even Sunny Day is going to get some cracks." Cheryl rolled to her side in her hospital bed and leaned on her elbow.

"It's a name people will remember. If she gets into the entertainment business with us, she's got a ready-made moniker to make her more recognizable."

"True. But will she hate us later for doing this to her?"

Aaron shook his head. "Not if she tell her her story. From the time she is little, she will know her name is perfect for her. She is Sunny May Day. Yeah," He sighed. "She's going to do big things with that name."

Cheryl chuckled and laid back on her pillow. "You might be right. It would be a great ingenue name. Maybe she can follow in my footsteps with the movies."

Aaron brought the baby to her mother and cradled her in the crook of Cheryl's arm. "She can do whatever she wants--music, acting, designing skyscrapers for all I care. I just want her to stay happy, our little sunshine girl. She'll be a success, I have no doubt."

Chapter 1

February 16, 1970
Indianapolis, Indiana

"Are you Sunny Day?"

Sunny glanced up at the delivery guy interrupting her concentration. These figures needed to be collated and organized before the governor's meeting in two hours. "Yes, that's me." She waited for the snicker or not-so-funny quip.

"These are for you." He handed over a vase overflowing with two dozen long stemmed roses.

She'd been so intent on nailing the poor kid for making fun of her name, she'd missed the giant bouquet in his hands that nearly took her breath away. "Thank you, these are gorgeous." After clearing a corner of her desk, she took the delivery from him and adjusted the flowers. "Oh, a tip. She tugged her purse from the bottom draw and dug out a couple quarters. "Thank you."

He nodded and moved to leave before turning back. "Your name really is Sunny Day?"

She fisted her hands, holding her temper in check. "Yes, I was born on a beautiful Southern California day, full of sunshine and promise so my parents deemed me Sunny." No need to get her middle name involved. "Born on a sunny day, named Sunny Day. There, now you know." She turned her back on him and swiped the card from the arrangement. Who would send her these beautiful…

No. Nope. No way. She tore the little card to pieces before pulling the roses from their holder and shoving them into the trash can. Then, after swiping the vase from her desk, she trotted off to the ladies to dump the water before chucking it in her wastepaper basket after the blooms.

Teresa Knept strolled past. "Saw someone was getting flowers —" Her gaze fell on the stuffed trash can. "What did you do that for?"

"They suddenly wilted." Sunny returned to her figures.

"What do you mean? They were stunning when he brought them up."

"Yeah, they were. Until I read the card. Not enough roses around to make up for what he did this last weekend. Some Valentine's day."

Teresa leaned a hip against the corner of Sunny's desk. "What did he do?"

In truth, she'd rather just forget about it. And him. If he couldn't be bothered to even call and say he'd be late or that there was an emergency or anything…After all, she'd given him the weekend to contact her. But this? Flowers and only a "love, Brock" scrawled on the card? Did he really think that was all it took? "I don't want to talk about it. Got too much to do right now anyway. Maybe when I cool off, okay Teresa?"

"Okay, Sunny. Let's talk at lunch." She pushed away from the desk, but after a step she turned and bent to whisper in Sunny's ear. "Don't look now, but someone is about to get blindsided."

Sunny laid aside her pencil and glanced where Teresa indicated.

Brock.

A big smile on his too handsome face while he waved at her coworkers like a campaign hopeful.

What was he thinking?

He arrived at her desk and planted one on her cheek. Totally clueless. "Hey beautiful. Did you get my…" Brock caught sight of the wastepaper basket. "Um, I guess you did. What's the matter? Didn't you like them?"

Sunny stood. This was too much. Her tempter was going to get the better of her if she didn't get it under control. She held her breath, starting her silent count while she rubbed her earlobe. There was no way she could explode in her work space, but this egomaniac was doing everything he could to get her to break that rule.

It took until thirty to put her in a frame of mind where she could speak calmly. "Brock, I think you have mistaken me for someone you can manipulate. I do not want to see your big grin or your flowers or your name ever again. I hope I have made myself clear."

"But, Sunny. I sent the flowers to say how sorry I was." He

had a little boy pout that was usually hard to resist. But this time it didn't work its charm.

"How was I to know that Brock? You only signed your name. Nothing about what happened, or where you were. If this relationship had a chance, you destroyed it by standing me up on Valentine's Day without a call or anything. It was the last straw. I am done. Goodbye, Brock."

"Sunny, baby, you can't mean that."

Before Sunny could answer, she spotted another visitor headed her way. What was it about trying to get your work done and suddenly getting popular? No one wanted her to finish this report. "May I help you?"

"Are you Sunny Day?"

Brock spun at the voice and his LA worthy tan drained from his face. "Venita."

Sunny watched the exchange between the woman and Brock. Something was off. "Yes, I'm Sunny Day."

"Really." The woman shook her head. "You couldn't even find someone with a normal name." She snorted and then turned her full attention on Sunny. "And you, stupid name girl. I would think anyone capable of getting a job in the governor's office would be smart enough not to get involved with a married man. But let's be clear. He is married. To me. This is your last mistake. And I will have your job for it." She spun on her heel, all one hundred pounds of her, and thundered toward the executive offices as if she were seven feet tall and all muscle.

"Brock, what did she mean?"

"Sorry, Sunny." He started to follow the woman.

"Brock? You are married?"

He stared at the floor but nodded before taking the same route as his wife.

Married? She'd been dating a married man? Ever since New Year's?

Well, one more reason she'd not forgive and take him back.

She didn't play that game. Marriage was sacred and she would not be the reason one fell apart.

She glanced about the room noticing for the first time all her coworkers—some stared openly while other merely stole peeks. Her cheeks bloomed with heat and she brushed her bangs from her brow before sitting back at her desk and picking up her pencil. With a swivel to the side so no one could see her shame, she tried to pull her mind back to her job.

But the numbers wouldn't add. They danced around, all the ones pointing at her, sharp little digits morphing into accusing arrows of condemnation as she tried to key them into the adding machine. She began the column again when her phone rang. "Treasurer's Office. Miss Day speaking. How may I help you?"

"Sunny, it's Belinda. Can you come to my office, please?" Human Resources?

"Sure. I'll be right there." She hung up, grabbed a stenographer's pad and pencil, and headed for the office on the next floor. After all the drama in her open office area, it was nice to step away from prying eyes. She didn't wait for the elevator, not when she could beat it by taking the stairs. A moment later she tapped at the closed door, then pushed it open. Only Belinda. Sitting behind her desk.

"Close the door, please, Sunny."

A chill went up her spine. This wasn't going to be good. "What's going on?"

Belinda stood and walked around the desk to her. "I wish I knew. Somewhere you've made someone upset. I'm to let you go. Now."

Sunny sank into the chair, her legs giving way. "Fired? Now?" It made no sense. Even if that woman followed up on her threat, Sunny's work had been without fault. Her boss told her so many times. She was even being groomed to step up to the next level in a couple months. "Why?"

"I don't know why. It makes no sense to me, but it comes from the governor's office. Like I said, you've upset someone. I need you to sign this paper and I'll cut you your final check. I'm supposed to get a guard to go back with you to get your things, but you won't cause a fuss, right?"

A guard? "I'm too confused to cause a problem. What do I do?" The sooner she got done what was required, the sooner she could get out of this nightmare.

"Just sign here. I pointed out that you've been a model employee and deserved a severance in addition to what you are owed. They agreed." A moment later Belinda handed her a check that was triple what she normally took home. Two weeks' severance then.

"I'm allowed to get my things?" Sunny tucked the check inside her steno pad, unable to meet Belinda's gaze.

"How about I walk up with you. That way it won't look so bad and I'm covered."

Sunny nodded. She'd never been so humiliated in her life. But she wasn't about to cry or cause a scene. Just get out of there. That's all she wanted to do. Get out.

She stood and Belinda held the door for her, following her out into the hall. "Can we take the stairs? Less people that way."

"Sure." Belinda walked to her right and got the door to the stairwell.

They climbed the steps in silence. What was there to talk about? All normal sounds were muted, muffled. Even the footfalls on the cement treads echoed as if far away. Sunny felt as if she were encased in a bubble that hushed the surrounding world.

At the top, Belinda opened the next door and let her hand rest on Sunny's shoulder a moment. Sunny knew she offered kindness despite being forced to do a hatchet job. It wasn't Belinda's fault.

It was Brock's.

If he'd been a faithful husband, none of this would've happened.

Or was she to blame for some of it?

Had she taken the time to look for telltale signs? Had she overlooked some signal that shouted "married?" What had she done that was so wrong they had to fire her?

At her desk, Sunny noticed the adding machine and financial books had been moved. Apparently word leaked back and someone else got put onto her task right away. Well, considering the governor needed the figures in little more than an hour, that made sense. But it was one more slap in the face.

She gathered her purse, tucking in the small family photo she had proudly displayed to anyone who stopped by. An extra tube of lipstick, a small hairbrush, a brown bag lunch, and her latest book purchases—*Jonathan Livingston Seagull* and *Love Story*. Neither of which she'd had a chance to start, seeing that it was just getting to lunchtime and she hadn't made up her mind which to read first. Then she remembered her steno pad.

Books and lunch in hand, her tooled-leather purse strap over her shoulder, she finally glanced up and caught Teresa's sympathetic gaze. With a forced smile, she wiggled her fingers in goodbye at the one friend she'd make in the office and walked with Belinda back to the stairs.

This time she heard the creak of the metal door as it swung on its hinge—like a cell door opening. Only she wasn't being locked in. They were about to lock her out.

At the next floor down, Belinda offered a handshake. "You're going to bounce back from this, Sunny. You have too much intelligence and talent. People who do things like this always end up getting theirs in the end. It was nice knowing you and if you need a reference, ask for me. I will give you a good one."

That was more than Sunny could take. A tear forced its way down her cheek. She swiped it away from her jaw before it dripped and cleared her throat. "Thanks. I appreciate that. Goodbye." Because if she didn't get out of there now, she wouldn't be able to see to do it. Tears were going to fall. If only she could hold them off until she got to her car.

Belinda headed to her office and Sunny continued to the first floor.

Just as her hand grasped the handle, the stairwell door was pulled away and someone bowled her over.

The next thing Sunny knew, she sat on her bottom at the base of the stairs staring into the most chocolate eyes she'd ever seen.

"Are you all right?" Pat held out his hand to help the lady to her feet. A petite blonde with big blue eyes that nearly swam with a sheen of moisture, he was sure he'd hurt her in some way. "Let me help you."

She took his hand but glanced away. "Thanks, I should have been looking where I was going."

The tingles racing up his arm thickened his voice. "No." Pat shook his head. "Entirely my fault. I was storming up the stairs, trying to go faster than that behemoth of an elevator." He reached for her shoulder bag whose contents lay scattered on the concrete floor.

"I'll get it. I don't want to hold you up. You're in a hurry." She stooped and reloaded her purse, flung the strap over her shoulder, and grabbed at her other items.

He picked up *Love Story*. She's a reader. But then about every woman over the age of fifteen was reading that book. He glanced at her other title. "Have you read *Jonathan Livingston Seagull* yet?"

She shook her head and accepted the paperback from him. "Not yet. If you'll excuse me. I'm sorry." Her face twitched as if she tried to control something, but she had yet to meet his gaze when she spoke. Instead she shoved out the door, and out of his life.

The words "what a shame" bounced through his brain. But he brushed them away and with one more glance at the now closed door, he resumed his trek up the stairs, sure he'd still beat the elevator to the third floor.

Childhood friend Trey Haynes worked there and as long as he had a lunch break today, he might as well see if they could eat together. Both had jobs that had them downtown, but somehow being able to catch up didn't happen that often. Pat decided to make an effort.

He exited at the third floor and found Trey's office, or open shared office. The man was focused over a column of numbers and punching keys on an adding machine.

"Hey, did you forget about lunch?"

Trey looked up, a blank stare at Pat. Then a light glowed in his eyes and his face showed recognition. "Oh man, I'm sorry. It's been crazy around here and I just got an urgent report dumped on me. I think someone got canned or moved or something but now I'm trying to figure out where he was and finish this in the next ten minutes."

Pat glanced at his watch, gaging how much time he had. "Want me to wait?"

"Nah. We can try again another time. But thanks. I'm really sorry."

"Hey, don't worry about it. I'll give you a call."

Trey waved but his attention was already back on the figures before him.

Pat started back to the hall. He still had some time and a little company for lunch would be nice. His other friends worked farther away, no way to meet up with them in the time he had.

Just as he rounded the corner toward the exit, he spotted someone else he knew. Did he want her to see him? Pat sighed. If he was ever going to smooth out their relationship, he first needed to stop ducking her.

Did he really want a relationship with her?

Yes, he had to admit he did. She was his big sister after all.

Though these days she was about half his size. Physically. In measured personality, she was gigantic.

"Hey sis, how about lunch?"

The woman with the trademark Whitcomb raven hair glanced over her shoulder. Her face pinched a moment, then she sighed. "Yeah, I think I could do with some lunch. Where do you want to take me?"

He chuckled at that. Well, he had invited her.

She clicked over in her heels that gave her a couple added inches in height and took his arm. "I need to talk to you anyway. Let's go to Mario's. It's close and I feel like Italian."

Pat covered her hand with his. So far things were pleasant and maybe a tasty lunch with good conversation might add to that. "Sounds great."

Rather than make her take the stairs in those shoes, he resigned to riding the elevator with her. With others in the car, she didn't start a discussion and he was gun shy enough about what might trigger an explosion that he enjoyed the quiet. Which lasted for the two blocks to the restaurant. But once seated, he could tell by her expression, she was about to start something big.

"I'm glad to see you. I've been meaning to call. I need a favor."

A favor? Well at least she wasn't going on about how he was the crowned prince and she a mere peasant struggling for notice. "What kind of favor, sis?"

"There's this parcel up in Kokomo. It's a beautiful setting for a new high rise. If I can acquire the land, I think I can push this project through. But I'm having trouble getting the owner to give me a definite deal. She keeps coming back with needing to think on it and other questions. I'm sure she's stalling, and I don't want someone else to get that property."

The waitress came over with water and bread sticks. "Are you ready to order or shall I come back?"

Pat gave his standard choice—spaghetti and meatballs. He

had no other meetings today and if he spilled on his tie, there was another in his office.

"I'll have the pasta primavera." His sister's standard order.

He could have ordered for them both, but she would have taken that as him thinking her not capable. Which was ludicrous. She was more than capable of doing so much. Part of him understood why she struggled so to prove herself. But the other part just wished she'd relax and not paint him with the same brush as their parents. He wasn't the problem. But the way their mother and father showed preferential treatment, made it look like he was the bad guy. And he hated that. He loved his big sister and wanted them to find some sort of, well, a way to get along and feel like siblings.

"So tell me more about this parcel."

"I've got a chance, Pat. A real chance. This deal looks to be big and will bring in steady income to Whitcomb. I should be able to get the land for a steal. The economy is such I think I can negotiate something that can go up quick and offer mid-level housing and a constant source of capital. Dad will have to admit I pulled off a great one and consider me for more than this token position."

"Sounds wonderful, kiddo. I'm proud of you." And he was.

"But…"

There's a but, and somehow she'd put his on the line. He knew it. "But?"

"I'm fairly sure the owner doesn't like me. I know I come off too gung ho, but I really need this deal. Can you drive up to Kokomo and talk with her?" Man, she was giving him the puppy dog look.

"Sis, I can't today. Got a brief to finish. And then there are two weeks of negotiation with Judge Maupin overseeing. Tell you what. I can try after that. Two weeks is the soonest my calendar is cleared enough to get out of the city."

She pouted. "All right. If that's the best you can do. I just know someone is going to snap that property up."

"Is it on the market or are you trying to talk her into selling?"

"No, it's not on the market. Yet. But she might get an idea. Oh, I hate to wait that long."

Pat sighed. "I know. If I had the time, I'd do it. As it is, I carved out this lunchtime to meet with Trey, but he got stuck on an emergency project. I was going to go back to the office and skip lunch before I saw you."

She smiled. "I'm glad you did. This is the nicest thing that's happened to me today. It's been pretty bleak."

He covered her hand. "I'm sorry. Want to talk about it?" Maybe she'd see he really cared.

She shook her head. "No, not really. I've already taken care of it. Just one more bit of fuel to add to mom and dad's fire that I can't do anything right."

"They don't think that." Well, maybe a little but not because of anything she'd done.

"Yeah, they do. That's why this deal is so important. If I land it, all by myself—and don't you dare mention that you sweet talked that old woman into selling to me—they'll have to finally admit I've got worth." She blinked fast and he knew her tears were close to the surface.

If he could just help. But anything he did for her only made her look weak. No, he'd never mention to his folks that he'd gone to Kokomo for her. But was there anything else he could do behind the scenes? Any strings he could pull to point his parents in the right direction?

It wasn't just that they doted on him and fed her the crumbs. They also wanted to control all his choices, including where he worked. Family first. Family is important. But the Whitcomb family took those adages to a whole new standard.

The Whitcombs were a first family in Indiana, with parts of their giant business holdings in all sorts of Hoosier endeavors from politics to construction to marketing to farming. It was hard to find a field where they didn't have some input. And income. Which was why they insisted on Pat bringing his legal credentials into the corporation. All in the family. That was their motto.

"They know you have worth. They're fighting generations of thinking where men do the business and women raise the kids. It's messing with what they know. That's all. Give them time. I mean, look around. The women's movement is fighting this all over. You just get to battle it at home, too." He smiled and hoped she saw him as an ally.

"You're right. But I do need you. Please, if you can do it sooner, let me know. I don't think my presence would help any. That old gal just doesn't seem to like me." She dabbed at her lips and pushed her more than half filled plate away.

"Not hungry?"

"Don't need the added weight. Tastes good, but a taste is enough. No need to give my husband more reasons to not be attentive."

Her husband was a slimeball, but he couldn't tell her that. He was the one thing her parents cheered. She'd married a good-looking charmer. The problem was, he didn't always remember he was married.

"You look great. Brock's an idiot if he's not paying attention to you."

She smiled, though it radiated sadness. "Thanks. After this morning I needed to hear that. I'm glad you asked me to lunch. Pat, I wish we had more times like this."

"Me too." And if she felt that way, maybe they would. He checked his watch. "I'd better pay the tab. Need to get back to the office and finish that brief." He raised his hand and the waitress brought them the bill. After leaving a tip under the ashtray, he stood and helped his sister with her chair.

"Thanks." She stood on tiptoe and kissed his cheek.

"What was that for?"

"For improving my day."

He wrapped her in a quick hug. "You are welcome. Let's do make this a regular thing. I miss just talking with you."

She nodded.

"And Venita, I promise to get to Kokomo first chance I get. I'll let you know."

"Thanks, Pat."

He paid the tab and walked her to her car before going back to his office. Now to finish that brief.

9 781954 986503